Praise for *This Earl of Mine*

"A book that begins with a Regency heiress seeking a bridegroom in Newgate Prison promises daring adventure, and Kate Bateman gives readers just what they're looking for . . . Pure fun."　　　　*—BookPage*

"Genuine romance that shines through . . . delightful leads and sexy capers."　　　　*—Kirkus Reviews*

"Delicious, witty, and ripping good fun! Kate Bateman's writing sparkles."

—USA Today bestselling author
Laura Lee Guhrke

"Dashing, daring, and deliciously romantic!"

—USA Today bestselling author
Caroline Linden

"A riveting new voice for Regency readers! Kate Bateman is now on my auto-buy list."　　*—Janna MacGregor,*
author of *The Good,
the Bad, and the Duke*

ALSO BY
KATE BATEMAN

This Earl of Mine

Kate Bateman

St. Martin's Paperbacks

First published in the United States by St. Martin's Paperbacks, an imprint of St. Martin's Publishing Group.

TO CATCH AN EARL

Copyright © 2020 by Kate Bateman.

For information, address St. Martin's Publishing Group, 120 Broadway, New York, NY 10271.

www.stmartins.com

ISBN: 978-1-250-30611-1

Our books may be purchased in bulk for promotional, educational, or business use. Please contact your local bookseller or the Macmillan Corporate and Premium Sales Department at 1-800-221-7945, ext. 5442, or by email at MacmillanSpecialMarkets@macmillan.com.

Printed in the United States of America

St. Martin's Paperbacks edition 2020

10 9 8 7 6 5 4 3 2 1

"It is only with the heart that one can see rightly; what is essential is invisible to the eye."

—ANTOINE DE SAINT-EXUPERY, *LE PETIT PRINCE*

Prologue

Only touch what you're going to steal.

Of the many rules of thieving her father had taught her, that one was key. Emmy Danvers broke it the night of Lady Carlton's masked ball; she touched Alexander Harland.

She had no intention of stealing him, except from the other eager women in the room. She was simply borrowing him for a single dance.

She was wearing a dress Camille had once worn to Versailles, a gorgeous concoction of watered blue silk adorned with gold braiding. A wig, powdered blue-grey and fixed with silk flowers, hid the true color of her hair. She'd added a coquettish patch to the corner of her mouth, the one the books called "the kissing." She was hopeful. And since it was a masquerade, she'd worn a cream leather mask which covered the top half of her face. Only her lips and chin were visible. Harland would never know who she was.

Emmy's heart pounded against her ribs. This was just

like a heist. The same nervous excitement as she eyed the prize, the same pulse-pounding fear of discovery. Harland drew her like the shimmering facets of a well-cut sapphire, a tug of attraction she was helpless to ignore.

He was standing with his two constant companions, Benedict Wylde and Sebastien Wolff. The three of them together were a sight to gladden any girl's heart, each one as handsome as the next.

With a fortifying breath, she stepped in front of the three men and executed a deep curtsey. They had been in the middle of a conversation, but Harland trailed off midsentence when he noticed her, and all three of them turned to stare, no doubt amazed by her shameless effrontery. Women were not supposed to approach men. Then again, women weren't supposed to steal jewels either. Emmy had never been terribly good at following the rules.

"Mister Harland," she said. "I believe this is my dance."

An intrigued smile touched his lips. He gave her a slight bow in return, and she willed him not to refuse her. His blue eyes, through the black mask he wore, regarded her speculatively.

"I don't recall agreeing to a dance, Miss—?" He let the end of the sentence hang, urging her to provide her name. She gave a light laugh.

"Oh, no! This is a masquerade. Names are forbidden."

"And yet you have mine."

"Yes. You are already at a disadvantage." He would hate that. He struck her as a man who would always want the upper hand. "Perhaps you'll be able to discover my identity during the course of the dance?"

Wolff nudged him. "You can't possibly turn down a challenge like that, Alex. Take the lady onto the floor." His appreciative gaze raked her, and he flashed her an easy smile. "Because if you don't, then I certainly will."

"How can I refuse?" Harland chuckled. He stepped forward and offered her his elbow. "You have intrigued me, my lady."

Emmy's stomach gave a little flip. He'd accepted!

With his slow, wicked smile and easy charm, he'd been her secret fantasy for so long. A few years older than herself, he'd always been part of a slightly different social set, a glittering, roguish, dangerously thrilling presence at any event he attended. She'd watched from the shadows as he danced with the prettiest girls and cut a swathe through the debutantes, flirting impartially but without serious intent. Having an older brother who was heir to the title, he was the quintessential carefree second son, free to pursue a life of youthful excess.

Emmy had stayed out of his way, wary of his reputation and of his keen intelligence. She'd been afraid he'd take one look at her with those piercing blue eyes of his and see right through the demure wallflower she played in public, to the reckless criminal beneath. She'd been content to watch him from afar and dream impossible dreams. Until she'd heard he was off to fight Napoleon.

What if he was wounded, as her brother, Luc, had been at Trafalgar? What if he was *killed*? The thought of a world without Alexander Harland in it, even on the periphery of her life, seemed very bleak indeed.

Seize the day, her grandmother Camille had adjured her. *Go after what you want, my love, but be careful.* Emmy gave a wry smile. Not carpe diem. Carpe *hominem*. She would seize the man.

She curled her fingers on Harland's sleeve and allowed him to lead her into the throng of couples forming in preparation of the next dance. The opening strains of a waltz sounded, and she almost laughed in delight. She couldn't have planned it better.

Harland put his hand at her waist, and her breath

caught as he tugged her close and lifted their joined hands to shoulder level. Good lord, he was tall.

"We've never been introduced," he stated with utter certainty as they whirled around the floor in a breathless spin. "I'd remember if we had. Tell me your name, princess."

Emmy laughed, blissfully aware of the thrilling nearness of his body, the warmth of his hand at the small of her back.

"I'm no princess, sir. For all you know I could be a scullery maid who's stolen her mistress's dress. I could be a criminal. A thief."

"A thief." He laughed softly. "Now that I can believe. You've stolen the breath right out of my lungs. Stolen the heart from my chest."

His teasing words, which he'd somehow made sound so sincere, made her ache with poignant longing. If only. But handsome princes never ended up with criminals. Not even in fairy tales.

"And you, sir, are a silver-tongued devil," she countered sternly. No doubt he said such things to every woman with whom he danced. And yet it was so tempting to believe him.

"Who are you?" he murmured. "And where have you been hiding? This can't be your first London season. You're no simpering miss of sixteen, just up from the country."

"That's true," Emmy conceded. She didn't need to think about the steps of the dance. With Harland, it was effortless, as if they'd danced like this a thousand times before. "I live here in town. And this is not my first season. But you are correct; we have never been formally introduced."

"Have we been *informally* introduced?" He chuckled, and his low whisper did funny things to her insides.

She shook her head. "No. You wouldn't recognize me, even without this mask and wig."

"That's something I'd like to remedy."

The dance ended, but he didn't let go of her hand, or return to his friends. He pulled her out onto the terrace, and Emmy followed, unresisting. Hand in hand, he led her down the steps and out into the moonlit garden. It seemed like something from a dream. They ventured through an iron gate set in a red brick wall and stepped into the kitchen garden, wreathed in shadows. He tugged her under an apple tree.

Suddenly nervous, Emmy twisted a half-grown apple from a branch and smiled.

"What's so amusing?"

"Hmm? Oh, this reminds me of a poem I once read about fairies who like to steal apples." She met his eyes in the dim light. Every one of her senses was alive, prickling with awareness. "It goes: *Stolen sweets are always sweeter: Stolen kisses much completer; Stolen looks are nice in chapels: Stolen, stolen be your apples.*"

His gaze dropped to her lips. They tingled in response.

"Stolen kisses, hmm?" he murmured. "Maybe we should try it?" He reached up and untied the ribbon holding his mask in place. "Since you already know who I am, I think we can dispense with this."

He took a step closer, and Emmy's heart pounded as she studied his face. Strong, straight nose, lips curved in gentle amusement. She dropped the apple and slipped her hands between the lapels of his jacket, flat against his chest. She could feel the warmth of his skin through his shirt, feel the unyielding strength beneath her palms. She had the oddest thought that this was home. The place she was destined to be.

He slid his hands around her waist, his long fingers

almost spanning the circumference. "Will you take your mask off, little thief?"

"That wouldn't be a good idea."

She lifted herself on tiptoe and pressed closer, tilting her head and offering her lips in shameless invitation. *Carpe hominem.*

Her heart almost stopped when he bent his head and kissed her. A light, almost questioning touch. He repeated the action, his lips soft yet firm, and Emmy closed her eyes, determined to savor the experience. This might be her one and only kiss with Alex Harland, ever.

His tongue traced the seam of her lips. Without thought, she opened her mouth and he slid his tongue inside to tangle with hers. Emmy stilled in shock, then realized the sensation was extremely pleasurable. She flicked her own tongue tentatively against his and was rewarded with a low groan of encouragement.

His hands came up to cup her face. He angled her head and kissed her again. And again. Deeper. Darker. Drinking her in. It was a revelation. A glorious, swirling taste and tease that turned her bones to jelly. Emmy almost swooned with pleasure. The scent of him filled her nose, the taste of brandy on his tongue made her insides molten.

Minutes, or possibly hours, later, he pulled back, panting. "Your name," he demanded roughly.

"No." She hadn't lost her wits entirely.

He expelled a huff of amused frustration. "If I had more time, I would discover exactly who you are." He brushed the edge of her jawline with his thumb, then stroked it over her lips in a shiver-inducing caress. "But I'm leaving for Portugal next week." His arms tightened around her, and his mouth thinned in displeasure. "God, I wish I didn't have to go. I wish we'd met sooner. I—"

Emmy placed her fingers over his lips to stop the flow

of words that mirrored her own feelings so precisely. She pressed her own lips together to stop herself from blurting out, *Don't go, then. Stay here. With me.*

Impossible. They were from different worlds, their lives on opposite trajectories. This was the only time they would ever intersect.

The next kiss was tinged with a bittersweet desperation, a mutual acknowledgment that this one, perfect moment was finite. Fragile. Unrepeatable.

"God, you taste so sweet," he groaned against her lips. "Smell so sweet. I want to breathe you in and keep you in my lungs forever. Does that sound mad?"

"Not at all."

It was harder than she'd ever imagined to pull out of his arms. Cool air replaced the warmth where his body had been. Tears stung her eyes beneath her mask as she took another step away from him.

"Leaving me, princess?" he murmured.

"I must."

"Will you turn into a pumpkin at midnight?"

She managed a watery smile at his weak attempt at a joke. "No. But I have to go."

A good thief always knew when to leave the scene of a crime. Kissing Alex Harland had been better than she'd ever imagined, but it might also prove the biggest mistake of her life. Because now she knew precisely what she was missing.

She started back toward the garden gate. He picked up his mask, which he'd dropped on the grass, and retied it. When they reached the steps of the terrace, he caught her hand and tugged her around to face him. He opened his mouth to speak, but she forestalled him.

"Don't say goodbye."

He inclined his head. "All right. Let's simply say good night, then. Until we meet again."

He kissed her hand, his lips warm on her skin, and her stomach clenched. She already missed him. How was that even possible? She pulled away and started up the steps.

"I'll find you," he vowed at her retreating back. "When I return."

Emmy bit back a bittersweet smile. He would only find her if she wanted to be found. And she had far too many secrets for that.

"No," she whispered, too softly for him to hear. "You won't."

Chapter 1.

"That blasted Nightjar has done it again!"

Alexander Harland, Earl of Melton, glanced up from his morning paper. Sir Nathaniel Conant, Chief Magistrate of Bow Street, dropped a sheaf of papers onto the table beside him and lowered himself into a vacant armchair with an irritated exhalation. "That devil—whoever he is—is a menace to society."

Alex concealed a groan of impatience. He'd barely finished breakfast. At this hour, the Tricorn Club's salon was usually empty. Benedict, having recently married, had moved out last month; "jumped ship," as Seb had wryly phrased it. And Seb himself, the third pillar of their unholy triumvirate, was doubtless still sleeping off last night's boisterous trip to the Theatre Royal. Alex had banked on a good hour of uninterrupted reading before being bothered by anyone.

Clearly, it was not to be. Mickey, the Tricorn's mountainous doorman, had been given strict instructions to admit Sir Nathaniel whenever he so desired. Alex twisted his head to glance at the clock on the mantelpiece. Events *must* be concerning to have roused the elderly peer at the ungodly hour of nine o'clock.

He carefully folded the newspaper and placed it on the table next to him. "Another jewel has been stolen?"

Conant's jowls wobbled as he shook his head. "The sneaky beggar's hit close to home this time, Harland. Pinched a bloody great diamond from Rundell, Bridge and Rundell."

"The Royal jewelers?" Alex raised his eyebrows as his mouth twitched in reluctant admiration. "You have to give the man credit; he never takes the easy route, does he? I'd have thought their security was tight as a drum."

"It is. But the Nightjar still managed to breech it. And that's not the worst of it." Conant gave a disgruntled sniff. "The blighter couldn't have stolen a worse piece. The diamond he took belongs to the Prince Regent himself. He'd asked Rundell to fashion it into a pendant. Prinny wants it found as soon as possible—and the culprit prosecuted to the full extent of the law."

Alex's pulse kicked up at the prospect of a new challenge. Since his return from the continent last summer, he, Benedict, and Seb had helped Bow Street investigate a number of sensitive cases. Two months ago they'd foiled an attempt to rescue Bonaparte from exile on the island of St. Helena via submarine, and the Regent had shown his gratitude by awarding all three of them with titles. Benedict was now the Earl of Ware, Seb had been made the Earl of Mowbray, and Alex the illustrious Earl of Melton.

Not that Sir Nathaniel paid it any heed. He still addressed Alex as Harland.

"Just when everything's quiet, and I think the sneaky devil's retired, or dead, he pops up out of nowhere and steals another gem. It's maddening, Harland. Maddening."

"What *do* we know about him?" Alex asked.

"Precious little, to tell the truth." Conant gestured at the file of papers on the table between them. "Whatever we have, it's in there. The mode of operation is always the same; he only ever steals one gem at a time, even when he has the chance to take more. The pieces he takes are always jewels of exceptional quality—but so are the ones he leaves. And the cheeky bugger always leaves a solitary black feather in place of the missing item, as a calling card." Conant took an indignant breath. "He's been at it for years. His crimes stretch back over a decade, at least. And I'm sure there have been times when his feather's been overlooked. Those bumbling clodpolls in the provinces aren't as meticulous as you and I, when it comes to preserving evidence."

Alex inclined his head in acknowledgment of the gruff compliment. "Presumably he leaves the feather because he wants the thefts to be known as his work?"

Conant scowled. "But why? Are those from whom he steals supposed to congratulate themselves on being members of an exclusive club? Those with the dubious honor of being one of the Nightjar's victims?"

"Who knows? But at least it gives us a way of linking the crimes. Perhaps there's a pattern, some logic to them? They're not opportunistic thefts."

"I should say not. Each one has to have been meticulously planned. No two are the same. And no evidence is ever left, save for the feather. It's as if the man's a wraith."

Alex's lips twitched in amusement. "Oh, he's flesh and blood, I guarantee it. And sooner or later, he'll make a mistake. Everyone does. Do you think we're looking for an older man, since he's been active for so long? Or a group of thieves working together?"

Conant grunted. "That's what I expect *you* to find out."

He steepled his fingers, resting his elbows on the arms of the chair. "The odd thing is, the gems he steals are the kind of stones that make jewelers sit up and take notice, but they never reappear on the market. We constantly check the pawn shops, jewelers, auctions, and gem dealers. They just . . . disappear."

"Maybe he doesn't sell them. He could be an avid collector who keeps them in a private collection somewhere for his own pleasure?"

Conant snorted. "Dammed odd thing to find pleasure in, I say. Rocks? What's wrong with cards and women, eh?" He chuckled heartily.

Alex drummed his fingers on his thigh, his mind already whirring with possibilities. He'd been praying for something to occupy his time, some challenge to enliven his current ennui. Here, at last, was an adversary worth pursuing.

"Maybe they're being smuggled out of the country? Or maybe money's not the Nightjar's primary goal. You say he could steal more but restrains himself? Perhaps he has some moral code about not stealing more than one piece from any individual?"

"Moral code? Ha! A thief like that has no morals, Harland. Nor any honor. Whatever his reasons, he'll get no mercy when he's caught, tried, and convicted. The law is the law. We'll see him hanged from Tyburn tree, you mark my words."

Conant slapped his palms on the arms of the chair and pushed himself to his feet. "Rundell and Bridge aren't keen to publicize this, obviously. They want you to investigate quietly, but I'm counting on you to catch the slippery devil. The Prince Regent demands it." He strode to the door. "I imagine you'll want to take a look at the crime scene. It's over in Ludgate Hill." He shot Alex a teasing smile. "I'm sure you already know that. No doubt you've purchased plenty of pretty baubles there yourself since your return from Waterloo."

Alex hid a wince at the man's uncanny perspicacity. He'd been at the jeweler's only last month to buy a parting gift for Alicia, his mistress. The discreet widow had been disappointed but pragmatic when he'd ended their month-long liaison. She'd been hoping for more than a casual physical relationship—a wedding band, in truth—but he'd never pretended to be looking for a wife. He doubted he'd *ever* be looking for a wife.

Not that there was anything wrong with the married state, of course; witness Benedict's current blissful existence with his heiress Georgiana. But unlike Alex, Benedict wasn't practically blind in one eye, nor as cynical when it came to women. As a second son, Alex was under no pressure to marry and produce heirs. He enjoyed women, their company, their bodies, but he'd never felt the need to limit himself to just one.

Except once. Almost four years ago, at a masked ball on the eve of his leaving for the Peninsular, he'd met the woman of his dreams. A woman who'd not only excited him physically but challenged him mentally. A woman whose husky laugh and intoxicating scent had wrapped themselves around his heart and ensnared it so completely, he'd almost forgotten his own name. *Un coup de foudre* the French called it. A thunderclap. And they were right. He'd felt a deep sense of inevitability, of utter rightness. An absolute conviction that, against all odds, here, finally, was the woman for him.

They'd talked. Danced. Flirted. They'd shared one perfect kiss.

Then she'd disappeared.

He'd never even discovered her name.

Alex closed the file in front of him with a snap and exhaled deeply. God, what a naïve fool he'd been back then. Three years in the King's Own Rifles had beaten such optimism out of him. He'd traipsed through Spain and Portugal, France and Belgium, and witnessed the true horrors of war, the brutal nature of both men and women. It had taught him the futility of such dreams.

He still dreamed of her, though. Not every night, but often enough. He'd wake with the lingering scent of her perfume on the breeze—an exotic scent he'd never encountered since. The feel of her lips on his. And a cock hard enough to hammer nails into solid steel.

It was ridiculous. He didn't know her hair color—she'd been wearing a powdered wig in the antiquated style of the French court some fifty years before. He didn't know the color of her eyes—they'd been hidden behind a ludicrous mask that covered the top half of her face.

The thought of her had nearly driven him to distraction. He'd been so frustrated, never solving the mystery, never knowing if she was someone's wife, someone's mistress, or someone with whom he might have considered a future.

Alex rolled his shoulders. He should have forgotten her by now. It wasn't as though he'd remained celibate over the past four years. He doubted she would have either. And yet, he'd found himself searching for her ever since he'd been back in town. He scanned every room he entered, every face, paradoxically convinced that if he just saw her—just once—he'd recognize her. His body would recognize hers. His *soul* would recognize her.

He huffed air out of his nostrils, irritated with himself. Bloody hell, what was wrong with him? As the co-owner of a gambling den, he was more than capable of calculating the odds of such a probability: long to the point of absurdity. She was doubtless a married matron by now with a parcel of brats driving her to distraction.

And he was blissfully free, a bachelor of means, with

a handsome face to match his handsome fortune. He could, within reason, have any woman he wanted with the lift of an eyebrow, the flash of a smile.

Except that one. The one that got away.

Was that it? Perhaps the reason his mystery woman still plagued him was the sense of unfinished business. He'd have tired of her within a month if they'd ever been properly introduced. It was merely the attraction of the unknown that allowed her to retain her unholy allure.

The same principle applied to the Nightjar; it was the challenge of the unknown. Alex hated to be beaten. His pride required him to outwit his opponent, to catch the prize, to win the game. He wanted to excel at whatever he put his mind to. His competitive nature would allow nothing less.

He stared deeply into the fire. The Nightjar intrigued him. Whoever the thief was, he was a master of disguise, of guile. Nobody had ever seen him, although his exploits had featured in many a column inch of newspaper print over the past decade.

He opened the thin file beside him and glanced at the report within. Brief, sketchy details about a number of high-profile heists throughout Europe. A remote chateau in Switzerland, halfway up a vertiginous mountain. A highly fortified villa on the shores of Lake Como in Italy. He shook his head. Conant had been right—nobody had the first clue how the Nightjar had managed most of his crimes.

Some of the details remained the same, however. Never any violence. No force of any kind, in fact. No safes had been cracked, no doors blown off their hinges. No servants drugged, nor guards harmed. The most striking characteristic was stealthy, quiet intelligence. Presumably disguise. In several instances, nobody had even noticed the gems were missing for several days after the

presumed theft; it was often impossible to say precisely
when they had been stolen.

Only once had the Nightjar deviated from leaving a
sole black feather at the crime scene. Alex smiled at the
report. The thief had inadvertently knocked over a silver
sugar bowl in the course of one of his robberies, but instead of stealing the silver, he'd taken the time to sweep
up the sugar with a piece of paper and then penned a note
of apology.

*Signor Locatelli. Please excuse the mess. I regret the
necessity of depriving your wife of her very beautiful
emerald earrings, but I am sure she will be delighted to
shop for their replacements. Pour la gloire de la France.*
                                                    —*The Nightjar*

Alex studied the brief handwritten note. An elegant,
sloping hand, obviously someone who'd received a formal
education. Was he looking for a gentleman thief?

The last reported theft had been four years ago in
1812. And then nothing. Conspicuous inactivity until last
night's little spree at Rundell Bridge & Rundell.

Alex shook his head, bemused. Why the long gap? Was
the Nightjar getting old? Losing his taste for adventure?
Either way, here, at last, was a problem to sink his teeth
into. The Nightjar, ancient or not, was a worthy opponent
against whom Alex could test his mettle.

"The law is reason, free from passion," Aristotle taught,
and Alex agreed wholeheartedly. He prided himself on his
relentless investigative skills, his ability to look at any situation objectively. He would bring the Nightjar to justice
using cool reasoning and impartial logic. Although he,
Benedict, and Seb got a financial reward for every case
they solved for Bow Street, the cash wasn't his primary
goal. It was the professional satisfaction he gained from
the victories that motivated him.

War had taught him that rules and laws existed for

good reason. Infantry soldiers formed into squares when under attack to present a united front and protect one other. Any man who broke rank not only made a target of himself, but endangered the lives of the men next to him. Infringement led to danger and anarchy.

In the Rifles, he'd been part of a large force, a cog in a vast machine. As a Bow Street operative, he had the opportunity to do something more individual, to be part of a much smaller team with Benedict and Seb. Any successes were entirely to their credit, any failures, theirs to own. Alex liked the accountability.

He'd fought for three years to protect the innocent inhabitants of this country. With Napoleon safely incarcerated on St. Helena, he would continue to uphold the laws of England, and guard against disruptive criminals like the Nightjar.

He called for Mickey, who arrived mere moments later.

"When Seb finally drags his thick head out of bed, tell him I've gone to Ludgate Hill. I'll be back for lunch."

Chapter 2.

"The British Museum? You cannot be serious."

Emmy Danvers, née Emmeline Louise d'Anvers, the daughter of Europe's most elusive jewel thief, dropped her forehead to the scarred kitchen table with a heartfelt groan. "Nobody in their right mind would attempt it. Why don't we break into the Tower of London and steal the *British* crown jewels instead? That way, when we're caught, the cells and gallows will be already set up for us. It's impossible!"

Luc, seated at the opposite end of the table, chuckled at her morbid humor. "That's what you said about Rundell and Bridge, and it went off without a hitch, did it not? It's not impossible, Em. Just difficult. A challenge worthy of our skills."

Emmy raised her head and shot her brother a withering glare. "I am sick of such challenges. We will be caught. And hanged. Or transported to the Antipodes. It's only a matter of time before our luck runs out."

Camille—who refused to accept the title Grandmère

on the grounds that it made her "feel terribly *old*"—took a delicate sip of her tea and nodded.

"Well, we are all in agreement there, ma chère. Your father, God rest his soul, may have been my son, but this quixotic dream of his has left you with a very dangerous legacy. The Nightjar!" She gave an elegant feminine snort. "What a name! I told him he should have called himself 'The Fox' or 'The Conjurer.' Something with a little more flair."

Emmy bit back a laugh of despair. That was typical of Camille. The fact that her son had repeatedly broken the law in at least six different European countries over the course of a fifteen-year career was less offensive to her sensibilities than the fact that he'd not done it more *stylishly*. In her grandmother's mind, there was very little that couldn't be forgiven provided one went about it in a suitably dashing manner.

With a family like this, how could she ever have hoped to lead a normal life? Was it any wonder they were in the tangle they were in now?

She glared at the letter that lay, unfolded, on the table between them. It was the latest in a string of similar missives, the first of which had arrived just over a year ago. "He is mad, this Danton," she said flatly. "How did he discover Father was the Nightjar? How did he find us?"

Luc's handsome features twisted in a grimace. "Does it matter? He can send us all to the gallows, as he says. We have no choice but to follow his orders."

Emmy groaned again. For four blissful years, since their father's death, they'd lived a blameless, crime-free life. Louis d'Anvers's patriotic whim—to recover the French crown jewels and store them until the Bourbon monarchy had been restored—had been, if not forgotten, at least suspended. Napoleon had been so secure in his rule over France that it had seemed unlikely his reign would ever end, despite the valiant efforts of Britain and her allies to quell his ruthless empire-building. Even exile on Elba had proved insufficient to stop him.

But with his downfall at Waterloo last summer, their father's dream of a Bourbon restoration seemed destined to become a reality. Luc and Emmy had just been discussing what they should do with the Nightjar's ill-gotten gains when the first letter from Emile Danton had arrived.

Danton's father had been the revolutionary leader Georges Danton, the man their father had publicly denounced for the theft of the French crown jewels. Having been deprived of his true target by their father's death, the younger Danton had turned his ire on the Nightjar's family. As far as Emmy could tell, Danton Junior was as corrupt as his sire. He'd demanded not only the cache of jewels their father had already stolen, but insisted they obtain three additional jewels—a white diamond, a blue diamond, and a ruby—that were still at large. She doubted very much that he planned to atone for his father's sins by returning them to the French government.

Failure to comply, he'd assured them, would result in most unpleasant consequences, not only for Luc and Emmy, but for those they loved. He'd specifically mentioned Camille as a potential target if his wishes were not carried out "in a timely manner."

Emmy and Luc had had no way of refusing, no way of communicating with their blackmailer. They'd thought to claim ignorance of where the treasure was hidden and tell Danton the secret had gone to the grave with their father, but there was no return address. His demands were always delivered by one of London's innumerable scrappy errand boys, who, when questioned, could only report that they'd been commissioned by "a dark-haired gentleman" with a "foreign accent."

With no other options, they'd begun to plan the Rundell & Bridge heist.

The Nightjar had been resurrected.

Emmy had been fourteen the first time her father had involved her in one of his "little jobs," and that had only been under duress. It had always been tacitly understood that Luc would inherit the role of the Nightjar, but when he'd turned eighteen, he'd insisted on enlisting in the Royal Navy under Admiral Nelson to "do his bit" in tackling Napoleon. He'd been wounded in the leg at Trafalgar only a few months later. His convalescence had been slow and painful, and his resulting disability had rendered him unable to take part in the physical element of the heists.

And so, for four years, from the age of fourteen to eighteen, Emmy had helped her father and brother track down and steal back the crown jewels of France.

She was singularly ill-suited for a life of crime. She was physically small, at only three inches over five feet, and while constant exercise ensured she retained a certain agility, no amount of practice could cure her dislike of heights. She steadfastly refused to steal anything that required being more than ten feet off the ground.

Father had maintained that stealing the jewels back was a moral imperative. If it happened to be contrary to the law, well, then, the law was simply wrong. Committing a few lesser, secondary crimes was necessary to serve justice for a much larger one.

Emmy agreed. The jewels belonged to France. They should undoubtedly be returned.

She just wished the role had fallen to someone—anyone—else.

Father had never asked his children to complete his task. Not in so many words. But Emmy had always felt the weight of his silent expectation on her shoulders. The pressure to finish what he'd started.

The back door banged open, interrupting her brooding thoughts.

Sally Hawkins, who'd left her job as a costumier at Covent Garden Theatre eight years ago to become their "cook-housekeeper," bustled in, looking artlessly seductive in a crimson shawl. As she dropped a basket full of fruit on a stool and unbuttoned her matching cherry-striped pelisse, Emmy suppressed an envious sigh at her friend's voluptuous figure. Sally needed neither corset nor stays to achieve that gorgeous hourglass outline.

"Mornin', all."

Sally slapped a folded newssheet onto the table in front of Luc, who made a valiant effort not to stare at the cleavage that appeared in front of his face as she leaned over. His Adam's apple bobbed as he swallowed, and his eyes closed as if he were in acute pain.

Sally settled herself on one of the kitchen chairs, and Emmy half smiled at her efforts to avoid touching Luc as she did so. Even a blind man could see the attraction between the two of them, but as far as Emmy knew, neither of them had ever done anything about it.

It had been Sally who'd helped Emmy nurse Luc during those terrible first few months of his convalescence. Sally on whom his gaze lingered whenever he thought she wasn't looking. And yet there seemed to be some intangible barrier between them, some tacit agreement to keep their distance.

Emmy sometimes wondered whether Luc thought of himself as less of a man because of his prosthetic foot, an unsuitable mate for the beautiful Sally. As an aristocrat, albeit a French one, he was socially her superior. Sally had been born in the roughest part of London's East End, and her voice still retained the accent of her youth. She was sharp as a pin, utterly unapologetic for the fact that she'd made her own way in the world, and possessed of a canny ability to read people's true intentions.

Their father had first encountered her as she fended off an armed assailant in a Covent Garden back alley. Sally had coshed her attacker around the head with a wooden sewing case and rendered him unconscious without any assistance. Impressed, Emmy's father had helped her move the body out of the road and escorted her safely home.

Sally's father, it transpired, had been George Barrington, one of London's most infamous gentleman thieves. As a child, Sally had assisted him in creating costumes and disguises for his various jaunts, but when Barrington was convicted of pickpocketing and transported to Sydney, she'd found work as a seamstress and makeup artist at the rowdy Covent Garden theatre.

Emmy's father had offered her a job—one that didn't require fending off unwelcome advances from drunk theatregoers on a regular basis—and Sally had quickly made herself indispensable in providing disguises for the Danverses' various criminal escapades. She was a genius with a needle and a pot of rouge. She could turn Emmy into a chimneysweep, a flower seller, or a duchess, at the drop of a hat.

And when Luc had returned from Trafalgar so badly injured, she'd proven an invaluable nursemaid too. Emmy was sure it had been Sally's gorgeous face and cheeky demeanor that had convinced Luc not to give up on life after all.

"*The Times* is reportin' the theft at the jewelers. Front page news too," Sally said. "Bow Street's been brought in to investigate."

Emmy's heart gave a leap, but she schooled her features into a polite mask.

Of course Bow Street was investigating the robbery. Ludgate Hill was within their purview. There were dozens of officers who could have been assigned to the case. There was no reason to think it would be *him*. The man she longed for and avoided with equal fervor.

Alexander Harland.

She pushed back from the table and stood.

"Where are you going?"

Emmy ignored her brother and turned to her grandmother. "Camille, do you fancy a trip to Ludgate Hill? I saw the prettiest little straw bonnet in the window of a shop there."

Camille took another sip of her tea and shot her a knowing glance. "Would that be the milliners next door to Rundell and Bridge, by any chance? This is a dangerous game, Emmeline. You would be far wiser to stay away. You know what they say: 'Curiosity killed the cat.'"

Emmy wrinkled her nose.

Curiosity was, undoubtedly, her most besetting flaw. As her father had pointed out on numerous occasions, a good thief does not have the *luxury* of being curious. He must be single-minded in his pursuit of the specific goal. He cannot allow himself to be distracted. He must take only that which he has come for and ignore everything else, or risk being caught. A thief should not indulge in curiosity.

She *knew* this. Being curious about Alexander Harland could only lead to trouble of the worst sort.

And yet.

Trouble was exciting, addictive. Alexander Harland drew her like a moth to a flame. He'd been her weakness for years and years, not that she'd ever admit it to anyone. The object of her foolish affections didn't even know her name.

"You risk drawing unnecessary attention to yourself, Emmy." Luc scowled.

She shot him a chiding glance. "Are you suggesting I can't blend into the background, Luc Danvers?" She'd been doing just that for years: hiding. She was an expert at becoming invisible. "I just want to find out who they've sent to investigate us, that's all. It's always good to know the enemy. I'll be careful, I promise."

Chapter 3.

Emmy's hired coach rattled down Fleet Street and passed beneath the ancient arched portal in the city wall that gave Ludgate Hill its name. Over the past few years, the area had become almost as popular as Bond Street for shopping, and the streets were bustling with well-dressed ladies and au courant gentlemen.

The stately grey dome of Wren's masterpiece, St. Paul's Cathedral, kept a benign watch over the area. Emmy caught a glimpse of the great brick walls of Newgate Prison as they neared their destination, and the sight of the looming ramparts dampened her excitement somewhat. The grim edifice was a sobering reminder of what could befall her family if they were ever caught.

She dismissed the morbid thought with a toss of her head.

The coach lurched onto Ludgate Hill and rocked to a stop, the driver having been instructed to deposit them at the far end of the street. Emmy helped Camille down, and together, they began a slow promenade along the thoroughfare.

To the casual observer they were two fashionably dressed women studying the contents of each shop window, and yet Emmy's awareness was entirely fixed upon the elegant white stone building at number 32. She'd been robbing its basement less than twelve hours ago.

Three stories high, the exterior of Rundell & Bridge was graced with elegant arches held up by fluted columns. The sign, hanging above the door, was of two golden salmon leaning against each other, the significance of which, for a diamond merchant and jewelers, eluded Emmy. She opened her parasol with a practiced flick of her wrist and ushered Camille a little closer.

Her stomach gave a little flutter of anticipation. Bow Street would send their best men to investigate this crime. She knew who it would be.

The delicious scent of strongly brewed coffee and the babble of conversation escaped from the front door of the London Coffee House, which took up two adjoining properties at numbers 24 and 26. Her stomach grumbled longingly. The next shop, Isherwood & Sons, House Decorators, held a display of hand-painted oriental wallpaper, and Emmy suppressed a smile at the odd name of the alley leading off it: Naked Boy Court. London's streets were a never-ending treasure trove of bizarre names. Surely there was an amusing story behind that one.

They still weren't close enough to see inside Rundell & Bridge. Emmy paused to inspect the bonnets displayed in the premises of Charles Vyse, straw hat manufacturer, then admired the silk stockings in the bow window of Ebenezer Flint, Hosier and General Outfitter. They passed the premises of Mr. Sharp, Perfumer to His Royal Highness the Prince of Wales, and finally stopped in front of

Mr. Blade's lighting emporium, directly across the street from the focus of her insatiable curiosity.

"I don't know what you hope to achieve by coming here, my love," Camille murmured. "Luc is correct. The theft went off without a hitch. Why return to the scene of the crime?"

Emmy barely heard her. A dark, masculine shape was inside the shop, talking to Mr. Rundell's mild-mannered nephew, Edmond. She squinted, using the reflection of the window and the shiny surfaces of the lights displayed in front of her to glimpse a tantalizing flash of broad back and dark blue tailcoat.

Tall, slim, brown-haired. Her heart skipped a beat.

The man turned, and her suspicions were confirmed; Alexander Harland's handsome reflection was magnified a hundred times, duplicated in the myriad faceted glass droplets of the chandelier before her. As if one version weren't dazzling enough.

She sipped in a breath. Harland always dressed immaculately. Crisp white cuffs, snowy cravat, beautifully cut jacket that outlined his impressively large physique. Buff breeches that molded almost indecently to his long, muscular legs. Black hessian boots polished to a military shine.

"Ah." Camille gave a wry, worldly chuckle. "*Now* I see the appeal."

Camille was, in her own words, a "connoisseur of gentlemen." Having been born into the French aristocracy, she'd been a friend of Queen Marie Antoinette and had spent her youth flirting and intriguing at the glittering court of Versailles. Entirely pragmatic about marrying for financial security, she'd wed her first husband, the wealthy Comte de Rougemont, thirty years her senior, when she was only seventeen. He'd died of an apoplexy three months after the wedding, leaving Camille a very rich, very merry widow.

Her second husband, Le Chevalier Hugo, had been "an

absolute rake, but impossibly charming." Camille had seemed genuinely fond of him. "There was never a dull moment with Hugo," she often said. "Of course, then he went and fell from his horse. I *told* him it wasn't wise to take that fence after a second bottle of Burgundy, but the fool wouldn't listen. Ah, well. I suppose it was all for the best. After all, if darling Hugo hadn't broken his neck, I'd never have met your grandfather, would I?"

Emmy's grandfather had been the last of the countess's husbands, and by all accounts, it had been *une affaire de coeur.* Her grandmother, having fled the Revolution and settled in England, had taken one look at Anthony d'Anvers—dashing diplomatic aide and fellow French exile—at the ambassador's reception and fallen "head over heels." Emmy's father had been born a slightly scandalous eight months after their wedding.

Having found bliss in the arms of a wonderful husband, Camille's goal in life was to see Emmy equally happily settled. She was entirely dismissive of powdered, fashionable dandies and held a great appreciation for rakes, rogues, and scoundrels of all kinds. She was especially fond of a man in military uniform.

Her sharp elbow jostled Emmy's ribs. "Enlighten me, Emmeline. Who is that wonderful specimen?"

Emmy sighed. She might as well make a clean breast of it. There was no keeping secrets from Camille. "That 'specimen' is Alexander Harland, Lord Melton."

Camille gave an appreciative sigh as she half-turned to study him covertly. "Ooh la la. I congratulate you, Emmeline. Your taste is superb. *Quel homme*!"

Camille always became more French whenever she was excited.

Emmy frowned at Harland's reflection. He was preparing to leave; he'd picked up his gloves from the counter. "Unfortunately, Lord Melton is an obstacle we must avoid if we wish to keep our heads. I've heard that he and his two friends, Benedict Wylde and Sebastien Wolff, are employed by Bow Street to solve crimes just like this one. I was afraid he would become involved."

Camille nodded sagely. "I see. We stand forewarned."

A glistening black carriage pulled up outside the jewelers and blocked their view. Unable to resist one final glimpse of her nemesis, Emmy tugged Camille across the street and around the back of the carriage. The coachman had already let down the step, and her heart almost stopped as the door to the jeweler's opened and Harland strode out.

In sudden panic, she lowered her chin so her parasol shielded her face. She grabbed Camille's elbow and swung them both away, feigning a rapt fascination in an enameled snuff box in the window. From the corner of her eye, she saw a flash of blue, caught a waft of masculine scent that made her stomach clench in agitation, before Harland jumped inside the waiting carriage and rapped on the roof to signal he was ready.

Her heart assumed an unnaturally fast rhythm.

What was she doing? She should be running away from the man, not trying to get closer. She had, after all, perfected the skill of walking away.

In a heist, there was always a moment when one had to commit past the point of no return. No matter how well-planned, every job contained an element of the unknown: a random passerby, an unexpected delivery, a servant who suddenly changed their routine. Every job was different, with its own personality, and Emmy had learned to trust her instincts when it came to assessing risk. Luck was as important as skill. There was nothing cowardly in retreating, in living to steal another day. On several occasions she'd abandoned a theft because something didn't feel right.

Everything about Alexander Harland warned her to run. Instinct told her that here was a man who would bring her nothing but trouble, not least because of the dangerous frisson of attraction that drew her to him utterly against her will. It was a matter of self-preservation, the very reason she'd walked away from him four years ago.

The day she heard he'd returned from Waterloo had been one of the happiest of her life. She was fiercely glad that he was alive, saddened to learn that he'd been injured. She'd managed to glimpse him across a crowded ballroom. Apart from a small scar by his right temple, there seemed to be very little physical evidence of his injury, but rumor said he'd lost a degree of peripheral vision in his right eye due to a cannon blast. That, at least, was the excuse he used for his current refusal to dance.

The Alexander Harland she'd kissed had been a cheeky, confident, young man. The Alexander Harland who'd returned looked older, wiser. He smiled less frequently. And he'd acquired a new cynicism, a certain hardness to his chiseled features. He had a bleak, weary look in his eyes, as if he'd seen far more of life than he'd ever desired.

His opening of a gambling club in St. James's had come as no surprise to her. Such a scandalous profession, skirting the very edges of what was socially acceptable yet pandering to the aristocracy's never-ending desire for novelty and entertainment, seemed entirely fitting with his character.

A few months ago he and his fellow club owners, Benedict Wylde and Sebastien Wolff, has been awarded earldoms by the Prince Regent for "services to the crown." Rumors had circulated in the *ton* for weeks that they were working for Bow Street, and those rumors had been echoed by Sally's network of friends and informants amongst London's criminal fraternity.

They were truly on opposite sides of the law now, the

Runner and the thief. And despite her undeniable attraction to the man, the more distance she put between them the better.

Emmy sighed. A Welsh acquaintance of hers had introduced her to the word *hiraeth*. It had no direct translation in English, but it seemed wholly appropriate to describe her feelings about Harland. The word expressed a bittersweet sense of missing something or someone that you'd loved, while still being grateful for their existence. A longing for home, or a time that felt like home.

Four years ago, at nineteen, she'd felt at home in Harland's arms. She'd imagined herself in love with him, but it had been a childish infatuation. She hadn't known the real Alex Harland. She'd loved an illusion, the handsome paragon she'd made up in her mind. Their dance, their kiss, was frozen in time like a perfect vision, a moment that would never be repeated.

She was older now, and wiser. A little more cynical about life and men. A little more realistic about fairy-tale princes.

The snap of a whip and the shout of Harland's carriage driver jolted Emmy back to the present. Amazed at her own inattention, she caught Camille's elbow, turned her back on Harland's conveyance, and marched them both swiftly away down the street.

Alex sat back against the seats with a deep exhale. When he breathed back in, a waft of feminine scent, something floral and unique, teased his nostrils and his heart gave an unsteady, disbelieving jolt. In the space of a single breath, he was transported to a moonlit garden, kissing the woman of his dreams.

His mouth dropped open. That perfume. Unmistakable. It was *her!*

He lurched forward and thrust his head out of the

carriage window, craning his neck to identify the source of the scent.

Had he just passed her on the street? There had been a couple of women looking in Rundell & Bridge's window, but he'd been so preoccupied with what he'd learned about the robbery that he'd barely glanced at them. The women had been on his right, in the black spot of his peripheral vision.

The carriage was pulling away from the curb. Alex cursed. Countless women thronged the street, a flurry of skirts and parasols in every pastel shade.

Which one was she?

He almost pulled the strap to stop the carriage, then imagined himself sprinting down Ludgate Hill, grasping each woman by the shoulders and spinning her around, peering into her face in some vain hope of recognition. Sniffing her wrist for evidence of that elusive, maddening perfume.

The image was sufficiently ludicrous to make him emit a laughing groan.

He was going mad. The possibility didn't seem unlikely, considering the things he'd witnessed during the war. Sometimes madness sounded like a pleasant escape from reality.

His mind was playing tricks on him. The woman he'd dreamed of didn't exist. Maybe she'd only ever been a figment of his imagination.

He inhaled again, but the scent was gone. All he could smell was coffee and horse sweat, tobacco and refuse. He sat back heavily against the velvet swabs and ran his hand over his face. He had work to do. A criminal to catch. A diamond to recover. He didn't have time for other distractions.

Chapter 4.

"So, what did you learn at Rundell and Bridge?" Seb asked as Alex strode into the Tricorn's private salon a short while later. "How did our thief get in?"

"He had himself delivered."

Seb, seated at the dining table with a plate of ham and eggs, raised his brows in silent question.

"The Belle Sauvage," Alex explained. "It's the coaching inn located directly behind the jeweler. The Nightjar hid himself in an empty beer barrel and had himself delivered to the Belle Sauvage on a vintner's wagon. According to the hostlers, the place is always teeming with people, so there's no way of knowing exactly when that was. Either way, the barrel was taken down to the cellar, the southernmost wall of which is shared with the basement of Rundell and Bridge."

Seb smiled, obviously impressed, and took another bite of ham. "Most enterprising."

"Our thief climbed out of his barrel, removed the few bricks that separated the wine cellar from the jeweler to make a small opening—which he concealed with another stack of barrels—and climbed through into the shop."

"Did you look at the barrel? A brewery name might help."

"I thought of that. It was sent from the entirely fictitious 'Black Feather Brewery.' Our thief has a sense of humor."

"Huh. How did he get into the safe?"

Alex shook his head. "Used a key, if you can believe it. When I questioned the irascible Rundell Senior and his far-more-pleasant nephew about any unusual incidents, they both recalled an elderly lady who'd fainted outside the shop the day before the robbery. The lady's companion asked whether they could sit inside while her friend recovered from her light-headedness. Rundell Senior produced some smelling salts and summoned a doctor. Rundell Junior, it seems, was more than a little taken with the companion. He gave me an excellent description of her ample bosom and charming dimples."

"I assume she was the distraction?" Seb chuckled.

"Indeed. It seems the Nightjar has some female accomplices. Since the key to the safe is still in Rundell's possession, the Nightjar must have used a copy. One of the women must have managed to make an impression of it in a piece of wax or soap while the men were distracted. At any rate, the lady 'recovered' before the physician arrived, and they left the scene in a hired hackney."

"So the Nightjar opened the safe, stole the diamond, and left a black feather in its place?"

"Precisely." Alex helped himself to a plate of eggs from the covered dishes on the sideboard and sat at the dining table next to Seb. "The owner of the stone was none other than our very own Prince Regent, although he hadn't actually paid for it yet. Rundell was quite tight-lipped, but I persuaded him to tell me what he knew. The

Prince was having it made into a necklace for his mistress Maria Fitzherbert."

"I thought he'd given her up long ago?"

"Apparently not. And that's not the half of it. According to Rundell, the *vendor* of the diamond is none other than Prinny's own wife, Princess Caroline. Both sides swore Rundell to secrecy. She told Rundell she was given it by her father, the Duke of Brunswick."

Seb let out a long, low whistle. "Now that *is* awkward.

"As you can imagine, Conant's keen to keep the whole thing under wraps to avoid any scandal."

Seb crossed to the bow-fronted sideboard and picked up a sheaf of papers. "He sent these over while you were out. Lord Sidmouth, at the Home Office, has been in contact with our counterparts across the channel. He asked for any information they had on the Nightjar, and got this from Eugène Vidocq."

Alex grimaced. "Not five minutes ago the French were our mortal enemies. Now we're swapping information like one big happy family." His tone was bitter. "It's as if the past ten years of bloody warfare never happened."

"It is hard to forget, when you think of all the men we lost—"

"Harder still when you've got a blind spot as a daily reminder of French 'hospitality.'"

Alex sighed. Enough. The war had been over for almost a year. The world was a different place. He had to move on. "What did the head of the Sûreté have to say about his fellow countryman?" he asked dryly. "As an ex-criminal himself, one can only assume he's all admiration for the man's skill."

The French head of police, Vidocq, was a most unusual character. He'd passed the first half of his adult life as a soldier, thief, smuggler, gambler, and convict. He'd escaped from one prison after another, often through the use of ingenious disguises. A decade ago, while still locked up in La Force, he'd begun to pass along cellblock gossip to the authorities. Later, when a set of emeralds belonging to the Empress Josephine went missing, Napoleon—under the logic of using a thief to catch a thief—tasked Vidocq with investigating the crime. Vidocq used his underworld contacts, his keen observational skills, and the previously unheard-of technique of undercover investigation, to track down Josephine's emeralds, the thieves, and their buyers, in less than three days. He earned both a formal pardon and the Emperor's continued favor.

In keeping with the man's rather warped sense of humor, he'd begun a new career with the Paris police, at first informing on his former companions in crime, then tracking down the culprits behind various robberies and killings. Within a year, he'd founded a plain-clothes unit called the Brigade de la Sûreté and become its first chief. He regularly hired ex-convicts and prostitutes as agents and attempted to prevent crimes, not just solve them. Under his command, the Sûreté had captured thousands of criminals over the past few years.

"Funny you should say that," Seb said, tapping the folder with his hand. "Conant seems to think that Vidocq never tried very hard to catch the Nightjar. Sounds like he has a certain professional respect for the man."

He paused, and Alex narrowed his eyes. Seb was deliberately withholding information for dramatic effect.

"And?" Alex prompted.

"He *did*, however, have a suspicion as to who the Nightjar might be. An aristocrat named Louis d'Anvers. The son of the Comtesse de Rougemont."

Alex exhaled slowly. "That's not a name I'm familiar with."

"He was born here in England. The family changed the name to Danvers to sound more English." Seb opened the file and selected a handwritten report. "Unfortunately, Louis d'Anvers died four years ago. So even if he *was* the Nightjar, he can't have committed the Rundell and Bridge job last night."

Alex held out his hand for the folder of documents and skimmed through them.

"What of the rest of the family?"

"Danvers's mother, the comtesse, is still alive. Danvers married one Emily Chadwyck, a gentleman's daughter from Leicestershire. They had two children, a boy and a girl. The wife died giving birth to a stillborn son when the daughter was only three years old. The children live with their grandmother in Waverton Street, between Hyde Park and Berkeley Square. The son is thirty, the daughter, twenty-three."

"The son could have reprised his father's role. Or this new theft could be a copycat crime."

"The Nightjar is dead; long live the Nightjar," Seb said wryly.

Alex extracted a yellowed newspaper clipping from the file. He began to read, and his eyebrows rose in surprise. "The man's identity isn't the only lead Vidocq's given us. We have a motive here too. Look at this."

He angled the page toward Seb. It was an excerpt from *La Mercure,* the Parisian newspaper, dated April 1800; sixteen years ago. The headline was *"J'accuse—!"*

The Nightjar had written an open letter to the editor, publicly denouncing revolutionary leader Georges Danton as a traitor to France. He claimed the theft of the French crown jewels from the Louvre had been an inside job, masterminded by Danton himself. The jewels, he said, had been used as bribes to purchase support for the Republique and, later, for the Emperor Napoleon, from foreign powers such as the Austrians and the Prussians.

"*I vow to steal back our country's bounty from those who have received it unjustly,*" the Nightjar had written. "*The jewels shall be recovered for the glory of France and held secure until the upstart Napoleon has been ousted and the Bourbons are once more restored to their rightful place upon the throne.*"

Alex sat back in his chair with a slow exhale. As a declaration of intent, it was certainly impressive.

On the following page Vidocq had compiled a list of the jewels missing from the national archives and correlated them with the gems the Nightjar was known to have stolen. They matched perfectly. The Nightjar had, apparently, been doing exactly as he'd promised.

"The thefts aren't random at all," Alex said. "He's stealing back the crown jewels of France."

"Exactly."

Alex pointed at one of the lines on the list. "The diamond taken from Rundell and Bridge must be this one the French call the 'Regent's Diamond.' Which means there are only three major jewels still unaccounted for. The blue diamond they call the 'Bleu Du Roi,' a ruby, and a thirty-carat sapphire known as the 'Ruspoli.'" He flipped through the remaining pages. "Do we know the location of these three jewels?"

Seb leaned back in his chair with a satisfied grin. "As a matter of fact, we do. Vidocq didn't discover where any of the jewels had gone until Napoleon declared a twenty-year statute of limitations on crimes committed during the Revolution. Since the original theft occurred in 1792, that meant nobody could be prosecuted for the crime after 1812. As the deadline neared, Vidocq told his agents to listen out for information regarding the gems. Sure enough, not two days after the statute of limitations expired, a London jeweler named John Francillon sold a forty-five-carat blue diamond to the diamond merchant

Daniel Eliason. Vidocq believes that stone is the 'Bleu Du Roi,' cut down and reshaped to disguise its origins."

"Where is it now?"

Seb tapped another piece of paper. "Eliason failed to find a buyer. Perhaps afraid of having it stolen from his own premises, he decided on what you might call the old 'hide-in-plain-sight' tactic. He loaned it to the British Museum. For the past three years, it's been on public display in their rocks and minerals gallery."

Alex couldn't prevent a chuckle. "Clever. And what of the others?"

"The ruby has been incorporated into a necklace that was purchased by Lord Carrington for his wife, Lady Sophia. She's worn it on numerous occasions in public. During the season, they reside on Park Crescent. The sapphire, according to Vidocq's sources, is in the possession of a disgraced Italian diplomat named Franco Andretti who now lives in a small village just outside Gravesend."

Alex took a deep draught of wine. "If this information is correct—and provided this new Nightjar has the same goal as his predecessor—then we have an excellent chance of predicting where he'll strike next."

"Indeed we do."

"All right, then. Tomorrow we'll investigate the security arrangements at both the British Museum and the Carringtons' town house. And I want to know more about the family of Louis d'Anvers. Especially his son. Do they ever attend any functions in the *ton*? Do we have any common acquaintances who might make an introduction?"

Seb shot him a cocky grin. "I knew you'd say that, so I strolled over to visit my great-aunt Dorothea, the Dread Dowager Duchess, this morning. She expressed amazement at seeing me clothed, shaved, and sober before midday. The old battle-ax knows everybody in the *ton*, and she has the memory of an elephant. Never forgets a thing. She's like a walking, talking Debrett's."

Alex gestured for Seb to get on with it.

"Turns out Dorothea is good friends with the comtesse. She couldn't believe I'd never made her acquaintance, although she did concede that being absent for three years 'fighting that odious Bonaparte' was a partial excuse. She confidently expects to see the comtesse and her grandchildren this very evening at Caroline Turnbull's soirée."

Alex smiled. "I'm sure Caroline will be delighted to see us."

Chapter 5.

Lady Caroline Turnbull's soirée was fashionably crowded by the time Emmy, Luc, and Camille arrived. The sound of animated chatter and a lively English reel greeted them, and Emmy wasted no time in finding a vacant chair at the side of the room for Luc.

After twelve years, he walked with only the slightest limp and required no one's arm for support. He did use an elegant silver-topped cane, but that was more for ornament than necessity. He was convinced it gave him a rakish edge. Sally mocked him about it constantly.

His injury had been caused by grapeshot—a bag of musket balls set on iron rings that when fired from a ship-mounted cannon resulted in a supersized blast. Luc was fortunate not to have bled to death on the deck, but thankfully the surgeon who'd operated on him had been experienced in dealing with such wounds. Emmy had read about many other poor souls who'd ended up with what they called a "sugar loaf stump," an amputation performed too close to the bone, resulting in a conical stump which was difficult to heal.

Since Luc was missing only the lower portion of his leg, Camille had instructed a Jermyn Street shoemaker to fashion him a prosthetic foot with a jointed ankle made from wood and leather. It had taken Luc some time to grow accustomed to the contraption—he'd spent many hours leaning heavily on Emmy or Sally and cursing his inability to balance—but now he walked with a confidence that showed little hint of the struggle he'd endured. Emmy had nothing but respect for the way he'd dealt with such a dramatic change in his life.

Even so, she had no doubt their father's criminal escapades, and her own "miseducation," had provided her brother with a welcome diversion during his long convalescence. He'd needed something to engage his clever mind. Helping to plan the next heist had stopped him from dwelling on his injury.

With Luc suitably settled, Emmy accepted a glass of champagne from a passing servant and proceeded to make herself inconspicuous.

In the animal kingdom, especially when surrounded by carnivores, one of the best strategies is to fade into the background and disappear. She had become adept at avoiding notice, like one of those color-changing lizards she'd seen at the Exeter Exchange. It was not that the *ton* itself provided any specific threat, but she was ever-conscious of the fact that she was unlike any other woman in the room. She had far more to hide than a penchant for gambling or an illicit assignation with someone else's husband. She couldn't afford to let anyone get too close, for fear they would uncover her secrets. Her family had to be protected.

Clusters of people formed, separated, and reformed

like the jewel-colored contents of a kaleidoscope. Camille came to stand beside her, and together they looked out over the crush of dancers.

"Lord Eversleigh is here," Camille murmured, and Emmy didn't bother to suppress a groan. The man was a corseted fool who persisted in pursuing her despite a complete lack of encouragement.

"He doesn't even notice when I'm being rude to him," Emmy whispered back. "He never listens to a word I say. He just stands there and stares at my décolletage."

"He's very rich."

"He's the most patronizing man I have ever encountered."

Camille cast a subtly scornful glance at the man who was still half the room away. "I quite agree. No amount of money could make up for having to face *that* over the breakfast table for the next thirty years."

Eversleigh considered himself a veritable tulip of fashion. His startling green-and-pink-striped waistcoat was festooned with fob chains and pocket watches. A sparkling diamond stick pin secured the cravat at his throat. Marcasite buckles dazzled on his shoes. Emmy liked to amuse herself by imagining precisely how she would deprive him of every item of jewelry he owned.

"I vow, if the Nightjar weren't such a noble thief, he would pay my Lord Eversleigh a visit," she whispered. She could retire for life on the fripperies with which he decorated his person. "He doesn't know me, nor does he have the slightest desire to do so. He just wants another ornament in his life, one without an opinion, who will not question, demand, or make scenes. I think we can both agree that I am *not* that woman."

"And what about Bantam?"

Emmy sighed at the mention of her sweet, persistent suitor. Edward Bantam was a thoroughly nice man. Utterly inoffensive, he'd hovered around her for years, and while not possessed of a rapier wit, he was still a perfectly decent catch. He could always be counted on to ask a lady to dance or to procure another cup of lemonade. He just didn't make her heart flutter and her stomach drop away.

The way Harland did.

"I wish I could feel more for him than friendship," she whispered. "But I can't. If I accepted him, we'd both be miserable. And besides, he would be horrified if he ever discovered the truth about me. He's an upstanding citizen. He's probably never broken a law in his life. Even if I *wanted* to trust him, how does one introduce such a topic into casual conversation? 'Oh, yes, I'd love a second cup of tea, and—did I mention?—I'm an internationally wanted jewel thief.'" She shook her head with a wry smile. "He'd probably turn me in himself."

"I want to see you settled," Camille murmured. "I'm not getting any younger. I want to see your children." She fanned herself vigorously. "The problem, of course, is that you are uncommonly beautiful."

Emmy almost choked on her champagne. "*You* are biased," she countered. "I'm pretty at best."

"Bah. I've seen half a century of beauties at the most glittering courts in Europe. Believe me when I say, even allowing for a little natural familial bias, that you are *très belle*, Emmeline."

Emmy felt her cheeks heat. "I'm sure that's why we've been almost trampled underfoot by the stampede of gentlemen all rushing to offer for me these past few years," she said dryly.

Camille shrugged. "Most men are fools. They're too blind to appreciate what is right in front of them. You're subtle. They overlook you because you downplay your beauty. But one of these days, you're going to encounter a connoisseur who'll see what you're trying to hide. Your aloofness will only intrigue him. He will be drawn to the mystery."

"I don't wish to be a mystery! We don't want anyone looking at me too closely. Think how dangerous that could be."

"It would be better if you were plainer," Camille agreed placidly. "Martha there"—she indicated a pleasant-faced woman to their right who was tapping her foot in time to the music—"she would be an excellent thief. Forgettable, nothing out of the ordinary. Interchangeable with a thousand nursemaids and governesses."

"My front tooth is crooked," Emmy persisted.

Camille gave her fan a dismissive flick. "That one tiny imperfection that only makes you more perfect."

Emmy was about to argue, but at that moment, the footman stationed at the top of the stairs announced in stentorian tones: "The Earl of Melton and the Earl of Mowbray."

Her heart leaped into her throat.

Alex paused at the top of the stairs. He disliked crowds, hated it when people approached him from his blind side. He didn't like being ambushed, especially by matchmaking mamas with empty-headed debutantes in tow, or bored married ladies looking for a little excitement. He'd taken to positioning himself with a wall, or Seb, on his right.

At least he didn't have to dance. The first time he'd attempted it, shortly after he'd returned from Belgium, he'd discovered that while he could see perfectly well straight ahead, his lack of vision to the right meant he was unable to see his partner's hand when she held it up to hold. He kept bumping into people if they happened to spin too close to him on that side.

The final straw had been when he'd accidentally

groped Lady Worthington's breast during a particularly lively reel. Lady Worthington hadn't minded one bit, and he'd spent the rest of the evening having to endure excruciatingly overt come-hither looks, right under the nose of her fiercely protective husband.

Alex had avoided dancing after that. He was damned if he'd be called out for besmirching the honor of some innocent young thing merely because his hand happened to fasten on somewhere inappropriate.

"God, what a crush," Seb muttered as they threaded their way toward the far wall, pausing to nod or exchange a few brief pleasantries with various acquaintances. They stationed themselves to the left of the orchestra, with an arched alcove at their backs, and surveyed the assembled crowd.

"I spoke to Caroline," Seb said over the din. "The Danverses are here. She said the son would probably be seated. And the countess is wearing a powder-pink gown."

Alex arched his head to see over the dancers and studied the chairs set up along the opposite side of the room. He dismissed several pink-gowned women as too young, and then his eye was caught by an elderly lady standing next to a handsome, seated man. The dowager's snow-white hair had been arranged in an upswept style, and while she was obviously of advanced years, it was clear she had once been a great beauty. She retained a certain ingrained elegance.

Seb followed his gaze. "That's them. The son's called Luc. And Vidocq's file omitted one crucial fact that puts paid to your theory he's the new Nightjar. The man's an amputee. Lost his right foot at Trafalgar."

Alex studied him. They were of a similar age, a similar height. Luc Danvers did not appear to be lacking a foot; he must have adopted a prosthesis, like so many others Alex had encountered since the war. A faint bump under his breeches, just below the knee, seemed to confirm that notion.

"He's almost as tall as either of us." Alex frowned. "And broad. Even if he wasn't missing a foot, he'd never have been able to fold himself into that beer barrel at Rundell and Bridge. Whoever we're looking for, they're smaller than that."

"What about the daughter?" Seb asked. "Standing next to her grandmother. Her name is Emmeline."

Alex moved his eyes to the right and froze.

Amidst the ever-moving gaiety of the ballroom, the woman was standing perfectly still, a sliver of darkness among all the frilly pastels. She was no debutante in ice blue or delicate pink, nor like the matrons in their somber greys and browns. Her dress was midnight blue, so dark it was almost black. Unfussy, unadorned with either ruffles or frills, it was striking in its elegant simplicity.

Alex narrowed his eyes, trying to discern her features. She'd chosen a place in the most shadowed part of the room.

She was a little over five feet. Her face was elfin, with a small nose, a softly pointed chin, and the hint of a smile at the edge of her lips. She looked playful, mischievous. As if she knew an amusing secret and didn't want to share.

A flash of desire quickened his pulse. The woman's sly merriment was oddly attractive. He couldn't make out the color of her eyes from this distance, but her teeth flashed white as she smiled at something her brother said.

It was clear that she and the man were siblings. They were both attractive, with the same tilt of eyebrow, high cheekbones, and brown hair. And yet one version was undoubtedly masculine while the other was unmistakably feminine.

Alex watched as the foppish Lord Eversleigh approached the trio. Eversleigh was rich; he regularly lost hundreds of pounds when he played at the Tricorn, usually because he was so often in his cups. His weaving course across the room suggested he'd already sampled Lord Turnbull's hospitality to the hilt.

He kissed the countess's hand with a flourish, then turned his attention to the younger woman. After kissing her hand too, he proceeded to address his comments to her bosom, waving his lace-edged handkerchief in the air for emphasis. Her mouth adopted a faint curl of disdain, and Alex felt his own lips quirk in response. She was not impressed with the boorish Eversleigh. An astute judge of character, then.

"*She's* small enough to fit in a barrel," Alex murmured.

Chapter 6.

Alex watched the young woman, trying to place her in the role of thief. It was unlikely that someone from the midst of the *ton* should have adopted such an unlawful sideline, but not impossible.

The fact that her family had wealth was significant, since the Nightjar didn't seem to profit from his crimes. His thefts were based on high-minded patriotic principle.

Three years of warfare had shown Alex that noble concepts like honor and justice were used only by those who could afford them. To a starving man, or a woman desperate for medicine for her sick child, the moral argument of whether stealing was wrong took second place to necessity.

Was Miss Danvers bored? In need of a challenge? Alex could sympathize with that sentiment. He worked for Bow Street even though he didn't need the money. His investment in the Tricorn too gave him a great deal of satisfaction. He relished the challenge of managing the place alongside Benedict and Seb.

Women of the *ton* had it far worse than men. Most of them were expected to do little else in life but attract a wealthy suitor—preferably one with a title—and settle down to a life of dreary domesticity while producing the next generation of aristocrats. He could hardly blame Miss Danvers if she craved a little excitement. But the law was the law.

Alex's mouth curved in a faint cynical smile as her gaze swept the room over Eversleigh's shoulder. She was cataloguing the exit points. As a soldier, a sniper, he automatically did the same thing, whether at the opera or a dockside tavern. He scanned for the highest vantage points too, the best place from which to take a shot. The stage, a balcony, a raised terrace. Seb and Benedict did it too. Old habits died hard.

Was it because she wanted to escape from the obnoxious Eversleigh? Or was it the ingrained habit of a thief? Alex watched her note the tall sash windows, the servants' door partially disguised in the papered wall to her left, the door to the dining room, and the double doors that led out onto the terrace.

A thief would hate to be cornered. A thief would always want to know his options for escape.

Her options, he amended silently. Her name was Emmeline. Emmeline Danvers.

Could she be the Nightjar?

The idea of being the one to corner her sent a shiver of excitement through him. It was more than the mere thought of bringing a miscreant to justice. The delicious possibility that his thief might turn out to be this attractive young woman gave him an almost sexual thrill.

Alex shook his head. He'd been too long without a woman. It had been almost a month since he'd given Alicia her marching orders.

He glanced over at the girl again and his blood surged

in anticipation. He'd never desired any of the criminals he'd been after before—not entirely surprising considering they were usually unwashed smugglers, pox-ridden whores, and toothless crones. His attraction wouldn't sway him or distract him from his goal, of course, but it would certainly add a little piquancy to the game.

"Do you know what a nightjar *is*?" Seb asked suddenly. "I looked it up this afternoon. It's a nocturnal bird. Its plumage is brown and speckled and resembles bark or leaves. It is exceptionally good at blending into its environment."

Emmeline Danvers was doing an admirable job of effacing herself on the other side of the room. She blended into the shadows beautifully.

"They're found all around the world," Seb continued, "and are mostly active in the late evening, early morning, and at night. That describes our thief rather well, don't you think?"

"It does indeed." Alex smiled.

Emmy could barely concentrate.

She'd followed Harland's progress through the room, watched as he directed that easy charm at everyone in his path. He knew just what to say. How to flatter, how to charm, and then skillfully extricate himself, leaving them wanting more.

He looked devastatingly handsome in his black evening jacket, a fact that irritated her no end. No man should look that good, especially one she was trying her best to ignore. She watched with hot envy as he bent his dark head toward a jewel-bedecked woman and laughed at something she said. Jealousy gnawed at her stomach when the woman's hand lingered playfully on his shoulder, then slid down his shirt front in a familiar caress.

When he stepped away, he took up a position almost directly opposite her.

Her skin pricked with an uncomfortable awareness.

He was watching her; she was sure of it.

Her heart began to pound in alarm. She felt his gaze like a touch all the way down her body, from her hair, over her breasts, waist, legs, and back up.

You're imagining things. He's not looking at you. He doesn't know you exist.

Almost against her will, she glanced up, certain she would find herself mistaken. His gaze would be centered on some other hapless female.

Her entire body jolted in shock as his eyes clashed with hers.

The intensity of his stare made her stomach knot and the hairs rise on her arms. A sense of dread squeezed her chest, as if she'd spotted a highwayman on the crest of a hill or the sails of a pirate brig on the horizon. She *knew* she would be the next victim.

She was being ridiculous.

She wanted to run, but she seemed incapable of looking away. Incapable of even blinking. Did no one else notice him staring at her so fixedly?

His brows rose in a subtle challenge, as if daring her to be the first to look away, and her own innate stubbornness kicked in. A modest young woman would have hidden her blushing face behind her fan. Emmy held his gaze, refusing to allow him to intimidate her.

Blood rushed into her cheeks and she experienced an odd, weightless feeling. Every instinct urged her to lower her lashes and escape the piercing concentration of his gaze. She felt pinned, like a moth on a naturalist's mountboard.

Then his lips quirked upward, and she watched in

astonishment as a smile transformed his face. In the space of a heartbeat he went from coldly austere, almost accusing, to breathtakingly handsome. Her heart missed a beat.

"Em! You're woolgathering again."

Luc's exclamation freed her from Harland's visual snare. She turned away, unaccountably flustered, as air rushed back into her lungs. She'd done nothing to attract his notice. Why was he singling her out now, after all this time? It couldn't possibly bode well.

"We should leave."

Luc raised his brows. "But we haven't even had dinner. I heard a rumor there was flan—"

"Lord Melton's watching me. He's over there, by the orchestra, with his friend Lord Mowbray."

Luc was too intelligent to turn his head and look. He merely nodded and smiled, as if still engrossed in conversation. "Ah. Do we know why?"

"It is entirely possible that her face and person have attracted his notice," Camille said. "From what I hear, Lord Melton is one of those connoisseurs we were discussing earlier."

"I don't think that's likely," Emmy breathed. "The man's been linked with some of the most beautiful women in town. I hardly think he'd spare me a glance. If I've gained his attention, it's because he's suspicious, not amorous."

"Did he see you at Rundell and Bridge this morning?" Luc asked sharply. "I told you it was a bad idea."

"I am certain he did not." Emmy maintained her smile despite her irritation. "Give me some credit. But still, I think it would be wise to leave now. I do not relish the thought of being cornered by him at the buffet."

Luc nodded. "Agreed. 'Discretion is the better part of valor,' as Shakespeare said. Help me rise. We can make our escape as soon as dinner is called. My desire for flan will have to wait."

With perfect timing, two servants appeared at the doors that led into Lady Turnbull's dining room and announced that supper was served. Emmy, Luc, and Camille used the mass exodus to wend their way across the ballroom. It was slow going; everyone was trying to go in the opposite direction. Emmy turned to locate Harland and discovered that he, too, was pushing his way through the crowd, making a beeline directly for her.

The thought was enough to give her steps an extra urgency. She ushered Luc up the stairs, silently cursing his slowness, and glanced back again, her heart in her throat, certain that Harland would be upon them.

But fate, it seemed, was on her side. The Dowager Duchess of Winwick, his companion's great-aunt, had waylaid them. Good manners dictated the two men stop and acknowledge the woman, and Emmy smiled when she saw the delighted dowager clasp the elbows of both Harland and her nephew in her gnarly fingers so they could escort her in to dinner.

She spent the trip home to Waverton Street trying to dismiss Harland's attention as mere coincidence. Doubtless he used the same tactic to put wallflowers such as herself out of countenance. It was probably a game between himself and Wolff, to see which ladies they could discompose the quickest.

The coach had barely pulled up at the front steps when Sally appeared at the door, looking uncharacteristically agitated. She must have been listening for the carriage. She ushered them into the front parlor.

Luc lowered himself into a chair with a grimace. "What's wrong, Sal?"

"We've had a visitor."

Camille glanced at the clock on the mantel. "At this hour? It's almost midnight."

"That's what I tried to tell 'im," Sally said, sinking into the vacant seat beside Luc. "But the gentleman"—she spat the word like an insult—"was insistent."

"Who was it?" Emmy asked.

"Yer blackmailin' Frenchie, that's who."

Camille sucked in a shocked breath, and Luc's hand clenched on the arm of his chair. "Danton? He didn't hurt you, did he? By God, if he did—"

Sally shook her head. "Nah. 'E were pleasant enough. Too pleasant, if you ask me. I seen 'is kind at the theatre. The quiet ones are always the ones to watch. They smile as they slip a knife between yer ribs."

"What does he look like?" Emmy asked.

"Middling height, smaller than Luc by a few inches, I'd say. Brown hair, cut short. Bit of a doughy face—makes his eyes look piggy. And 'is mouth is girly-looking. He has a pretty cupid's bow on top and a pouty lower lip. Looks like a spoiled child."

"What did he say?"

"'E was sorry to have missed you." Sally curled her lip. "He'd read about the Rundell and Bridge job and wanted to congratulate you."

Luc snorted. "Did he ask for the diamond?"

"'E asked if I had anythin' to give him, but I told 'im I didn't know nothin' about nobody. Said 'e should come back at a more reasonable hour." Sally grinned, but then her expression sobered. "'E said he'd be back. And that he wanted to be readin' about the British Museum as soon as could be, or people might get hurt."

Luc's head snapped up. "He threatened you?"

Sally rested her hand on his sleeve. "I'm a big girl, Luc Danvers. I've dealt with worse than 'im in Limehouse."

Luc clenched his jaw, and an angry flush pinked his

cheekbones. He touched his fingers to the back of Sally's hand.

"I hate that he tried to scare you," he said softly. "I'm sorry I wasn't here."

Sally covered his hand with her own and smiled back at him, and for a moment the two of them seemed to forget Emmy and Camille were in the room. Then Sally rose, brushing her skirts in a brisk, no-nonsense manner. "Well, I'm glad you weren't 'ere. You'd probably 'ave skewered 'im with that sword-stick of yours and then where would we be? None of you lot know 'ow 'ard it is to get bloodstains out of a cream carpet."

Emmy rubbed her throbbing temples. Danton's sudden appearance, combined with her unsettling encounter with Harland, had resulted in a pounding headache. "Surely Danton knows we can't just rob the museum without weeks of preparation? What does he think we are? Magicians?"

Camille sighed. "That, I'm afraid, is the curse of being the Nightjar—a reputation for achieving the impossible."

Luc caught Emmy's eye. "Even so, we'd better get planning. Emmy, you and Camille can go to the museum tomorrow. The sooner we get those last three jewels, the sooner we'll have that bastard off our backs."

Chapter 7.

The British Museum was housed in a sprawling French-style edifice on Great Russell Street. The building had been constructed for the first Duke of Montagu but a subsequent duke, alarmed by the decline of Bloomsbury from fashionable aristocratic enclave to distinctly middle-class district, had abandoned the house in the mid-eighteenth century and moved to Whitehall.

"The building was sold to the trustees of the British Museum and used to house the collection of the Irish Physician and scientist Sir Hans Sloane."

Alex nodded dutifully as he followed curator Henry Franks through the museum's echoing halls.

"The lower floor, where we are now," Franks explained, "contains our extensive library of printed books." He gestured vaguely toward a wing that disappeared off to the right. "The upper floor, which we shall see in a moment, Lord Melton, is home to our impressive collection of insects, worms, corals, vegetables, birds and quadrupeds—stuffed, of course, not live"—

he chuckled at his own humor—"snakes, lizards, and fishes."

Alex shuddered. He'd seen quite enough lizards and flies during his time in the Peninsular. Those damned mosquitoes had plagued the entire regiment. He made a noncommittal sound. "And where might I find a blue diamond that was loaned to the museum a few years ago?"

Franks pushed his wire-rimmed glasses up his nose. "Ah. You refer to the Eliason jewel. That would also be on the second floor, in our minerals, shells, and fossils room. This way."

Alex let out a relieved exhale when he saw the jewel in question was still resting in its velvet-lined cabinet. The Nightjar had not already paid the museum a clandestine visit. "Who has the key to this cabinet, Mister Franks?"

"I do, my lord, although I don't carry it around with me all day." Franks held up a jangling metal ring upon which resided eight or so keys. "I keep the keys to the main doors here on my person, but all the cabinet keys are stored in my office downstairs, on hooks. Each one is labelled with a room and a cabinet number to avoid confusion."

"I see. And what other security measures do you have in place?"

"Well, I myself live in an apartment in the east wing, my lord. I make a nightly patrol at eleven, just before I retire, and another at nine in the morning, just before opening time. And of course, there's Brutus."

"Brutus?"

"Our guard dog. He's half Doberman. I let him loose in here at night. He'd let me know if we had any intruders."

"Aren't you worried he'll relieve himself on one of the exhibits?" Alex chuckled.

Franks sent him an offended look. "Brutus wouldn't do that. He knows he only receives his morning beefsteak if he waits to use the gardens."

Alex nodded.

"Can I ask why you're so interested in the museum's security, my lord?"

"I expect you've read about the break-in at Rundell and Bridge a few days ago?"

Franks nodded. "Indeed I did, sir. A most worrying state of affairs. I do hope Bow Street don't think the British Museum will be another target."

"It's a possibility," Alex hedged. "You should stay alert."

More like a certainty, if his theory was correct.

Franks drew himself up. "I am conscious of the fact that we house a great number of valuable objects here at the museum, sir. Rest assured that I shall be most vigilant when it comes to the security of our collections."

Alex clapped him on the shoulder. "Good man. I'm sure Bow Street can count on you to keep an eye out for anything suspicious. Now, I have a mind to visit the sculpture gallery before I leave. Lord Elgin tells me the friezes he brought from Greece are worth a look."

"The diamond is upstairs," Camille murmured as she and Emmy strolled through the British Museum's Greek and Roman sculpture gallery. Their skirts swished softly in unison against the polished parquet floor. Emmy counted the number of steps it took to reach the staircase, twenty-eight.

They paused to admire a marble depiction of a gladiator, and she tried to imagine the athletic figure dressed in clothes. It would be impossible to fit shoulders that muscled into the confines of a modern tailcoat. And what cravat would wind around a neck so thick? For one brief, startling moment, she wondered what Alexander Harland might look like without *his* clothes on, and her entire body begin to glow. Would he look like *this*? Both hard and smooth? All ripples and curves?

"Oh, look. There's Lord Melton."

Emmy swirled around in horror. Sure enough, the subject of her feverish imaginings was standing at the far end of the gallery.

She ducked behind the statue and closed her eyes. It was as if her outrageous fantasies had actually summoned him into existence, like some terrible, far-too-handsome genie. She tried to will him away, but when she braved a peek from around the gladiator's thigh, there he remained, stubbornly, attractively present.

The one small mercy was that he hadn't noticed them—he seemed to be inspecting a frieze of wall-mounted panels. They could still escape.

Since they were at a safe distance, Emmy allowed herself a moment to study Harland's physical architecture in the same way she might study the floorplan of a heist, taking in every pertinent detail. Certainly he was built along monumental lines. Tailoring couldn't disguise the bulk of muscle in his biceps, nor the breadth of his shoulders. His breeches conformed so faithfully to his thighs that she could actually see the ripple of muscles beneath. And the tails of his coat were undoubtedly hiding a remarkable posterior—

"We really should go and introduce ourselves," Camille trilled.

Emmy clutched her arm. "Are you mad? Why would we want to do that? I thought we'd agreed to *avoid* his notice?"

"Oh, pish. He'll turn around and see us at any moment. It will be far more noticeable if we don't acknowledge him. We must be brazen. Confident. And besides, I knew his mother. I'm sure he's a lovely man."

"He is the *enemy*," Emmy hissed as if she were the

wicked stepmother in a badly acted play. "He works for Bow Street! He is *the law*."

Camille waved her hand in a dismissive gesture.

"And he is not a 'nice man,'" Emmy added. "He is a rake and a gamester. He might be an earl, but he is thoroughly disreputable. He owns a gaming club. In St. James's."

"And where else would one open a gaming club?" Camille asked tartly. "Blackheath? Limehouse? Is he rich?"

Emmy narrowed her eyes. "Well, yes, by all accounts. Not that it makes—"

"There you go, then." Camille smiled. "Handsome, rich, *and* charming. The perfect trifecta."

She began to sidle forward, using the sculpture of a recumbent Apollo as cover. Emmy tried unsuccessfully to pull her back.

Alex was not impressed by Lord Elgin's marbles. They seemed to consist of an endless procession of headless riders dressed in little more than bath sheets trying to control overly frisky mounts. If the Greeks wanted them back—and he wasn't sure why they would—they were welcome to them.

He was about to return to the Tricorn when his nose detected the same scent he'd experienced outside Rundell & Bridge. He stilled in shock. His heart began to pound against his rib cage, and for one moment, he experienced an almost overwhelming surge of happiness.

The girl from the garden. She was here! Fate was giving him a second chance.

She must be remarkably close. It had been months since anyone had managed to sneak up on him without attracting his attention; he was usually far more conscious of people coming at him from his blind side. The marble sculptures must have concealed her approach.

He was almost afraid to turn around. "Never meet your

heroes," the old adage said, and the same was doubtless true for mysterious dance partners. What real-life flesh-and-blood woman could hope to compete with three years of dedicated fantasizing? She was bound to be a disappointment. Married. Or plain. Or cross-eyed.

Still, he had to know.

Bracing himself as if for a blow, Alex turned and encountered a froth of brown hair done up in an elaborate feminine style. He readjusted his gaze downward—the owner of the hair was a good foot shorter than himself—and found himself looking into a pair of wide grey eyes set in a pale, elfin face.

The same face he'd studied across Lady Turnbull's ballroom last night.

He experienced an instant's confusion and then a wave of bitter disillusionment incinerated every last ounce of optimism in his soul.

He'd always suspected fate was a perverse bitch, but even *he* couldn't have predicted this cruel twist. *Of course* his mystery woman would be the prime suspect in a series of impossible crimes. And *of course* she would be beautiful, in that subtle, understated way that had always appealed to him most.

Alex bit back a cynical laugh and narrowed his eyes. It made an awful kind of sense. How much energy had he wasted, dreaming of her? He should have known she was too good to be true.

This close, he could see details he hadn't noticed at Lady Turnbull's. Her eyes were grey, with pale, silvery flecks. Her nose was small and tilt-tipped—the word "impertinent" sprang to mind—and the bridge of it was unmistakably freckled. She had a beauty spot half an inch below her left eye.

He let his gaze drop lower and almost groaned. Her lips were exactly as he remembered. Those lips had laughed at him from beneath a Venetian mask. Those lips had pressed against his in innocent ardor and left him panting for more.

Those lips were utter, pink perfection.

"Lord Melton?"

Alex blinked. A throaty female voice to his right interrupted his self-flagellation.

"Good morning! I am Camille Danvers, Comtesse de Rougemont. It is a pleasure to make your acquaintance. I knew your mother, years ago. Such a charming lady. I still miss her terribly."

Remembering his manners, Alex lifted the older lady's hand to his lips. "A pleasure, madam. And thank you, but I barely remember her. She died when I was but six years old."

The countess gave him a studied appraisal. "She was a handsome woman, and I must say you've certainly inherited her good looks." She gestured to the tiny traitor beside her. "Allow me to introduce my granddaughter, Emmeline."

Alex took the hand that was offered, amazed at how small it seemed within his own. They were both wearing gloves, but the shock of the contact still sent a sizzle of something—anger, definitely anger—all the way down to his toes.

He brought her hand up to his lips, and at the last moment, seized by a wicked impulse, twisted it and pressed his mouth to the inch of exposed wrist between glove and sleeve.

The scent of her robbed him of breath, and he took a perverse satisfaction in her shocked gasp as his lips touched the bare skin over her fluttering pulse.

"It is a pleasure to meet you, Miss Danvers," he growled.

At last.

Chapter 8.

Emmy was quite certain her heart was about give out. She snatched her hand back as Harland straightened and resisted the urge to thrust it behind her back. The skin on her wrist tingled.

Harland's reaction was confusing. When he'd first turned around, he'd been smiling in welcome, but an instant later his expression had changed to one of cynical animosity. He was glaring at her now as if she'd committed some unpardonable sin. Which she had, of course, many times, but there was no way *he* could possibly know that.

A chill swept over her, immediately followed by a flash of heat. Her stomach turned over in panic. She'd forgotten the impact of him close-up. His eyes were remarkable, a steely, inky, fathomless blue. The precise color of the diamond she was going to steal.

The only other time she'd been this close to him had been the night they'd danced, and then the full effect of those eyes had been hidden behind his black half mask. Now, he was staring at her openly, as he had done last night, and the effect was truly unnerving. Did he focus such attention on everyone? Or was she, in particular, of interest? She sincerely hoped not.

Good lord, he was tall. The top of her head barely reached his shoulder. She had to tilt her neck to see his face. A strange mixture of danger and excitement swirled in her belly. How easy it would be for him to catch her around the waist with those huge hands and lift her up. Her mouth would be level with his—

No! She didn't like tall men. He was the enemy.

"I heard a rumor that you work for Bow Street, Lord Melton," Camille said easily. "I do hope you're not here to investigate a crime?"

Emmy opened her eyes in a wide, innocently amused expression and found her voice. "One wonders where you will start."

Harland's brows rose. "What do you mean, Miss Danvers?"

"Why, only that I suspect a good ninety percent of everything around us, from the Rosetta Stone over there"—she waved toward the Egyptian room behind them—"to these marbles Lord Elgin 'rescued' from the Parthenon in Greece, have been pilfered from somewhere."

"One could argue that they're safe in here," he said. "Being preserved for future generations."

She gave him her widest smile. "Hmm. Is stealing something for a noble reason ever an acceptable excuse? Is stealing something that's already been stolen truly a crime? They're interesting moral questions."

His eyes flashed grey-blue from under his lashes. "The general principle in criminal law, Miss Danvers, is that theft is theft, regardless of the status of the object itself. Two wrongs don't make a right."

"I quite agree. It is pleasant for people like me to be able to enjoy these items here in London, but it would be even better to see them in their original environment. They should be returned home, don't you think?"

"Perhaps you're right." He inclined his head in polite acknowledgment and turned to Camille. "And to answer your question, ma'am, no. I am not investigating a crime here. Mr. Franks has the security arrangements well in hand. But I do, on occasion, lend my services to Bow Street. As part owner of the Tricorn Club I have a number of useful connections. You may have read about an incident at Rundell and Bridge in which I have become involved?"

Camille fanned herself gently. "Ah, yes. *The Times* suggested it was the work of that notorious criminal the Nightjar." She placed her hand at her throat, as if her pearls were in imminent danger of being snatched. "How dreadful! One hardly feels safe in one's bed. Do you think you will catch him, Lord Melton? When so many others have failed?"

Harland's smile was almost predatory. "Oh, I *know* I will, madame. I will chase him to the ends of the earth if need be. There will be no escape. Justice will be served."

He sent Emmy another strange sideways glance, and she suppressed a shiver of foreboding. This man was a hunter. His languid exterior belied a steely inner determination; if he set his mind on something, he would be relentless in his pursuit. She turned away and feigned interest in a pair of statues flanking the door.

"You're a fan of Italian sculpture, Miss Danvers?" he asked, moving so they stood side by side. He leaned forward to read the information card, and his cuff rode up his arm as he extended his hand.

Emmy's mouth went dry as she glimpsed a scant inch of masculine wrist. Hairs, veins, sinews. It made her feel light-headed. Good lord, if this was how she reacted over the tiniest bit of skin, imagine what it would be to see him—

"These are by Buonarotti. Dying slaves, apparently," he murmured.

She forced her attention back to the sculptures. Parts of the white marble had been left rough and unfinished; the figures seemed to be emerging from the rock as if they were coming to life before her eyes. The first slave's head was thrown back, his eyes closed, his arm raised above his head. The muscles in his torso rippled and bulged.

Emmy swallowed. Instead of tortured, the figure looked almost . . . aroused. Exhausted by a surfeit of loving. She lowered her gaze—and smothered a gasp at the realistic depiction of his private parts, which were unashamedly on display. Her cheeks warmed in mortification. She heard Harland make a constricted noise, almost a snort, above her head.

"Clearly there was a shortage of fig leaves in Rome during the sixteenth century," he said mildly, but she could hear the laughter in his voice. "No wonder they don't admit children below the age of ten in here. It's a veritable den of iniquity. Mister Franks should post a warning for ladies of a nervous disposition."

"Indeed, he should," Camille said lightly. "He can't want impressionable young debutantes fainting all over his museum. Come along, Emmy. I think we should go and look at something a little less . . . stimulating. Fossils, perhaps. Or rocks."

Harland gave them a polite bow. "In that case, ladies, I shall leave you to your visit. Good day."

Emmy bobbed a curtsey. As Harland walked away, the click of his boot heels echoing down the hall, she realized her knees were shaky. She took a deep, calming breath through her nose and exhaled through her mouth.

She and Camille mounted the stairs and made their way to the rocks and minerals section. She knew the way; she'd memorized the route.

The diamond, along with other examples of precious and semiprecious stones, was housed in a solid oak display cabinet. It would have been too heavy for two people to move, even if it hadn't been bolted to the floor. Emmy leaned over so her nose almost touched the top of the display case. Her breath fogged up the glass as she spoke.

"Why was Harland here? It cannot be a coincidence. If he's made the connection between the Rundell and Bridge diamond and this one"—she pressed her gloved finger onto the glass above the sparkling gem—"then we are in serious trouble. If he knows which jewels the Nightjar is stealing, then all he has to do is set a trap and—"

Camille bent to study a crystalline geode beside her. "I expect Bow Street is merely warning anyone who houses expensive jewels to be on alert."

"I don't like it," Emmy said. "We should put it off for another week until interest dies down."

"You know we can't do that. The fact that Monsieur Danton has decided to show himself to us, or at least to Sally, is not a good sign. He could have continued to blackmail us perfectly well by letter. He could have collected the jewels without any of us ever seeing his face. I do not think we should disregard his command for urgency. I think he could prove an extremely unpleasant man."

Emmy sighed, acknowledging that as the truth.

"Besides, everything is ready for tomorrow night," Camille murmured soothingly. "Mister Franks has agreed to meet Sally at the White Lion at five o'clock. You know the floor plan by heart. The delivery's all set up." She patted her reticule. "And I have another delicious treat for Brutus, when we pass by the gardens. He's such a sweetheart."

"He weighs the same as me," Emmy grumbled. "And he's slobbery."

Camille gave a wistful sigh. "Oh, darling. If I were twenty years younger, I'd come with you."

"You'd probably be better than me."

Her grandmother had nerves of steel. Nothing flustered her. She could stare people out of countenance at the drop of a hat. Whereas Emmy quite often veered between elation and terror, between resentment that such a career had been forced upon her, and resignation that stealing the jewels was, morally at least, the right thing to do.

If she were perfectly honest, she often experienced a thoroughly wicked rush of pleasure from robbery too. Instead of feeling guilty, she felt a confusing delight in the danger and excitement, at least once it was all over. It was the thrill of a job well done. The gleeful sense of getting away with it.

Perhaps she was more like her father than she'd thought.

Camille gazed down at the grey-blue gemstone between them, and her expression softened. "I remember this before it was cut down, you know. It used to be twice this size. The Sun King, Louis's grandfather, used to wear it as a hat pin, but Louis had it set in a sash for the Order of the Golden Fleece. He wore it at all the ceremonial functions. Marie Antoinette used to tease him that he out-glittered the stars in the sky." She sighed. "Ah, such happy days."

Emmy straightened and squeezed her arm. "Come on. I've seen enough here. I need some food before I get into that ridiculous coffin."

Chapter 9.

The worst thing about the British Museum plan was the sarcophagus. Emmy forced herself not to think of its previous occupant as she lay down in the cramped wooden space and glared up at Luc.

"How does it feel?" he asked.

"Uncomfortable."

Her brother grinned. "Well, it wasn't meant for live people, you know."

"Don't remind me."

"You only have to be in there a short while. And it's better than that beer barrel. At least you get to lie down flat. And you'll be transported a lot more respectfully."

"The beer barrel didn't once belong to a dead person," she said. "And it smelled considerably more pleasant."

"I've made you plenty of air holes. Try it."

Emmy gave a resigned sigh and folded her hands across her chest. Luc, with Sally's help, slid the heavy lid across her field of vision. It made a horrid grating noise. As the light was cut off, she forced herself to breathe slowly through her nose. It smelled musty, like being entombed inside a hollow tree trunk, and she was glad she'd compensated by giving herself a few additional dabs of perfume to mask the smell.

When her eyes became accustomed to the darkness, she realized that numerous small round holes pierced the lid; she was speckled all over with a smattering of tiny light spots. She moved, trying to see how much space she had. Her elbow bumped painfully on the side.

Luc's muffled voice filtered through the thick wooden lid. "See? It's a good thing you're so small, Em. I'd never have been able to fit in there. Now push the lid off. You have to be able to move it on your own."

Emmy wriggled and cursed, pushing sideways and upward with her palms on the underside of the lid. It was a struggle, but she managed to shift it enough to get her fingers through a gap at the side. She pushed the lid off completely and sat up. Sally gave her a round of applause, and Luc nodded approvingly.

"Perfect."

Camille entered the kitchen and smiled at seeing Emmy sitting inside the ancient sarcophagus on top of the table. The fact that this wasn't the strangest thing Emmy had ever been cajoled into doing was indicative of just how odd her family truly was.

"It's time," Camille said. "The cart is waiting in the mews. Sally, you look wonderful!"

Sally gave a sarcastic curtsey. She'd made an effort to look even more ravishing than usual, since she was meeting Henry Franks, the museum curator, for a post-work tipple in a tavern across the square from the museum. Her hair had been left partly down, and one stray lock curled enticingly over her rounded shoulder. Her milky-white bosom was shown to devastating effect in a pale blue cambric dress. A more perfect distraction would be hard to find.

Luc narrowed his eyes. "Franks had better not try anything untoward," he growled.

Sally gave him a wide, confident grin. "I can 'andle 'im, don't you worry."

"The thought of you 'handling' him is precisely what concerns me, madam," Luc muttered.

Sally chuckled. She stroked a light caress across his jaw and bent to press a playful kiss on his cheek. "You have nothing to worry about, my lovely."

For a brief moment they stared at each other, and Emmy held her breath, hoping they would finally give in to their obvious mutual attraction and kiss properly, but Sally pulled back with a flustered laugh and the moment was broken.

Luc turned back to Emmy, all business. "Right. Let's go. You should arrive just before closing time. Franks won't have time to look at you, much as he would like to. He won't want to be late to meet Sally."

He winced and Emmy bit her lip to stop a smile. The thought of sending Sally out to flirt with another man while looking so delectable was clearly torture for him.

Sally had worked her magic on him too. Instead of an attractive thirty-year-old, she'd made him look much older, with greying hair, a bushy fake mustache, and grizzled sideburns. A wide-brimmed hat pulled low over his forehead disguised the top part of his face, and a lumpy greatcoat hid his athletic form.

"You'll be placed in the store room or the dust room," Luc said. "It's closest to the back door. As soon as you're sure Franks has locked up, push off the lid and get to work. The keys to the cabinet will be hanging on a hook in his office."

Camille tucked a small brown paper-wrapped package down near her feet. "Don't forget Brutus." She leaned forward and gave Emmy a hug. "Bonne chance, ma chère. I have every faith in your skill, of course, but a little extra luck never hurt anyone. Now off you go."

A flat-backed delivery cart was waiting outside, a raggedy urchin holding the horse's bridle. Emmy and Sally placed the sarcophagus inside the wooden packing crate they'd prepared, and Emmy climbed back in, leaving the top half-off so she could breathe. Sally packed the rest of the crate with straw, then threw a woolen blanket over the whole thing to disguise it. The springs rocked as Luc climbed onto the front seat and took the reins.

"Let's go."

Emmy braced herself as the cart lumbered out into the street and rattled over the cobbles. It was only a ten-minute ride from Waverton Street to Bloomsbury, but she felt every bruising jolt and teeth-rattling bump. She was going to be a mass of bruises by tomorrow.

It was uncomfortably warm beneath the blanket, and dark. The sounds of London were muffled, almost dream-like, and her mind began to wander. What kind of life was this? Other women were getting ready for a walk in Hyde Park, or preparing for an evening of entertainment. They were out there enjoying themselves, flirting, trying to find a partner. How on earth was she ever going to meet someone when all she did was sneak around mostly abandoned buildings? The only single men she was likely to encounter in her near future were police constables and jailors.

Or Bow Street Runners.

She banished the thought.

Frustration bubbled within her. She wasn't just trapped in this stupid crate, she was trapped in this stupid *life*—bound by her father's legacy and by Danton's greedy demands. The only way out of it was to see the blasted thing through to the end. This sarcophagus could serve as a fitting metaphor for her life; the painted facade on the outside bore no resemblance to the person beneath, just as the image she presented to the *ton* was nothing like reality.

Was it too much to wish for a normal, relatively uneventful life? A life with a home and a husband and, God willing, children? She couldn't see it happening. Marriages should be based on trust. She would rather die an old maid than enter into a lifelong union with untruths between herself and her husband. How could she marry a man if he knew only the lies she'd told him? And what man would marry her if he knew the truth? Her dream to find a man who knew every one of her flaws, all her past misdemeanors, and who loved her anyway, was impossible.

A corner away from Russell Street Luc pulled the carriage to a halt, turned in his seat, and flicked aside the blanket. Emmy blinked in the sudden onslaught of daylight.

"Time to put the lid on," he said cheerfully.

He slid the sarcophagus closed, and Emmy heard him push the top of the wooden crate into place overhead. She tried to regulate her breathing as he pulled up at the back entrance to the museum and went to summon the curator.

Her heart sounded unnaturally loud in the enclosed space. She forced herself to think of wide, open spaces, long fields of wheat rippling to the horizon.

"I was not expecting any sort of delivery." Franks's confusion was evident in his brusque tone. "Where did you say this had come from?"

Luc, who could emulate Sally's East End accent perfectly, pulled out a sheaf of crumpled papers from his greatcoat; Emmy heard them rustle. "I told yer, guvn'r. Blackwall docks. Ship called the *Zenobia* just come from Alexandria. Captain ordered me to bring this 'ere box straight to a Mister Franks at the British Museum."

"This is the first I've heard of a bequest from a lord—who did you say it was?"

"Lord Burlington, sir. Least, that's wot this 'ere paper says. Been working with a chap called Belzoni out there in Egypt, diggin' up all kinds o' moldy stuff."

"How odd. Do you know what it is?"

Luc sniffed. "A 'gyptian sarco—scarc-uh—a coffin, sir."

Emmy could practically hear Franks's curiosity get the better of him. Luc's casual mention of the infamous archaeologist Giovanni Belzoni was a stroke of genius. Franks would be intrigued.

She gave a mental shake of the head at his gullibility. Honestly, hadn't the man ever read about the Trojan horse? The classics were full of pithy warnings like "beware of messengers bearing gifts." Luc's Lord Burlington was entirely fictitious; a glance at Debrett's last night had confirmed the title had died out with the last earl ten years ago.

But people were always impressed with aristocratic titles. Emmy wrinkled her nose. Just look at Harland, he was a prime example. He might be the Earl of Melton, but a fancy title didn't change his core nature—that of irritatingly handsome cynic.

Franks, however, clearly subscribed to the maxim: Never look a gift horse in the mouth. "A sarcophagus, you say. How marvelous. Well, you'd better bring it in, then."

"Can't 'elp you there, guv'," Luc said with cheerful regret. "Me back's gone, see? Can't lift anyfink 'eavier than a tankard o' beer. That's why I drives a cart, see?"

Franks sighed. "Oh, very well. You there, lad." He was obviously calling to one of the many urchins loitering in the street. "Give me a hand with this crate."

Emmy braced herself as she was slid off the back of the cart. She prayed whoever was helping Franks wouldn't drop her—not only would that be extremely painful, but the game would most certainly be up if she spilled out of the sarcophagus. She swayed and bobbed, then her feet tilted upwards as she was carried up some steps, and then she was righted with a bump as the crate was, presumably, deposited on a table inside the museum.

The darkness lifted as Luc or Franks removed the outer lid of the crate. Pinpoints of light freckled her face.

"My goodness, that is extraordinary," she heard Franks breathe. "I do believe it's Middle Kingdom. Just look at that painted decoration!"

Emmy held her breath as something touched the lid of the sarcophagus, but Luc stepped in to avert disaster.

"If that's all, sir, I'll be goin'. Got myself an appointment wiv' a laydee, if you know what I mean."

"Oh, no, of course," Franks said distractedly. He bustled away from the case. "Here's for your trouble. And my goodness, what time is it? I, too, am meeting a lady."

"Ten to five, sir," Luc said. "Sounds like we'd both best be off. Don't do to keep a woman waitin'."

"No, no, you're quite right." Franks gave one more longing sigh. "I suppose this can wait until morning."

"That's the spirit. Ain't no dead 'gyptian more interesting than a handful o' live muslin, now is there? Whatever poor bugger's in there, he'll still be dead tomorrow." Luc cackled at his own joke, then turned it into an impressive fit of coughing. Emmy silently congratulated him on his performance. He really did sound as though he were a frail sixty-year-old cab driver with bad lungs.

With a wash of relief, she heard the scuffles and footfalls of the men fade away. A door clicked. She waited an extra few minutes, just to be sure she was alone, then pushed aside the lid and took a grateful gulp of cool, fresh air.

She was in.

Chapter 10.

After a brief glance around, Emmy deduced her location—the mysteriously named "dusting room," beneath the northeast stairwell. It seemed to be a storeroom. A bizarre array of items in various stages of restoration sat on wooden benches and shelves. A glassy-eyed taxidermy zebra head gave her a reproachful glare as she stretched her arms above her head to relieve her cramps. She stuck her tongue out at it. At least she wasn't stuffed and mounted on a shield.

Not yet, at least.

She climbed out of the box, glad that she was wearing her usual thieving attire of shirt, breeches, and stockings. She envied the men of this world; breeches were far more practical than acres of billowing skirts and petticoats.

Camille had designed the outfit. Emmy might be a thief, so practicality was tantamount, but there was no reason she could not also be stylish. According to Camille, black, while slimming, was "not at all the thing," despite being a great favorite with highwaymen. Brown was not to be considered; "Not with your complexion, darling."

So Emmy wore midnight blue for her nocturnal adventures. Dark enough to disappear into the shadows, flattering to dark hair and grey eyes. Father had approved, as had Luc, so Emmy had bitten back the sarcastic retort that nobody would care what she was wearing when they clapped her in irons and put a rope around her neck.

The one piece of Father's advice Emmy had failed to follow was his moratorium on soap. He'd warned her to bathe only in hot water and to eschew powder and scent before a job, but Camille had disagreed. She said a woman was "as good as naked" if she left the house without perfume.

Emmy smiled in fond memory. For her sixteenth birthday, Camille had taken her to Floris, her favorite parfumier in St. James's. She'd helped Emmy choose her own customized scent, a combination of peony, rose, neroli, and orchid. Emmy had felt so grown-up. She'd worn the same perfume ever since; each spray was an extra layer of invincibility, of feminine armor.

It was time to get to work.

A door led into Franks's office and Emmy smiled in triumph as she spied the perfectly labelled row of cabinet keys mounted on the wall. She pocketed cabinet 4A—Rocks and Minerals.

Thieving was an odd profession, rather like being a soldier, she imagined. It consisted of long periods of boredom interspersed with brief moments of terrifying activity. She waited an extra ten minutes, just to be certain that Franks had really gone to meet Sally, and then untied the brown paper packet Camille had given her. She cracked open the door that led into the main wing of the museum and whistled.

"Brutus! Here, boy!"

The rhythmic click of canine claws scrabbling on polished wooden floor ensued, and Emmy kept her body behind the door, using it as a shield. Thus far, her acquaintance with Brutus had been conducted with the confidence-inducing iron bars of the museum's garden railings between them.

A low growl made her insides curdle as the huge dog skidded around the corner. He was fearsome, some kind of hound, a Doberman perhaps? Black and tan, with pointy ears and a full complement of extremely sharp teeth. He looked like the jackal-headed deity painted on her sarcophagus.

Emmy wasn't a fan of any dog larger than a dachshund. A dachshund she could outrun or escape by climbing on a chair. Brutus was a good seven stone of pure muscle. She doubted the door could stop him.

The beast stopped a few paces away and regarded her suspiciously.

"Hello, Brutus, my lovely," she cooed. "It's only me. Your friend Emmy. The one who brings you tasty presents." She produced a strip of steak from her package and threw it toward the dog's front paws. "Look what I've brought for you today."

Brutus bent his head and sniffed the steak.

"I bet you're hungry, aren't you?" Emmy coaxed. "Of course you are. Men are always hungry." At least, Luc always was.

Brutus finally recognized her. His entire demeanor changed, and Emmy sagged in relief. With a bark of welcome, he gulped down the steak and trotted forward, his tail wagging expectantly. She opened the door and gave him another steak, careful to keep her fingers well away from his snapping jaws.

"Good boy!" She breathed shakily. If only all large, intimidating males of her acquaintance could be subdued in such a manner. She set off down the corridor toward the main staircase with Brutus, either hopeful of more steak or having appointed himself her temporary guardian, trotting at her heels.

The blue diamond was in exactly the same place as it had been earlier, and Emmy reached inside her pocket and produced the Nightjar's signature black feather.

The small handwritten card she'd also brought was doubtless a mistake. She could hear her father's voice in her mind: *Just steal the jewel—only the jewel—and get out.* This note would break the rules. It would bring all sorts of complications. But some wicked imp compelled her. She simply couldn't resist.

Emmy unlocked the cabinet, lifted the hinged lid, slipped the blue diamond into her shirt pocket, and replaced it with the feather. Then she studied the rest of the rocks, searching for the perfect one with which to tease Alexander Harland.

Obsidian, volcanic glass? She bent to read the description. An igneous rock. Derived from the Latin *ignis*, meaning fire, formed by the solidification of lava. Alex Harland certainly raised her temperature by a few hundred degrees, but that wouldn't do. The comparison was far too flattering.

She glanced at the next lump. Granite? A hard stone. His eyes were certainly hard—glittering and accusatory. His heart, at least where women were concerned, was doubtless just as petrified. His thighs, and the muscles of his chest—*Stop that.* No, he was not granite. Granite was common, and there was nothing common about Harland.

What about amber? The name came from the Greek word *elektron*, because it held a static charge. Father had shown her the trick of rubbing an amber bead against her hair and then using the charged stone to pick up a torn-off scrap of tissue paper, as if by magic. Alex Harland exerted the same invisible pull on her. She felt that static shock, that quick snap of awareness when their eyes met, when his body brushed hers. She shivered.

At the next rock she paused, read the description, and quelled the desire to giggle like a lunatic. Oh, that was perfect! She withdrew the official museum card and replaced it with her own. What she wouldn't give to be a fly on the wall when Harland saw what she'd done.

Luc would be furious at her for taunting their nemesis in such a manner, but if one couldn't have a bit of fun in life, what was the point?

Brutus followed her as she relocked the cabinet, slipped back down the stairs, replaced the key in Franks's office, and straightened the lid of the sarcophagus.

It was always far simpler to leave a building than to enter one. With one last pat for Brutus, Emmy used a statue of Cupid and Psyche embracing to reach the clasp of a window and pulled herself up and through, dropping the few feet into the back alley that led to Montagu Place.

Luc had positioned the cart across the entrance of the alleyway to prevent anyone else coming in. He gave her a cheeky grin from underneath his hat as she climbed up onto the seat beside him and donned a flat cap of her own. "All done?" he asked casually.

Emmy slouched back into the seat, suddenly overcome with exhaustion. She always felt drained after the excitement of the heist left her.

"All done. Let's go home."

Chapter 11.

Alex frowned. It had taken Franks almost an entire day to discover the loss of the diamond. He'd been so engrossed in studying some new Egyptian sarcophagus that he hadn't noticed it missing on his morning tour of the museum. Alex quelled a spurt of irritation as he and Seb listened to the man's bumbling attempts to understand what had happened.

"Indeed, it was only at around four o'clock that a gentleman pointed out that it was missing and asked whether it was being cleaned." Franks wrung his hands in obvious agitation. "I sent to inform you directly, Lord Melton."

Alex nodded. "Thank you. But what happened to your guard dog? You assured me he was a veritable Cerberus." He glared down at the animal in question, who was trotting amiably beside them. Brutus whimpered, as if he recognized the accusatory tone. He tucked his tail between his legs and dipped his muzzle in a perfect canine grovel.

Franks's neck turned pink. "Ah, well, it seems the

thief discovered Brutus's fatal weakness. The clever devil bribed him with steak."

Seb rolled his eyes. "Whoever would have thought of that?"

"Et tu, Brute?" Alex chided the dog, but neither of his companions appreciated the Shakespeare reference.

"There's more, my lord." Franks cleared his throat as they neared the minerals gallery. "It seems the crook has taken a personal interest in *you*."

"In what way?"

They stopped in front of the cabinet. The glass was still intact. There was no evidence of forced entry, but the diamond was notably absent. A lone black feather lay in its place. Franks pointed to a folded ridge of card, propped up next to another specimen nearby.

"The thief not only took the diamond, they also replaced that particular label."

Alex bent to read the note and his brows rose in affronted disbelief.

Specimen: Meltonium Harlandii. Locale: London and its environs. Defining characteristics: Inert. Dull in appearance. Particularly dense. No practical uses. Almost worthless.

"What kind of rock is that?" Alex asked very softly.

"A meteorite," Franks supplied. "It is, in all probability, the oldest thing on this entire planet."

Behind him, Alex heard Seb snort, then give up any pretense of trying to quash his laughter. "Oh, that's priceless! Alex Harland: old and thick and not of this world!"

Alex reminded himself that Seb was one of his best friends. It would be bad form to knock his bloody teeth out. He glared at the handwritten note. It was not the same hand that had written the Nightjar's previous message about the sugar. It was equally neat and educated, but more sloping. Slightly—dare he say it—more *feminine?*

Seb wasn't finished. "Is this how the Nightjar sees us at Bow Street? Big, hulking lumps with no more intelligence than a misshapen rock? I believe we should be insulted, Alex. Or, you should be."

Alex ground his teeth. One eyelid began to twitch. If he'd had any doubt about the identity of the Nightjar, this taunting little note quashed it. Emmeline Danvers's cheeky face rose up before him, those lips curved in a teasing smile, those damnably alluring freckles peppering her nose, and his blood began to boil.

Franks unlocked the cabinet and handed the feather to Alex. Alex brought it to his nose and his stomach clenched in recognition. It smelled of her. His mystery woman. Emmeline Danvers. The Nightjar.

One and the same. Damn her.

Anyone who said women weren't capable of such things was a fool. Women were capable of anything. He wasn't yet precisely sure of how she'd managed it—although he'd bet the sudden appearance of that sarcophagus downstairs had something to do with it—but he was sure of one thing: she was his thief.

"One thing I've always wondered," Seb said to the room in general. "How come ladies are always referred to as diamonds of the first water? Is that a gemological term?"

Franks nodded, glad of the distraction. "It is indeed. 'First water' denotes the highest quality. Diamonds are assessed by their translucence; the more like water, the better. It means they have a perfect cut, color, and clarity, and lack internal flaws."

"We all have internal flaws," Alex growled. "And external ones too." He touched the scar at his temple, then turned on his heel and strode toward the entrance.

"Where are we going now?" Seb demanded cheerfully.

"To the Danvers residence. Good day, Mister Franks."

Alex jogged down the stairs, out of the main entrance, gave directions to the driver, and jumped into the waiting carriage.

Seb scrambled in after him. "You really think it's her?"

"Without a doubt. I even met her here yesterday when I was talking to Franks. That woman has some gall."

Seb gave a crooked smile. "There's something incredibly attractive about competence, don't you think? I find it almost . . . arousing. In certain circumstances, of course."

Alex shot him a disbelieving look. "You think we should admire her sangfroid?"

The little imp certainly had a cool head in a crisis. He had it himself, gained from his years in the Rifles, an ability to think clearly when bullets were whistling past his head. In a colleague, it was an excellent trait. In an adversary, it was irritating beyond measure.

Seb's expression grew serious. "She might not have had a choice, you know. There may be extenuating circumstances."

"Everyone always has a choice," Alex said grimly. "She knows the difference between right and wrong."

"Maybe her only option was choosing the lesser of two evils?"

"Stop playing devil's advocate," Alex growled. "You sound as if you're on *her* side. She's a bloody criminal."

Seb shrugged. "I just think it's odd that you're so angry. You've never reacted like this with any of the other criminals we've been involved with." His face took on a slyly innocent expression. "Maybe it's because none of the other criminals had such perfect breasts."

"You shouldn't be noticing her breasts!"

Seb chuckled, delighted to have drawn a response. "You just seem, I don't know, *emotionally invested* in this one. I've never seen you so animated. There's more to this than upholding the law."

"You know what they say: Keep your friends close and your enemies closer . . . especially if they're female."

"That should be the Harland family motto." Seb chuckled. "Maybe we should get it carved above the fireplace at the Tricorn?"

Alex winced. Seb made it his business to know everything about everyone. His personal motto was "knowledge is power." And for all his teasing, he'd hit the nail on the head. Emmeline Danvers's involvement felt like a personal betrayal, the shattering of all his foolish dreams. He'd held a false image in his heart for all these years, fostered stupid longings that should have been quashed long ago. The image of purity, of innocence, of that laughing shimmering girl, had been an illusion.

"I *will* catch her. I always get my man."

Seb spread his arms along the back of the seat with a grin. "See, that's where you have a problem. Because in this case, your *man* is a woman. A very attractive woman."

"Whether or not she's attractive is neither here nor there. Justice will be served. Let's not forget what happened the last time I gave a pretty woman the benefit of the doubt."

Seb levelled him with a direct stare. "This is nothing like Spain, Alex. Not the same at all."

It had been one of Alex's blackest moments, an experience he'd never been able to forget. They'd been escorting a group of French prisoners of war through the mountains and had stopped near a small village. As usual, a group of locals had appeared, offering food and drink. A young Spanish woman carrying a basket of flowers had approached the group of bound prisoners, who were resting on the ground.

She was beautiful; her unbound hair was wild around her face, her eyes flashing brown. The fringed edge of her burnt-orange shawl fluttered as she walked. All heads turned to follow her progress.

Alex's commanding officer had just motioned at her to move away from the men when she reached into her basket and pulled out a grenade.

The entire camp stilled. Alex had been on lookout; his rifle was already in his hands. Someone shouted an order to shoot, but he'd hesitated. He didn't want to shoot a woman. He couldn't believe she would carry out her threat.

The explosion, when it came seconds later, killed the woman and the two Frenchmen closest to her and wounded a dozen more. It transpired that her husband had been killed by the French the week before.

Alex closed his eyes. It still rankled. He'd been naïve, blinded by her attractive appearance, still clinging to the faint hope that the world wasn't as brutal as he already knew it to be. His gut had warned him of danger, but he'd ignored his instincts and allowed emotion to override his training. Innocent men—even if they were technically the enemy—had died because of his weakness.

In hindsight, the situation had a certain dark irony. Back then, he'd still had full vision; he'd been blinded by hope and inexperience. Now, he was blinded in truth, at least partially, but never again would he be fooled by a pretty face. He'd learned his lesson.

"We can't just walk in there and search the place," Seb said, interrupting his brooding thoughts. "We need a warrant from Conant."

"I know that."

"Then why—?"

"I don't know," Alex said irritably. "I just want to take a look at her. In her home, the place she feels most secure.

She'll be confident there. Relaxed. She might let something slip that incriminates her."

He couldn't explain it logically, but he was convinced that if he just looked her in the eye he'd *know*. He'd see it in her face. The guilt. The amusement. The spark of challenge in her eyes.

"Besides, there are plenty of ways to get what we want without a search warrant. Sometimes all you have to do is ask nicely."

Chapter 12.

Harland's timing was unfortunate.

Emmy, Luc, and Camille had just sat down to an early dinner so they could go and watch one of Sally's friends, Molly, perform at the Haymarket Theatre.

An impatient pounding on the front door had Emmy and Camille glancing at one another in wide-eyed alarm. Emmy's first thought was that it was Danton, come to demand not only the Rundell & Bridge diamond but also the blue one she'd stolen the previous night. Both lay on the white tablecloth between them.

Quick as a flash, Emmy seized the blue stone and dropped it into the bowl of soup in front of her. It was, thankfully, leek and potato, and therefore opaque. Beef consommé would have been a disaster. Camille, with a chuckle, did the same with the clear diamond. It made a distinct splash just as Sally reappeared in the doorway and announced, "Lords Melton and Mowbray to see you."

Emmy was certain her face must be an incriminating shade of pink, but Camille merely dabbed the corners of her mouth with her napkin and said loudly, "At *this* hour? How singular. Still, I suppose it must be something important."

"Shall I put them in the salon, ma'am?" Sally asked.

"Heavens no. You may show them in here. If they will come visiting at dinnertime, they should expect people to be eating dinner."

A wave of excitement that bordered on nausea rose up as Harland and his friend appeared in the doorway. Camille gave them both a radiant smile and batted her eyelashes. Emmy almost rolled her eyes. Sometimes her grandmother acted more like a girl of sixteen than a woman of seventy. "My lords, what a pleasant surprise."

"Good evening, Countess. Danvers. Miss Danvers."

Harland's voice did fluttery things to her insides. Emmy tried to keep her eyes on the soup but failed. The instant she looked up, his blue gaze bored into hers, and she pressed her lips together to stop a completely inappropriate smile. He looked harried. Angry. Harassed. He'd definitely discovered the note, then.

Camille rose from her seat, and Emmy did the same. Luc, however, remained seated. "To what do we owe the pleasure, gentlemen?"

"I apologize for interrupting your dinner." Harland swept the table with a brief glance and Emmy quelled the urge to cover her soup bowl with her napkin. He made a motion with his hand. "Please, sit down."

Camille sank back into her chair, as did Emmy, although she would have preferred to remain standing. Harland loomed over her at the best of times. There was no need to add to the height difference.

"I was wondering if I might have a brief word with Miss Danvers?"

Luc's eyebrows rose. "I wasn't aware the two of you were acquainted."

"We met at the British Museum yesterday," Camille supplied brightly.

"And what do you wish to speak to her about?" Luc asked, in the tone Emmy had long ago christened his protective-big-brother voice.

Harland shot her an indecipherable glance from under his lashes. "This is not a social call. I'm sorry to report that shortly after Miss Danvers and the countess visited the museum, it fell victim to the thief known as the Nightjar. A stone of some considerable value was stolen from one of the galleries."

Camille made a convincing little gasp of shock. "Oh, dear. But what can that possibly have to do with us?"

"I have reason to believe that the thief may have been present in the museum at the same time as you, preparing for the heist."

Emmy bit her lip. He knew. He knew it was her. He was just playing with them, like a cat with a mouse.

"I was hoping you might be able to furnish us with descriptions of the other visitors you encountered."

Camille nodded. "Of course. We would be delighted to help. But my memory is not what it once was. I'm sure Emmy will be able to provide you with a more complete list of those she remembers."

Emmy shot her a furious glance. She didn't want to give Harland an example of her handwriting. She'd made some effort to disguise it when she'd penned that taunting note, but why give him something with which to make a comparison? He might use it as evidence.

"We'll send it over to Bow Street tomorrow," Camille said. "Will that be all?"

"There is one more thing," Harland said silkily. "I was wondering if I might visit Miss Danvers's bedchamber."

Luc glowered at him. "I fail to see what bearing that could have on your investigation, Lord Melton."

Harland gave him a smile that was both innocent and, to Emmy's mind, utterly diabolical. He reached into his waistcoat and withdrew two familiar black feathers. "The Nightjar left these at his last two crimes."

He lifted them to his nose and inhaled, and Emmy felt a cold wave of dread sweep over her.

"They have a very distinctive scent. Almost like a woman's perfume. When I met Miss Danvers yesterday, I couldn't help but notice that her perfume is very similar to that of these feathers. A happy coincidence, you might say."

Emmy narrowed her eyes. *A happy coincidence, my arse.* He knew. But at least he wasn't accusing her of being the Nightjar directly. Not yet, anyway.

"I had no idea you had such an excellent nose, Lord Melton," Luc said acidly.

Harland's smile was wicked. "I daresay I've had some experience in recognizing female perfumes."

She didn't want to know about his experience with other women, the fiend.

"If Miss Danvers would be so kind as to show me the scent she uses, I'll know what I'm looking for. It may be that the Nightjar is, in fact, a woman."

"It could just be a man who gets his feathers from a woman's fan or headpiece," Camille suggested. "What are they, anyway? Ostrich feathers?"

Harland stroked them back and forth along his jaw. Emmy couldn't tear her eyes away from the mesmerizing sight. There was something horribly sensual about it.

"I believe ostrich feathers are larger. These are goose feathers, dyed black. Unfortunately, they're too common to track down their source. They're used in everything from pillows to hats. But the scent is rather distinctive. Identifying this particular perfume might well be the key to identifying the culprit."

Damn. Damn. Damn. She should have listened to her father. She'd never imagined feathers could absorb scent to such a degree. Or that Harland would have such a delicate nose.

Emmy finally found her voice. "Of course. If you'll just excuse me, I'll ask Sally to go and get a bottle of my perfume from my room."

Camille shot her a wicked, laughing look. "Oh, Sally's far too busy in the kitchen. You go, Emmy dear."

Emmy and Luc shot her identical incredulous stares. Surely Camille wasn't *matchmaking* at a time like this? But one glance at her grandmother's wide smile and sparkling eyes confirmed it. The woman was meddling.

"Well, we can't let Lord Melton go, can we?" Camille said with mock innocence. "That would be most unseemly, to have a gentleman poking around in your drawers."

Emmy glared at her for the deliberate innuendo.

Wolff, Harland's companion, smiled broadly, and Emmy had a sudden vision of Harland searching through her very French, very lacy underthings. The thought of those big hands touching the delicate silk of her negligees made her feel molten inside. She stood with a decisive motion. "All right, then."

Harland watched her every move as she rounded the end of the table. He and Wolff stepped aside so she could pass through the door.

She'd already dressed for the opera. Her gown was a watered silk, royal blue with black velvet trim and black-dyed lace at the half-sleeves. It made a lovely satisfying swish when she walked.

Harland's gaze bored into her back as she ascended the stairs. For a panicked moment, she considered giving him a bottle of Camille's perfume instead.

No, she couldn't do that. He'd already managed to

identify her scent from hundreds of others. The thought was disturbing. How was that even possible? It was akin to finding a needle in a haystack. The man must have an almost supernatural gift. Had his sense of smell somehow become more acute since he'd lost some vision, in compensation?

Emmy glanced around her bedroom with new eyes, imagining she were Harland. Would he think it strange? Decadent? She adored the hand-painted wallpaper she'd chosen. The flowering branches, blossoms, and birds were lush and exotic; she always felt as if she were sleeping in a jungle, instead of a town house in Mayfair. Flecks of real silver leaf had been added to the panels and reflected the candlelight to give a magical feel.

She'd imagined him in here. Would the real man sit on her bed? Touch her sheets? Leave the scent of his cologne hanging in the air?

Stupid.

There was an almost-finished bottle of scent on her dressing table. Emmy snatched it up and hurried out, keen to have him out of the house.

He was waiting in the hall. She thrust the bottle at him with a jerky movement.

"Here. Not that it will be of much use. The ingredients aren't listed on the label. It's made for me by Floris. They keep the precise recipe at their shop."

Harland's gloved fingers touched hers as he took the small glass bottle. It looked ridiculously delicate in his hands. "Thank you, Miss Danvers."

To her amazement he un-stoppered it and lifted it to his nose. For a brief moment, he closed his eyes and her heart turned over in her chest. It seemed so *intimate*, somehow. He was breathing in her essence, drawing it down into his lungs, inside himself. She felt a little lightheaded, as if she were the one inhaling so deeply. When he opened his eyes, they seemed all pupil, almost entirely black. Emmy couldn't look away.

Camille's voice floated in from the dining room. "Won't you stay for dinner, my lords?"

Harland's gaze dropped to her lips, as if he were contemplating taking a bite of *her*. "Thank you, but I'm afraid we must decline. I have what I came for."

"Perhaps we'll see you at Lady Carrington's annual ball next week?" Camille called.

His dark gaze bored into hers. "Perhaps." It was a promise and a threat.

Wolff stepped into the hallway, breaking the charged moment, and Harland executed a neat bow. "Good evening." He turned on his heel and left her standing in the hall.

As soon the front door closed, Emmy let out a relieved *whoosh* of breath and stalked back into the dining room. She glared at Camille, the septuagenarian matchmaker. "What was all that about? Are you *trying* to get us arrested?"

Camille chuckled and fished the diamond out of her soup with her spoon. "We could hardly refuse his request, could we?" she said reasonably. "And the man can't arrest you for owning a bottle of perfume."

"He *knows*," Emmy said. "He's just biding his time, gathering evidence before he pounces."

Camille dried the diamond on her napkin and placed it on her bread plate. "He is delicious. Emmeline, if you do not snap him up immediately, I shall be exceedingly cross. What a fine specimen!"

Emmy gave her an exasperated frown. "He's not a horse."

"I should say he is. A stallion." Camille chuckled bawdily. "I'd take a canter on him any day of the week."

Luc looked scandalized. "Really!"

Camille took a sip of wine. "Pish. You youngsters these days are far too straitlaced. There's nothing wrong with appreciating the opposite sex. If I were twenty years younger, I'd have him myself."

Emmy gave an appalled laugh. "You're welcome to him."

Chapter 13.

Emmy couldn't concentrate on the theatre performance. The acting was good and the story was full of drama, but she was bored and restless. Without Harland's electrifying presence, the whole evening felt like flat champagne that had lost its fizz. Life was no fun without someone to annoy. Or evade.

When the lights came on to signal the intermission, Camille leaned over and caught her fan, which Emmy had been tapping on her knee. "Why don't you go home? Or better still, why don't you use those tickets Lord Mowbray sent over?"

Luc leaned forward in his seat. "To the Tricorn?" He shot Emmy a questioning glance.

Barely an hour after Harland had left Waverton Street, a note had arrived for Luc containing two admittance cards for the Tricorn. The accompanying sheet had simply been signed "Mowbray."

Whether Harland knew about the invitation or not was impossible to guess.

Camille nodded. "Don't pretend you haven't been dying to try your hand at the Tricorn's tables ever since it opened, Luc Danvers." She turned to Emmy. "And don't *you* pretend you haven't been burning with curiosity to see what kind of place Harland inhabits." She patted their hands with her own and gave them each a gentle smile. "I know you both too well, *mes enfants*."

Emmy bit her lip. Camille was right; she'd dreamed of getting a peek inside the hallowed portals of the Tricorn for months. She wanted to see Harland's lair. "What if someone recognizes me?"

Camille reached into her reticule and pulled out a black silk half mask with a thin ribbon tie. She blinked in mock innocence. "Oh, look. I must have left this in here after the Colcroft's masquerade."

Emmy took it with a dry snort. "How convenient. Some might even say *unbelievably* convenient. What are you up to, Camille?"

Camille shrugged. "There's nothing wrong with doing a little reconnaissance on the opposition, darling. Just to see what we're up against. He's already called on us, remember. We're simply returning the favor."

Emmy fidgeted in her seat, plagued by indecision. The night was suddenly alive with possibility, but common sense dictated she keep her distance. This could be a trap, although how, exactly, she couldn't imagine. There was nothing she planned to steal from the Tricorn. And it wasn't as if she was going to get caught cheating at cards; she didn't know how.

Camille waved her fan. "Don't worry about me. I can share a carriage home with Lady Sutherland."

Emmy glanced over at Luc. "Why not?"

She'd take care not to be identified by anyone. And the chance to gain some insight into Harland's private world was too tantalizing to resist. Knowledge was power and all that. She wanted to see him on his home turf.

Luc gave a resigned sigh. "Oh, all right, then. Come on."

Alex suppressed a yawn as he gazed out over the main room of the Tricorn from his favored position up in the minstrel's gallery. It was warm up here near the ceiling, but the elevated position made him feel comfortable, master of all he surveyed. Well, one-third master, as least.

He'd squandered plenty of his own fortune in gaming hells like this one before he'd left for the continent. He'd been adrift in the *ton*, gambling and drinking, with no real aim in life save for having fun. The structure of the army had come as a welcome change; every mission had been clearly defined. *Storm that citadel. Secure the mountain pass. Protect those townspeople.* He'd thrived on the challenge.

Running the Tricorn gave him a similar sense of satisfaction, a feeling that he was doing something worthwhile with his life, instead of squandering his talents and time. It was a legacy, of sorts. Something he could pass down to the next generation.

Not that he was anywhere close to *producing* that next generation, of course. He'd have to find a woman he could stomach as a wife first. Some hope. The only woman he'd ever seriously considered might well be a criminal mastermind.

His stomach rumbled—he'd skipped dinner, chasing after little Miss Miscreant. He should have accepted her grandmother's offer of food. *That* would have annoyed her.

Unlike White's or Brooks', the Tricorn provided its members with a decent supper in addition to high-stakes games of chance. Benedict had convinced Alex and Seb to hire an outrageously expensive French chef, Rene

Lagrasse, to run the kitchens. Given the fact that they'd done nothing but try to kill Frenchmen for the previous three years, the two of them had needed some convincing, but once they'd tasted Lagrasse's mouthwatering fare, they'd been in full agreement.

Now, almost a year since the Tricorn had opened its doors, there was a waiting list of two hundred gentlemen clamoring for membership, both aristocrats and wealthy cits. The three of them were well on the way to making their fortunes.

Alex smiled thinly. The Tricorn was an equal-opportunity club. Everyone, whether banker, mill owner, tradesman, or duke, was equally welcome to throw their money his way.

As a second son, he would inherit no title or property from his father's estate. That would all go to his older brother, James. And yet Alex had never resented his brother's position. James had no ability to choose the course of his own life. There had never been any question that he would attempt to join the army and fight against Napoleon. Their distant, unloving father would never allow his heir to endanger himself in such a manner.

Alex, however, had always been the "spare," an insurance policy against the extinction of the illustrious Harland name. Ironically, that made him free.

Did his brother resent the cage of his seniority? Did he feel emasculated by his lack of choices? Alex had, after all, been able to prove his mettle in the army, both to himself and to his disapproving father. He'd made his fortune on his own.

The earldom that had recently been bestowed upon him by the Prince Regent had been the icing on the cake. Alex was justifiably proud of it; he'd earned that title, not simply been handed it for being born first.

Perhaps that was why the thought of the Nightjar

getting away with it annoyed him so much. Stealing jewels wasn't the same as *earning* them.

Alex shook his head and checked the various employees down on the floor. Everything seemed to be running smoothly. Each gaming table had an operator to deal the cards and two croupiers, who watched the play and ensured the players didn't cheat the operator. Mickey, the ex-boxer, doubled up as both doorman and, on occasion, dunner, to collect any debts owed to the bank. A couple of waiters hovered between the tables to offer the players plenty of drink from the Tricorn's excellent wine cellar.

It was crowded tonight. A couple of tables hosted noisy hands of whist and loo, while others dealt macao. Fortunes changed hands with alarming speed.

Most of the women on the floor were courtesans in the company of male members. Their brightly colored silks and satins glowed like so many precious jewels amongst the dark evening attire of the men. Fans fluttered and feathers bobbed from outrageously elaborate hairstyles. A couple of the women wore masks to add to the air of mystery. Or perhaps to hide less-than-perfect complexions, Alex mused cynically.

He took an appreciative sip of his brandy, enjoying the burn as it slid down his throat, and felt the tension begin to leech out of him.

It had been a mistake, opening that bottle of perfume again in his room. The tantalizing scent had filled his nose, filled his lungs, invaded his private domain. It had been far too easy to imagine *her* lying naked on his sheets, that sweet mouth curved in welcome. Alex growled as the blood pooled in his groin, a heavy ache of frustration. He turned to go back downstairs, but a flash of navy blue caught his eye.

It couldn't be. She wouldn't dare!

It was.

He drained the rest of his brandy in one gulp.

She was threading through the crowd in the wake of a man who, from his silver-topped cane and slightly uneven gait, could only be her brother. Danvers wasn't a member. How the hell had they gained entry?

Emmeline Danvers was wearing the same dress she'd had on earlier, at dinner. It left her shoulders deliciously bare and provided a tantalizing glimpse of the pale mounds of her breasts, especially from Alex's lofty vantage point. Her waist was tiny—he was sure he could span it with his hands—and he'd watched that pert bottom of hers swish up the stairs. His imagination had dutifully supplied all manner of depraved ideas. Like following her up and discovering exactly what the inside of her bedroom looked like. Like discovering if those freckles covered the rest of her body.

Alex scowled down at the pestilent woman. She'd added a black half mask that covered her from her eyebrows to the tip of that ridiculous nose, but he'd recognize her anywhere, even in the dark. *Especially* in the dark. He seemed unnaturally attuned to her presence.

A hot ball of anger formed in his gut. The last time she'd been masked, he'd imagined himself in love with her. Now, four years later, he almost hated her for putting them both in such an impossible position. If she was the Nightjar—and he was almost certain that she was—then he would have no choice but to turn her in. Her capture at his hands was inevitable. He was too good at his job not to prevail.

She would be prosecuted. She would lose not only her freedom, but quite possibly her life. What the hell was she thinking, coming here, flaunting herself in his kingdom? Did she think herself invincible? Did she think he was a fool?

Christ, if she was as guilty as he thought she was, she should be taking a carriage to Scotland or catching a boat across to France. She should be removing her sweet, thieving behind from the country, getting as far away from him, and Bow Street, and justice, as possible.

Chapter 14.

Emmy wanted to look everywhere at once, but she kept her head down and tried to look inconspicuous.

She'd never been inside a gentleman's club before, never imagined the noise, the luxury, the smell. Dice rattled in cups, roulette balls bounced and clattered in their wooden wheels, cards snapped and scraped over green baize. The air was an almost tangible fog of alcohol, tobacco, and warm bodies. Masculine shouts, curses, cheers, and groans formed a constant wave of sound, augmented by the odd feminine laugh. It was a world away from the staid formality of Almack's with its lukewarm lemonade.

Emmy was amazed at the colossal sums being transferred at the tables. She gambled with her life every time she stole something, and it seemed that the stakes were equally high here. The whim of a single card could make or ruin a man.

A wave of anger toward the players seized her. *She* had good reasons for risking it all. She did it reluctantly, against her will. What excuse did they have? Why choose to skirt ruin, merely for fun, for the thrill of it? It seemed an irresponsible way to find pleasure.

Luc joined a game of whist, and she stood behind him, feigning interest. She'd never liked cards. She lacked the patience. She passed an idle glance around the room, her heart in her throat, searching for a familiar face.

Did the owners of the club spend much time on the gaming floor? Or did they stay in their private apartments, ensconced in solitary splendor? If the private half of the Tricorn was anything like the luxury of this public side—the place positively exuded subtle yet expensive taste—then they must live like kings.

Out of habit, she catalogued the exits. The main door led to the curving flight of stairs they'd taken from the marbled entrance foyer. A dining room branched off to the left. A billiard room, judging from the occasional crack of ivory balls from within, on the opposite side. She glanced up. A minstrel's gallery, with a balcony like an opera box, overlooked the room, fed by a single door. That was where she would stand, given the choice.

Emmy recognized a few of the gentlemen in attendance. Eversleigh was impossible to overlook, in his pocket watches and a lurid yellow-striped waistcoat. He looked like a boiled sweet and seemed impressively inebriated. Lord East was there too, with an orange-haired woman who was most definitely not his wife.

Emmy's spirits drooped a little. There was no sign of Harland, nor his friend Wolff. She hadn't expected to see the third owner of the club, Benedict Wylde. He'd recently married Georgiana Caversteed, the shipping heiress, and it was rumored to be a love match. Emmy rather hoped he had better things to do with his evenings than oversee a crowd of intoxicated thrill-seekers.

Perhaps Harland was having dinner. Perhaps he wasn't even in the building.

Perhaps he was with a woman. She clenched her teeth.

Luc pushed back his chair. "I need to go to the necessary, but I don't want to leave you alone," he murmured. "I should never have let you and Camille to talk me into this. I dread to think what will happen if somebody recognizes you. Come with me. It's downstairs."

Emmy nodded, and together they made their way back to the staircase. Luc was clearly enjoying himself. He had a formidable intellect; he could probably devise a method of breaking the bank if he put his mind to it, but she was just glad to see him having fun. He'd missed out on several years' worth of evenings like this when he'd been an invalid.

The Tricorn's giant doorman, a man named Mickey, pointed Luc in the direction of the bathroom, and Emmy took advantage of his momentary inattention to palm the key that he'd left on a table near the door.

For all she knew, it opened something completely useless, like the Tricorn's wine cellar, or coal shed, but if she were lucky, it might prove more interesting—like the key to the back door, for example. Or to the private apartments. She slipped it into her reticule. No telling when something like that might come in handy.

As Luc lumbered off in the direction given, Emmy loitered at the far end of the corridor, feigning interest in the surprisingly good paintings that hung on the burgundy damask walls. A paneled door to her right opened, and she turned, expecting to see a servant, but instead, she encountered a familiar pair of slate-blue eyes.

Of all the—

She opened her mouth to say something—anything—but Harland took one swift glance down the deserted corridor, caught her elbow, and tugged her through the door.

Emmy was too surprised to do more than gasp as he

closed it behind them with a heavy click and swung her round so her back was pressed against the wall.

The noise from outside decreased to a dull hum, and she registered, dimly, that they were in some kind of secondary hallway, illuminated at regular intervals by a series of glowing wall sconces. He stepped up close, his huge chest inches from her own, his shins pressing against the front of her skirts.

Irritation mingled with shock. She was masked; he couldn't know who she was. Did he make a habit of abducting female strangers in this manner? Was this how he conducted all his interactions with women? He just pulled them into dimly lit corners whenever he felt the need to—

She tugged her elbow from his grip and went on the attack, even as her heart thundered in her ears. "Lord Melton, you seem to have made a—"

"What are you doing here? How did you get in?"

"You have me confused with someone else, sir."

He sent her mask a scathing look. "Do you think I'm *completely* blind?"

Emmy made one last-ditch effort. "My name is—"

"Emmeline d'Anvers," he supplied smoothly, and Emmy stilled in shock at the unexpected perfection of his French accent. From his lips, her name sounded liquid, seductive. As if he'd said it a thousand times before. Only Camille and her father had ever used that version. Luc and Sally used the clipped, Anglicized style—Emmy Danvers.

He crossed his arms over his chest. "I'll ask you again. How did you get in?"

Emmy looked him in the eye. "Your friend Mowbray sent my brother tickets."

His jaw tensed, and she thought she heard him mutter a curse. His gaze flicked down to her mouth—about the only part of her face he could see beneath her mask—then back up.

"You shouldn't have come. This is no place for a lady. It could be dangerous."

Emmy almost laughed aloud. Oh, yes, dangerous. The danger wasn't out there, though, in the card room. It was right here in front of her. Six foot two of bristling, infuriated male.

"You'll be ruined if someone from the *ton* recognizes you."

She managed an offhand shrug. "My reputation, or lack of it, is not your concern."

An inch of white cuff flashed as he braced his hands on the wall on either side of her head. He leaned forward, crowding her with his height, and a thrill of something that wasn't quite fear flashed through her. It had been a mistake to come here, to taunt him. But she'd never felt so alive. Being near him elicited the same nerve-wracking rush as participating in a heist.

"You're in my club, Miss Danvers. That makes you my concern."

Emmy pressed herself back against the wallpaper in a vain attempt to create some space between them. The air seemed thick, throbbing with tension. They were almost nose to nose. The light from the nearest sconce outlined the harsh line of his jaw, the bulge of his shoulder. She caught a hint of brandy on his breath, and it warmed her, curled her stomach.

His eyes narrowed. "You are the most aggravating woman I have ever had the misfortune to encounter."

"And you are the most irritating man."

She forced herself to hold his gaze. She understood this game; to close her eyes would be to admit defeat, and she refused to flinch first. She kept her eyes on his as he brought his hand to her cheek and spread his fingers along her jaw, just daring her to move. His hand was so large, he touched both earlobes at the same time.

She shivered.

"Do you find this irritating, Miss Danvers?" he murmured. His thumb stroked her chin, then slid to the corner of her lips.

She found that she was breathing hard, little pants against his skin. Her stomach swooped as he slid the pad of his thumb to the center of her lips and snagged her lower lip, folding it down. His eyes darkened.

In a sudden move, he yanked the ribbon that held her mask. It fell to the floor, and Emmy felt instantly exposed. The tiny piece of cloth had given her more confidence than she'd realized, the illusion of safety.

"Better," he murmured. "I see you, Emmy Danvers."

Was that a threat? A warning?

"Considering you're half blind, that's quite ironic," she managed on a shaky exhale.

His eyes were slate blue behind a tangle of dark lashes. Emmy regarded him with suspicion as he slid his hand around to the nape of her neck.

His lips touched hers with a static jolt that made her gasp. He pulled back, just a fraction, as if gauging her reaction, and then closed his eyes. He seemed to be waging an internal battle with himself. Emmy held her breath.

"Sod it," he breathed.

There was no hesitation this time. No uncertainty. His mouth molded over hers confidently, the perfect weight, neither too soft nor too aggressive. Heat curled inside her. He increased the pressure, and her lips opened at his silent command. She gasped as his tongue tangled with her own.

Brandy and sin.

Emmy closed her eyes. He traced her lower lip

then slid back for more, angling, pressing, repositioning; an endless slow burn that grew more and more urgent with every swirl of his tongue. Reason slipped away.

Madness. This was madness.

Nothing had ever felt so right. His mouth was even better than she remembered. Hot and insistent. Addictive. Her blood was a dull roar in her ears, blocking out the sound of the club only feet away.

Pretend. Just for a few moments. Pretend we're enemies who kiss. Pretend we're not enemies at all.

Another kiss. A deep, wet slide. Slow and languid, as if he had all the time in the world. As if he were savoring the taste of her.

Don't stop! Don't ever stop.

Seized with a reckless desperation, Emmy captured his lower lip between her teeth. He groaned, a low sound of appreciation deep in his throat, and her pulse leapt with delight. Interacting with him made her feel stingingly, achingly alive. She wanted to ruffle his feathers, to goad a reaction out of him.

You're supposed to be avoiding him!

Don't care. Closer. More.

She flattened her palms against his chest. His skin was hot beneath the cotton, his heartbeat strong. His delicious masculine weight pushed her up against the wall and an aching heaviness pulsed between her legs.

His hand slid to her ribs then up the side of her breast in a wicked slow caress. Her nipples peaked inside her bodice, and she gasped in dazed wonder. His kiss became a challenge, a gauntlet being thrown down. Who would stop first? Who would pull away, admit defeat?

Not me.

Air whooshed out of her lungs as he caught her waist and lifted her, pressing her hard against the wall. Emmy wrapped her arms around his neck and marveled at his strength as he grasped her bottom in both hands and crushed her to him.

"God—" He sounded breathless, almost pained.

"Emmy!" Another voice, Luc's, sharp and insistent.

Harland froze. And then cursed. He loosened his arms, and she slid back down to the floor, the wall at her back the only thing keeping her upright. Cool air rushed between them.

Emmy stared at him in astonishment. What had just happened? She could barely catch air into her lungs. Her legs felt like jelly. She placed one shaking hand over her heart and took as deep a breath as her stays would allow. *Good God.*

He stepped back, straightening his shirtsleeves, then ran a hand through his hair.

"Emmy!" Luc's voice echoed through the thick door, fainter this time.

Harland caught the handle of the door and swung it wide. Light flooded in. He shot Emmy a fierce look. "Go home, Emmy Danvers. And stop playing with fire."

Emmy scooped up her mask from the floor and ran.

Chapter 15.

Seb wrinkled his nose when Alex entered the Tricorn's private sitting room the following afternoon.

"Phew! Where have you been? You smell like a tart's boudoir."

Alex raised his sleeve to his nose, sniffed, and grimaced. "I've been at Floris, the parfumier over on Jermyn Street."

"Still trying to pin down our fragrant thief?" Seb surmised. "Any luck?"

"Indeed. Monsieur Fargeon confirmed what I'd suspected—that the scent on the feathers left by the Nightjar is the same as the one provided to us by Miss Danvers."

"And?" Seb shrugged. "What does that signify? She can't be the only woman in London with that particular perfume."

"As a matter of fact, she probably *is*. It's a rather unusual scent, by all accounts. As individual as personalized snuff." Alex pulled out his penciled notes. "It was invented by a Frenchman named Houbigant, who made perfumes for Marie Antoinette and the Empress Josephine. According to Fargeon, he's been making the same scent for Miss Danvers ever since her sixteenth birthday. He makes it only for her."

Alex squinted at the paper, trying to read his own handwriting. "He says it evokes 'a classic French garden' with 'headnotes of bergamot and lemon, a midrange of jasmine, rose, and orange blossom, and base notes of sandalwood and ambergris.' Whatever that means."

Fargeon had been quite the character. He'd maintained that every scent told a story, weaved a spell. He claimed that just by un-stopping a bottle, he could transport a man to Arabia or the shores of the tropics.

Or to a moonlit garden, with an armful of fragrant, deceitful woman.

Alex frowned. The scent of her still haunted his bedroom, thanks to the bottle he'd commandeered. The taste of her still lingered in his mouth, even after a day. What in God's name had he been thinking, to kiss her like that? He was deranged. He should have been trying to trick a confession out of her, not kissing her senseless up against a bloody wall.

Seb raised his brows. "A heady concoction. But can he be certain it's exactly the same? Beyond reasonable doubt?"

"He's an expert. His opinion's good enough for me," Alex said grimly. "When you put it together with her family history and Vidocq's deductions, it seems clear that she's the Nightjar."

"Well, hell," Seb sighed. "I suppose you're going to catch her now?"

Alex nodded. "There are only two of the major jewels left to steal. Lady Carrington's ruby, and the sapphire in Kent."

"I don't mind taking a trip out to Kent," Seb said easily.

"I'm getting a bit sick of London. I'll see if I can drag Benedict away from marital bliss to accompany me. "

"All right. You go; I'll talk to the Carringtons."

"You'll never guess who I just saw in Covent Garden," Sally said as she breezed into the salon with her arms full of freshly cut flowers. "Your Lord Melton."

Emmy's teacup clattered back into her saucer, but she managed a frown. "He's not *my* anything."

Camille raised her own teacup to her lips and exchanged an amused glance with Sally, which made Emmy want to grind her teeth. "Of course not, darling."

Emmy hadn't been thinking about him, or that earth-shattering kiss, for the better part of two days. Not at all. She definitely hadn't woken that morning from the most wickedly erotic dream of her life with her body throbbing on the verge of climax because she'd been imagining herself beneath Harland. On a bed instead of against a wall.

Do you find this irritating, Miss Danvers?

Not. At. All.

She cleared her throat. "What was he doing?"

Sally fluffed the flowers in a vase. "I was on my way to Floris, to get you another bottle of scent, since he took the last one, and he was just leaving."

The image of such a masculine man in such a feminine place was an amusing contradiction. A lesser man might have been overawed, but Emmy couldn't imagine Harland being intimidated by anything. He was the kind of man who made himself at home in a modiste's dressing room and calmly dictated which underwear his paramour should buy.

Her heart sank. Bother the man. She hadn't had any perfume for two days, because of him. She felt naked without it. A little less feminine. A little more vulnerable. The thought of him having her scent in his house, of being able to smell it whenever he felt like it, made her feel a little strange.

Neither Luc nor Camille seemed particularly concerned by his ongoing investigations. They believed she was wily enough throw him off the scent. But Emmy could sense the net closing in. The sword of Damocles hovered above her head, held aloft by only the thinnest of threads. Any moment, whenever Harland decided, it would come crashing down upon her neck.

She glanced over at Camille. "I don't suppose it will make any difference if I say we should postpone stealing the ruby?"

Camille took a dainty bite of teacake. "I do understand your concerns, Emmy, but time is of the essence. Danton has been suspiciously quiet, which worries me. Harland might be suspicious of you, but he will want enough evidence to obtain a conviction before he makes his move. The fact that he hasn't done anything yet suggests he doesn't have enough proof."

"He knows what we're after," Emmy urged. "He's going to try to catch me stealing the ruby."

"Let him try. You are clever and forewarned. And really, the opportunity on Thursday is too good to miss."

Emmy sighed. The ruby Danton had demanded was owned by Lady Carrington, who lived on Park Crescent. In two days' time, her neighbor, the Spanish Ambassador, would be holding a ball in honor of the Russian and French Court. Close to six hundred people would be in attendance; it was one of the most anticipated social events of the year. It would provide an excellent distraction.

"It would be nice," Emmy said wearily, "to have normal concerns. Like trying to decide which dress to wear, which gloves to purchase. Not which *window* to climb through."

Camille smiled. "You are not normal, Emmeline."

"A phrase every girl longs to hear."

Camille waved her hand. "If you weren't a thief, you would be like all the other girls out there. Unforgivably dull. You'd have no conversation at all. You're so much more interesting this way, darling."

"How can I be interesting when I can't talk to anyone about it? I must pretend to be vapid and almost mute and suffer idiots explaining things badly to me. It took every ounce of willpower I possessed not to empty my glass of champagne over Lord Bolton's head when he tried to tell me that rubies and spinels were the same."

"Don't forget that diamonds are only produced under immense pressure. It can be the same for people. You have produced your greatest work, attained your greatest potential, because you were put under pressure."

"Yes, but—"

Camille's eyes took on a roguish twinkle. "I've discovered it's often the case with husbands too. A combination of applying pressure—and the right amount of heat—usually produces diamonds. Necklaces mainly." She gave a throaty chuckle. "And what fun it was to provide the heat! Ah, me. I do miss your grandfather."

"Grandmère!"

"Bah. Don't tell me you haven't felt an equal amount of heat for your Lord Melton."

Emmy groaned into her teacup, wishing she could deny it.

"It is rather an inconvenient attraction." Camille sighed. "Considering your respective professions."

Emmy gave a cracked laugh. "It is not *inconvenient*. Inconvenient is snapping your parasol on the hottest day of the year. Inconvenient is being unable to find a matching pair of stockings. This is a disaster."

"I know how you like to collect words that have no English translation, Emmeline. So here is one for you:

the Russians call what you have *tosca*." Camille nodded sagely. "It is a melancholy yearning, a longing, a love
sickness. An unbearable feeling that you need to escape
but lack the hope or energy to do so. It is an awful feeling.
But without *tosca*, there cannot be delirious happiness."

Emmy frowned into the tea leaves that swirled at the
bottom of her cup. "I don't want to be attracted to him.
He's not a man, he's a bloodhound. Sniffing us out. Hunting us down. He is relentless. He will catch us and rip us
to pieces—"

"How terribly bloodthirsty." Camille laughed. "But I
have seen the way he looks at you. It is not ice in his veins,
but fire. There is passion beneath the hauteur. A man like
that is slow to kindle, but when he does? Ooh la la." She
raised her brows. "You distract him, Emmeline. And that
gives you power. Distracted, he will make mistakes. If
you rile him enough, he will snap."

"I don't want to see him snap," Emmy said, quite honestly. "He's dangerous."

Camille tilted her head. "Au contraire, I think it could
be extremely exciting. But it takes a brave woman to deal
with that kind of man. You must meet him head-on. He is
not comfortable, I think. But he would be so very worth it."

"He will show me no mercy if he catches me."

Camille nodded. "Sometimes the chase is such fun that
the catching is quite a disappointment." She took another
bite of teacake. "On the other hand, sometimes being
caught is only the start of the adventure."

"Being caught would be the start of a trip to the gallows," Emmy said sharply. "Nothing more."

Sally's reappearance at the doorway precluded any further argument. "Ready for a trip to Park Crescent?"

Emmy gave a resigned nod.

Chapter 16

Emmy put both hands on the small of her back and arched her spine—the universal movement of a heavily pregnant woman trying to relieve the weight she carried in front— then took hold of the bottom of Sally's ladder to steady it.

Luc had driven around Park Crescent late last night, flicking white, watery paint at several of the first-floor windows. This morning Sally and Emmy, happily disguised as itinerant window washers, were doing a brisk trade cleaning off the "pigeon droppings."

Sally had excelled this time. Tied to Emmy's waist by an ingenious series of straps and buckles was a pig's bladder—thoroughly cleaned—filled with water. It gave the realistic appearance of a pregnant belly; the weight of it added to the authenticity of her posture.

Sally always said that for a disguise to be truly effective, the wearer must have an attitude to match. If you were supposed to be a ballet dancer, every movement, every action had to mirror that belief. You should keep your head up, chin high, be graceful. Conversely, if you were supposed to be a vagabond, you should hunch, and drag your feet, and scratch as if you had vermin. She'd learned such things from her days at the theatre.

Emmy felt very much like a woman who wanted to sit and relieve her aching feet. An apron tied over the top of her skirts added to her apparent bulk, as did the scratchy wig she wore beneath an unsightly bonnet that shielded her face.

Lady Carrington's servants had been all too happy to delegate the task of window washing to Sally, who had turned herself into a strapping young lad. She was currently whistling tunelessly at the top of the ladder, gaily swiping at the "droppings" with a wet rag.

They'd done what they needed to do. While washing the back of the Carringtons' house Sally had deformed one of the window latches just enough to prevent it from fully closing. Everything was set. Emmy had wanted to leave at once—Luc was waiting for them with the carriage just around the corner in Harley Street, but Sally had insisted they wash a few more windows along the street to allay suspicion.

Emmy cursed softly as a splash of water from Sally's bucket landed squarely in her eye. It stung. Sally maintained the secret to a perfectly shiny window was vinegar in with the water.

"Get a move on!" Emmy muttered at Sally's breeches-clad bottom.

Sally glanced down, and her white smile split the grimy oval of her face. "Almost done, missus." She chuckled. "Don't want to leave no streaks."

Emmy cast a wary glance down the stately curve of Park Crescent. The row of elegant terraced houses had been designed by Prinny's favorite architect, John Nash.

They formed a gentle semicircle around a central green park. A couple of the upper-class residents were strolling along the well-kept paths toward the verdant swathe of Regent's Park a little farther down the street.

Emmy ducked her head as she recognized Lord Denman, Chief Justice of the Court of Queen's Bench, leaving his house. After the Lord Chancellor, Lord Denman was the second-most important judge in England. She had no intention of gaining *his* notice, either inside or outside a courtroom.

When she glanced up again, she almost swallowed her own tongue. Alex Harland was striding along the crescent, heading directly toward her. She pressed herself to the foot of the ladder with a whispered curse.

"It's Harland!" she hissed.

Sally turned to look and gave an appreciative sigh from her elevated vantage point. "Good lord. Just look at those shoulders. Camille's right, that man is—"

"Come *on*!" Emmy whispered.

He was almost upon them. Emmy ducked, bending over her large belly with difficulty, and nudged the bucket of water closer to the foot of the ladder, ostensibly to get it out of his way. She felt a swish of air behind her as he passed by and breathed a sigh of relief when he spared herself and Sally only the briefest glance. He turned into the gate of the Carrington residence.

Emmy's palms began to sweat. She'd been right! He knew they were going to steal the ruby, although how, she couldn't fathom. True, her father had once proclaimed the Nightjar's intentions in print, but that had been sixteen years ago, back in Paris. How likely was it that Harland would have stumbled across something so obscure? And yet his sources must have managed to dig it up. How irritating.

Sally, finally, seemed to catch her urgency. She descended the ladder, tossed the wet rag in the bucket, and joined Emmy as she started to waddle down the street.

The pregnant woman was a good disguise, but it was useless for a speedy escape.

Emmy reached into her apron, flicked open the small folding knife she carried, and made a nick in the water-filled sack. She was immediately treated to a slow, unpleasant trickle of liquid leaking down her right leg. It soaked into her stocking, then slithered into her shoe. Her belly began to deflate. Still, better wet than arrested.

Still whistling, Sally put her arm solicitously around Emmy's shoulders and bent her head as if murmuring something comforting.

"As soon as we're 'round that corner, run," she muttered.

Alex took the steps to the Carrington residence two at a time, then stopped halfway. Something niggled at him, a sniper's sense that something wasn't right.

He shot a glance down the street, wondering what had prickled his attention. A carriage rattled along. A child played with a yappy dog over in the park. And a tuneless whistling floated back to him from the young window washer who was escorting his pregnant wife along the road.

Alex frowned. The boy's ladder was still propped up against the front of the house. The bucket was still there. Why were they leaving without their equipment? Alex narrowed his eyes. That boy had a suspiciously rounded pair of hips. And that pregnant woman seemed to be walking faster with every step.

He checked his pockets for his watch. Had he been pickpocketed? No.

Still suspicious, he bounded back down the steps and started after them.

"Hoi! Madam!"

The pair started walking faster. Neither of them looked around—a sure indication of guilt. Alex quickened his pace. They turned the corner. He broke into a trot.

He rounded the last house just in time to see the "pregnant woman" standing in a puddle of water, and suddenly as slim as a reed. Alex let out a shout. He heard a distinct feminine gasp as she hitched up her sodden skirts and bolted down the street in the wake of the shapely window washer.

He hastened in pursuit.

The two of them dodged nimbly through the pedestrians on Harley Street, dashed across the road in front of a draper's cart, eliciting a flurry of abuse from the driver, and dived into a nondescript black carriage. The driver—an elderly cove with grizzled sideburns and an apparent hunchback—whipped the horses with a shout and the whole lot galloped off before Alex could catch up.

He stopped, panting, in the middle of the street and made use of every single swear word he'd ever learned. He hadn't seen the woman's face, but he was convinced that expectant mother had been Emmy Danvers.

Bloody, bloody hell.

The fact that she was here, quite clearly studying the location for her next crime, should have filled him with a deep sense of satisfaction. He'd correctly predicted where she would strike. He would catch her. He doubted she'd be sensible enough to abort the plan to steal the Carringtons' ruby, even knowing he was close on her tail. Whatever her reasons—and he strongly suspected a touch of insanity at this point—she seemed unwilling to stop her larcenous hobby.

A wave of impotent fury balled his hands into fists as he stalked back to Park Crescent. Bloody woman! Could she not see how this would end? What did she think was going to happen when she was caught? That her pretty face and aristocratic name would protect her from the full weight of the English judiciary system? It would not.

The punishment for stealing was harsh. A person could be executed for taking anything worth more than five shillings, be that a handkerchief or a sheep. Did she think if she made those stardust eyes fill with tears that a judge would be moved to clemency? Would those irresistible lips spout lie after lie?

Alex shook his head. Or did she think that *he* would be the weak link? That she could somehow sway him from turning her in? A muscle ticked in his jaw. Did she plan to seduce him into letting her go? His groin throbbed in an enthusiastic *yes!*

God knew, he would be tempted.

He frowned, irritated at himself. No. He would *not* be swayed, however persuasive that sweet body and those glorious lips might be. The law was the law. Reason free from passion. Just as Aristotle said.

Half an hour later, having spoken to Lady Carrington, Alex had learned two things. One, that Lady Carrington deserved to have her ruby necklace stolen. When he'd asked to see where she kept her jewels, the woman had complied willingly; the endeavor required a trip to her bedchamber. Licking her lips—which were thin and not at all tempting in the way that Emmy Danvers's lips were—she'd casually mentioned that her "incredibly dull" husband would be "away for hours at some stuffy parliamentary debate." Perhaps Alex would like to see her newly redecorated boudoir? Alex had politely declined.

The second thing he'd learned was that the Carringtons' neighbor, the Spanish Ambassador, would be holding his annual ball on Thursday night. Which meant the odds were high the Nightjar would use the crowds and confusion to strike.

Alex bounded down the steps with a spring in his step, his pulse thumping in anticipation. Emmy Danvers was going to get caught.

Chapter 17.

Emmy's dress for the Ambassador's ball was dark-blue silk, an exquisite French-inspired creation that skimmed her shoulders and waist before falling in artless swirls around her legs. It felt as decadent, as smooth, as double cream.

Sally had pinned her hair up in elaborate coils on the top of her head, with a trio of black feathers and a diamond-studded clip, which added inches to Emmy's diminutive stature. The feathers matched her black satin gloves and ostrich-feather fan.

Camille also looked magnificent, very much "la Grande Dame" in a gown of pale-green brocade shot with gold thread that shimmered when she turned in the light. Her upswept hair highlighted her excellent bone structure and piercing blue eyes.

"Well, don't we look marvelous?" Camille laughed, her eyes sparkling. "The men of London should guard their hearts tonight."

"Let's just hope Lady Carrington isn't guarding her

ruby," Emmy muttered. "If she's wearing it, we'll have to come up with another plan."

Luc, handsome in a black satin evening jacket, shrugged. "You're good at improvising, Em. You'll think of something."

Park Crescent was teeming with carriages when they arrived. Light blazed through the open front door of the ambassador's house as a stream of people waited to be admitted by the liveried servants. Since the Prince Regent was rumored to be attending, along with several of the royal dukes, members of the cabinet, and Wellington, a squadron of the Royal Horse Guards had been placed on duty in the street in case of any disturbance.

Emmy glanced over at the Carringtons' house. As expected, only a few lights burned in the upstairs living quarters. Some of the staff had been given the night off, since they weren't needed to attend to their master and mistress, and the rest were gathered in the basement kitchen, peering out between the railings to watch the fantastic creatures arriving next door.

As she ascended the staircase to the huge ballroom that occupied the front of the house, Emmy was relieved to catch a glimpse of Lady Carrington wearing a sparkling diamond choker. She'd left her rubies at home. Thank goodness.

Luc made his way to the room that had been set aside for cards and took a seat, while Emmy left Camille talking to some friends and made her way to the ballroom.

Couples, with elbows high and hands clasped, swirled around the inlaid wooden floor to the accompaniment of a string quartet playing Schubert. Conversations rose and fell in rhythmic cadences like the sea. Fans fluttered, jewels flashed, turbans bobbed. It was a dizzying, glorious spectacle. Emmy took up position between a decorative wooden pillar that had been painted to look like marble and a side table held aloft by a grotesque gilt dolphin.

She became aware of Harland when the back of her neck prickled in warning. His huge, warm body materialized behind her, a solid masculine presence impossible to ignore. He must have learned such tactics in the army; how to sneak up on an enemy unobserved. How to take advantage of the terrain and natural cover to gain an advantage.

She tamped down a delirious sense of anticipation. She'd known he would seek her out. His presence just added another level of excitement, of danger to the game. She had the feeling he would always be within arm's reach. Was that a desirable thing or not?

His low voice came from over her shoulder. "Miss Danvers. Fancy seeing you here." His tone was drier than a desert.

Her whole body seemed to light up, like a breathed-upon ember. "Lord Melton," she said coolly.

Had she really kissed him senseless a few days ago? It seemed impossible. She wanted to do it again.

"Tell me one thing about yourself that very few people in this room know," he said.

Emmy kept her gaze on the dancers. *I'm a brazen, unrepentant jewel thief.* She shouldn't even be talking to him. Every piece of information might be used against her. But politeness won out.

"Very well. I enjoy discovering foreign words that have no direct English translation." She glanced over her shoulder and caught his look of mild surprise. Any other woman would have told him she liked embroidery or playing the pianoforte or sketching.

"Hmmm." The sound he made was encouraging, as if he'd received the pleasantly satisfying answer to a puzzle that had been plaguing him for some time. Emmy decided to elaborate.

"The French have several of them. *L'esprit de l'escalier*, for example. It literally means 'staircase wit' and is used to describe that perfect, clever retort you think of only after someone's left and you're going back upstairs."

Harland smiled—a wide, genuine smile that lit his eyes—and her heart seized in her chest. His smile was a thing of beauty, something rare and wonderful. She wanted to make it appear again.

"*Sortable* is the adjective to use for friends and family members you can take out in public without fear of being embarrassed," she said.

He was *très sortable*. Any woman would preen to have him on her arm.

Now that she'd started, Emmy couldn't seem to stop. "The Scots have a good one: *tartle*. It's that panicky hesitation just before you have to introduce someone whose name you cannot quite remember."

"That *is* a good word," he said. "I have definitely been tartled, on occasion." He tilted his head, still not looking at her. "I've travelled extensively on the continent—Bonaparte's unofficial Grand Tour. I must have picked up a few words to add to your collection. Let me think."

He gazed out across the dance floor, apparently deep in thought, and Emmy stole a glance at the clean line of his jaw and firm lips. Her skin tingled.

"I have one," he said finally. "See that annoying fellow over there? In mustard-yellow pantaloons."

"Lord Eversleigh?"

"Indeed. The Germans have a word for him."

She raised her brows in silent question.

"*Backpfeifengesicht*," he supplied.

"Bless you," she said, straight-faced.

He shot her a chiding sideways glance. "It means 'a face badly in need of a fist.'"

Emmy quelled a snicker of amusement. "Interesting."

"The Russian soldiers I met had plenty of entertaining phrases too. Most of them were related to drinking. They have a whole host of words to convey various levels of intoxication. *Soosh-nyak*, for example, is that dry feeling you get in your throat when you wake up after a night of heavy drinking."

"I wouldn't know," Emmy said virtuously. "But no doubt you're intimately acquainted with the sensation."

He ignored that little jibe. "They have another word that describes the disappointment of seeing a woman who appears pretty from behind but not from the front. I can't remember what it is, though."

"That's very helpful," she said with faint irony.

The realization of how much she was enjoying herself crushed her chest. This easy, teasing banter was a tantalizing glimpse of what could have been, had circumstances been different. But any friendship between the two of them was an impossibility. These brief, forbidden moments were all she could ever have.

The dance ended, and another set began to form. Harland stepped past her and caught her hand. "We should dance."

She didn't have time to voice an objection. He led her onto the dance floor and turned her neatly in his arms. The heat of his palm warmed through her glove where their hands were joined. His left hand settled easily at the small of her back.

She braced herself to look him in the eye, and the predictable flash of lightning sparked between them. *What an unreasonable attraction.*

His gaze rested for an instant on her mouth, then flitted away. Emmy was aware of curious glances being sent their way, a flurry of speculative whispers. Any woman with Alex Harland would be an object of envy. With his height and sinfully dark good looks, he was utterly compelling, and her heart fluttered at being the center of attention. The cattiest amongst them were probably wondering how a freckled little thing like her was dancing with a demigod like him.

"Wait, you don't dance!" she recalled belatedly. "You haven't danced since you returned from the Peninsular."

His eyebrows rose, and she could have bitten off her tongue for betraying how much she knew about him. His lips quirked. "It's true I haven't danced, but that doesn't mean I cannot do so. I've just chosen not to. Until now. I never found a suitable partner."

Her pulse fluttered. What did *that* mean?

"You'll have to help me, Miss Danvers," he murmured. "I cannot see our joined hands, nor the couples in our periphery. If it looks as if we are about to cause a collision, do let me know."

She glanced round in alarm. "Really, there's no need. We should—"

"Afraid?" he taunted softly.

That did it. She lifted her chin. "Of course not."

His chuckled exhale sluiced against her temple. He pulled her tighter into his embrace and squeezed her hand. "In that case, try to keep up."

The music started, another Viennese waltz, and Emmy's breath lodged in her throat. Her first steps faltered, but Harland spun her out and back into his embrace with consummate skill.

Had she truly imagined that he would be clumsy? His footwork was perfect, his body straight and tall. He seemed to be touching her everywhere: his hand at the small of her back, gently guiding, at her elbow, around her waist, sliding easily around her hip.

The ballroom dissolved into a breathless succession of dips and swirls, advance and retreat. Heat spread throughout her limbs. Her skin began to glow. Every nerve in her body was attuned to his presence. She wanted to press herself closer still, to feel the extraordinary breadth of his chest against her cheek, the rippled muscles of his stomach beneath her palms. The press of his mouth on hers.

No. No. No. She was becoming befuddled by his nearness. She couldn't trust him an inch. He was here to catch her in the act of stealing the ruby. Why else would he have been at the Carringtons' house two days ago?

Had he warned them? Had they moved the ruby? Was she about to walk into a trap?

She'd been plagued by visions of opening Lady Carrington's jewelry case and finding nothing but a taunting black feather. Of turning to see Harland's huge hands and triumphant face materializing from the darkness, blocking her only escape.

Last night, she'd awoken from a hot, confusing dream of being chased and caught, of being held against a rock-hard chest, her wrists manacled by unrelenting fingers. She'd been begging, sobbing, but for what? For freedom? For forgiveness? For more of that wicked, forbidden heat? She'd been simultaneously aroused and terrified.

She couldn't wait until this was over. When Danton was appeased, she could start chasing her *own* desires, her own dreams. Except the only thing she'd ever truly desired was this man who'd stop at nothing to see the Nightjar brought to justice. Ha.

"You're playing a dangerous game, you know." Harland's murmur jolted her back to the room.

"I don't know what you mean."

"Oh, I think you do. You're very good at hiding, aren't you, Miss Danvers? You pretend to be stupider than you are. You disguise your beauty behind drab colors. But not tonight," he conceded, flicking an appreciative glance down at the silk of her dress. "Tonight you look like a jewel, ripe for the plucking."

She stepped on his toe in surprise. What a choice of words. Deliberate? Or mere coincidence? She didn't believe in coincidence. Everything this man said had a deeper meaning.

He glared down at her as if he could see into her soul. As if every misdeed and wicked thought lay naked to his gaze. Emmy bit her lip against the insane urge to confess everything. Good lord, no wonder this man was so successful at Bow Street. He only had to look at a perpetrator to have them spilling their secrets.

He bent his head and his breath tickled her cheek. "A word of advice, Miss Danvers. Only play a game if you are certain you can win."

"That's an interesting comment, coming from a man who owns a gambling club."

He shrugged. "An individual might encounter a streak of luck, it's true, but sooner or later, that luck will run out. The odds are always stacked in the bank's favor."

Her own luck couldn't possibly continue. But did he think she had any choice in the matter? She had to play the game. "I stand forewarned, my lord," she said lightly.

The waltz ended on two final, joyously uplifting chords. *Enough.* She needed to stop torturing herself with the pleasure-pain of his proximity and get on with the real business of the night.

"Thank you for the dance, my lord. And the advice." She bobbed him a curtsey then sent him a sidelong look full of mock sympathy. "Oh dear. I see a whole raft of ladies expecting a waltz, now you've finally set foot on the dance floor. You've opened Pandora's box."

His alarmed glance at the flock of women hovering on the periphery of the room was a joy to see. Emmy used his momentary distraction to step away. She had a ruby to steal.

Chapter 18.

It was easy enough to slip into the library at the back of the house. The room, although not officially open to guests, had not been locked. Emmy unlatched the tall doors that opened onto the narrow wrought-iron balcony and slipped through. The cool night air brought goose bumps to her skin.

Below her, the indistinct shapes of well-tended trees and bushes disappeared into the darkness of the garden. She clutched the rail and forced herself to look down. To her right, only a few feet away, an identical balcony belonging to the Carringtons protruded from the dressed stone. Pushing down a wave of nausea, she lifted her skirts and climbed over the metal rail. It was cold, even through her gloves.

She hated heights.

The French had a phrase, *l'appel du vide*, "the call of the void." She felt it, always, that intrinsic urge to jump from high places, despite her fear.

With a heart-stopping stretch, she reached over and

caught the other railing, first with her hand, then her left foot. For an awful moment she froze, suspended like a starfish over the drop, one foot and one hand on each balcony. The sudden ridiculous thought of someone happening to come outside and glance up—they would see right up her skirt to her scandalous navy silk underthings—made her stifle a snort of nervous laughter.

A push, a lurch, and she transferred her weight to the opposite side and climbed gratefully over the rail. It would have been a lot easier if she'd been able to wear her breeches, but the cut of her dress had not allowed for her to wear them underneath.

There. Worst bit over.

Her palms were damp inside her gloves but the window catch Sally had bent out of shape ensured the window opened easily. Emmy strained her ears, listening for any hint of sound from within, but heard nothing. She slipped through the narrow window.

The Carringtons' house was a mirror image of the ambassador's, but their library didn't have half as many books. Every one of her senses stretched as she made her way through the house. What trap had Harland laid for her? Since he himself was still on the dance floor, he couldn't be lying in wait, but that didn't mean he hadn't arranged for other Bow Street agents to be here.

Emmy crept forward, studying every lumpy sofa, every suspiciously billowing curtain, but failed to detect any other presence. Her blood was a pounding rush in her ears as she crept up the stairs to Lady Carrington's bedroom.

The ruby was exactly where Luc had said it would be, in a red leather–covered box at the back of the armoire. The key, as promised, under the Meissen parrot on the mantel. How Luc had discovered this information Emmy had no idea, but since Lord Carrington was known to turn a blind eye to his wife's blatant flirtations, she suspected there were plenty of gentlemen with intimate knowledge of her bedroom who might have been persuaded to share the information.

She was sure her brother hadn't felt the need to make a personal investigation of Lady Carrington's "valuables" himself. He was too dedicated to Sally.

The claw setting of the ruby snagged her glove as she twisted the pendant free from its place in the center of the necklace, and she quashed a faint twinge of guilt at the destruction of the piece. The ruby didn't belong here.

Emmy lifted her hand to her hair, plucked one of the black feathers from her coiffure, and placed it neatly inside the jewelry box. She considered pushing the ruby into her cleavage, but since her breasts weren't as abundant as Sally's, it would make an obvious, uncomfortable lump beneath her corset. She reached up and poked it into the center of her intricate topknot instead. Her hair had always been thick, like a horse's tail. It would be safe up there.

Still unable to believe that Harland hadn't set some fiendish trap, she made her way down the stairs, her slippered feet silent on the thick carpet runner. Instead of going back across the balconies, she planned to descend another level, to the entrance hall, and leave via the garden. She listened, alert for the slightest noise, unable to beat down her innate suspicion.

Where was Harland? His men? This was too easy. It was impossible that he'd planned nothing, especially after his verbal hints that he was on to her—

The door to the servant's quarters opened, and she stilled.

Blast the man. She'd been right.

She ducked behind a pillar, her heart pounding, but instead of Harland's mocking voice ordering her to give herself up, she heard a hushed female giggle and a corresponding masculine rumble, then the swift patter of shoes on the marble hallway tiles below.

"William, we can't!" the female whispered, in a breathless tone that quite clearly said *William, we must!*

"Of course we can," William growled. "They won't be back for hours. And besides, do you know how many times I've watched you bend over that hearth to set the fire and wanted to catch you in my arms?"

"A hundred?" the girl guessed teasingly.

"A thousand."

"Oh, *William!*"

Emmy grinned as the unmistakable silence of kissing ensued.

"Come on," William groaned. "Let's see if 'is lordship's desk is as sturdy as it looks."

More rustling, the click of a door, and the metallic tumble of a lock being turned. Emmy sent the amorous couple a mental toast, glad they were enjoying their evening. She envied their freedom.

The laughter and murmured conversation of the remaining servants below stairs floated up from the basement kitchen. They seemed to be having just as much fun, if not more, than the guests in the ballroom next door. Emmy smiled. One of the reasons the Nightjar always left a feather behind was to ensure that none of the menial staff were ever accused of stealing. That, at least, was one thing she didn't have on her conscience.

With a swift glance left and right, she made her way to the back of the house and let herself out into the Carringtons' garden. Music and laughter from the ambassador's house spilled out the open windows, but the weather was too cool to have tempted guests onto the terrace. Only a low stone balustrade separated the two gardens, and she stepped over this final hurdle with a little bounce of triumph.

Take that, Alexander Harland, with your veiled warn-ings and your oblique threats! Tonight, the game is mine.

Emmy approached the tall glass structure at the rear of the house and slipped inside. The ambassador's con-servatory was almost overflowing with tropical abun-dance. It was as if her own bedroom wallpaper had come to flowering, riotous life. A midnight forest, in three di-mensions.

Wafts of sultry air made her shiver as she padded along one of the narrow brick pathways toward the main part of the house. It was quite dark. A couple of small Chinese-style paper lanterns had been placed at odd in-tervals along the narrow walks, but their tiny puddles of light were swallowed up in the gloom. Moonlight filtered through the glass panes high above, but the dark slash of leaves, palms, or tropical ferns, created a shivering lattice overhead, obscuring the light.

Emmy inhaled deeply, trying to calm her residual nerves. The scent of the place was strangely comforting: warm earth, rich vegetal fecundity, sweet flowers, and mossy loam. A wave of belated relief overcame her, and she sank onto one of the knee-high brick walls that di-vided each section. Her hands were shaking.

Silly, but this always seemed to happen. During a heist, she was completely focused, able to control her nerves. But afterwards, when she was safe, and alone in her bedroom, *then* she became scared. She shook. Sometimes she cried. She'd think of everything that could have gone wrong, even as she hugged herself in elation.

The door at the far end of the conservatory opened, admitting a brief blast of raucous noise, and her head snapped up. A blast of cooler air stirred the damp hairs at her neck. She shrank back onto the foliage, glad that her dark dress would prevent her from being easily seen.

Someone must have wanted a break from the party. Probably a drunken reveler needing some air.

Boot heels, definitely masculine, clicked on the pathway, and Emmy tensed as they came closer. Damn it. Why couldn't he have chosen a different path? She hadn't gone through all this to be caught in some ridiculous, compromising situation with a stranger.

A figure appeared, tall and menacing, and all the hairs on her arms rose in warning. An awful trickle of foreboding ran down her spine. Emmy stood, not caring that it gave away her position, as the unmistakable, *inevitable* voice of Alex Harland rumbled through the darkness.

"Ill-met by moonlight, Miss Danvers."

Chapter 19.

Emmy frowned in the darkness. Shakespeare? She vaguely recalled the scene. It was from *A Midsummer Night's Dream*: Oberon and Titania, the feuding married couple of the underworld. Very apt. Except, of course, she was nowhere near married to Harland, thank the lord.

She pressed her gloved hand to her throat, not having to feign her jittery shock. "Lord Melton. You startled me. I was just getting a little air. I was about to leave."

He tilted his head. "Whereas I have just arrived. It seems we're destined to be forever at odds, Miss Danvers. Adversaries, if you will."

She managed a nervous laugh. "Oh, I wouldn't go that far, my lord."

"Would you not?" He paused a moment, as if considering. "What *would* you say we are, then? I don't think we can really class ourselves as friends."

Emmy ignored the twinge of hurt at his easy dismissal of friendship and managed a careless shrug. "I'm sure I don't know. I'd have thought you have more than enough adversaries from your work for Bow Street, however."

He took another step closer. She tried to retreat, but the low brick wall behind her prevented her escape.

"That's true." He sounded relaxed, gently amused. "But there's definitely something to be said for a good adversary. There's something . . . *invigorating* about it, don't you think?"

"I've never thought about it," Emmy lied.

"I have. An enemy keeps you on your toes, brings out your full potential. I'd never have honed my sharpshooting skills, for example, if I hadn't been forced to fight Napoleon's troops for so long. I'd never have learned how to chase down criminals if I didn't work for Bow Street."

A diamond is only produced under great pressure. He and Camille were of the same mind.

"You sound as if you enjoy the chase," she said, and hated the way her voice quavered. She needed to be bold and flirtatious, not reeking of guilt and nerves.

His smile flashed in the darkness as he took another step closer. A shaft of moonlight illuminated one half of his face, caressing his cheekbones, the straight line of his nose, the wicked curl of his lips.

"Oh, I do. Catching a criminal elicits a wonderful sense of triumph—all the better if I've been led a merry chase." His low murmur, almost a purr, sent a shiver through her. "Things are always so much more satisfying if you've had to wait for them, don't you think?"

His gaze dropped to her lips and without thinking, Emmy pulled in her lower lip, biting it with her top teeth. His expression became almost pained. He glanced back up and slanted her a look from beneath his lashes that made her insides liquefy.

"Do you know how long I've dreamed of having the Nightjar at my mercy, for example?"

Her heart began to pound. *He knew.*

No! He didn't know for sure. He was just trying to goad her into saying something incriminating. She pressed her lips together to stop words spilling out.

He answered for her. "A *long* time. And I know exactly what I'm going to do when I catch him."

Emmy let out a silent sigh. *Him.* He'd said *him.* She was only imagining the double meanings to his words. She was still safe. For now. "What will you do?"

"Exact retribution," he sighed dreamily. "I've fantasized of the moment over and over again. I cannot wait to have him in my power."

Oh, God. The heat of him was mere inches away. Emmy inhaled his scent and entertained a brief, startling fantasy of stepping forward and letting her body soften and curve into his, of resting her head against all that masculine warmth and strength. She sidestepped instead. "I really must be getting back to the ballroom."

He moved to the side to block her and her heart gave a panicky squeeze in her chest. The rich scent of earth and hothouse flowers made her head reel.

He leaned forward conspiratorially, as if the darkness engendered confidences. "So, what are you doing out here in the dark? Here to meet a lover?"

Emmy gasped. "No! I'm not meeting anybody! I just needed to catch my breath. It's so crowded in there."

Flustered, she turned and sniffed at the nearest flower, a peony in full bloom. Peonies were her absolute favorite, with their extravagant abundance of petals and gorgeous sweet scent. She closed her eyes. How on earth was she going leave, with him blocking the path?

Alex frowned at her tempting profile. The woman was utterly infuriating. Why couldn't she be like all the other vapid, *innocent* women out there in the ballroom?

He bit back a growl and studied the charming tilt of her nose, the satin softness of her sweetly lying lips. Why the hell couldn't he be attracted to any of those other women?

Her presence out here had nothing to do with meeting a paramour. The only illicit assignation she'd arranged tonight was with Lady Carrington's jewelry case.

Oddly, the thought of her meeting another man annoyed him just as much as the fact that she was a thief, but he didn't want to examine that contradiction too closely. He didn't care how many men she kissed in dark corners. Really.

He narrowed his eyes. Wearing those feathers in her hair was practically flaunting the fact that she was the Nightjar. She must think him as dense as the rock she'd labelled at the museum. She'd only been out of his sight for a few minutes, but he'd bet his life that if he ventured next door, he'd find one of those feathers in Lady Carrington's jewelry box.

Fury burned in his chest, both at himself and at her. She was a scheming little liar, as guilty as he suspected. So why was he so reluctant to unmask her? Why did he want to stop time and stay in this state of *not* knowing just a little longer? Why did he feel the insane urge to hold her in his arms one last time before everything went wrong?

Self-loathing lashed him like a whip. He never learned, did he? He still wanted to ignore the facts, to believe in the innocence of a beautiful face, just as he'd done in Spain. He wanted to be blind to her sins. He choked back a bitter laugh. Maybe the injury to his eye was the perfect poetic justice, the physical embodiment of his greatest flaw: willful blindness.

She was stroking the waxy petals of an orchid now, and he tried not to remember the way those fingers had felt against his skin.

Concentrate.

She turned back to him, with those big wide eyes, and he experienced the usual jolt, that strange humming awareness of being alive. He'd felt the sensation once before, from an "electro-static machine" Lord Braxton had hired as a parlor trick. It had made his nerves tingle. Emmy Danvers produced the same reaction.

He couldn't allow himself to feel anything for her. She was a criminal and he was sworn to uphold the law.

Yet here he was, breathless with desire.

The faint strains of a quadrille drifted in through the doorway, but he felt disconnected from it all, as if they were in another, more elemental world, one that consisted of darkness and earth. Her pupils seemed enormous, her skin luminous against the near-black of her dress, and he curled his fingers into his palms against the urge to put them around her throat. He couldn't decide whether he wanted to strangle her or ravish her.

He felt positively medieval, freed from the trappings of polite civilization by the shadows and the heat. There was no point in denying he wanted her. No point in pretending he wasn't going to kiss her either. He'd thought of little else for days. Craved it like the laudanum they'd given him when he'd first been wounded.

She'd hidden the jewel somewhere on her person, he was certain. Finding it was going to be an absolute pleasure.

He closed the distance between them and the lush scent of her filled his nose, headier than all the flowers surrounding them. He slid his hand around her nape. She sucked in a surprised breath and started to object, but he didn't want to hear excuses.

"Don't say another word."

His lips found hers with unerring precision. He half expected her to push him away, but with a muffled groan she lifted herself up on tiptoe and returned the kiss as if she were as desperate to taste him as he was to taste her.

Hellfire. This woman was always a surprise.

Alex closed his eyes and kissed her deeply, extravagantly. He let her taste his hunger, taking her breath and giving her his in a sinful, erotic exchange. Her heart pounded against his chest as he pulled her close, the same heartbeat that throbbed in his ears, a deafening drumbeat of sound.

You're supposed to be finding the jewel.

The sensible thought struggled to surface against the drowning tide of pleasure. Alex forced his hands from her nape and stroked down her arms, then slid them back up over her ribs to her armpits. She made a little whimper of pleasure against his lips; the sound went straight to his cock. He kept on kissing her, claiming her attention while he drew his thumbs down the center of her bodice, feeling for the telltale bump of a hidden gem. But all he could feel were the stiff whalebone strips of her corset and the soft, yielding woman beneath.

His hand skimmed over her breast and she arched up into his touch with a groan that made him feel invincible. Unable to resist, he slipped his fingers inside her bodice and bit back a groan of his own. God, she was so soft. The perfect weight in his hand.

Time lost all meaning. There were no seconds or minutes. Only decades luxuriating in her mouth, eons of pleasure as he tugged down the front of her dress and lowered his lips to her skin. Her fingers tightened in his hair as he flicked her with his tongue, glorying in the contrasting textures of hard, ruched nipple and satiny curve of breast.

A reckless wash of desire swamped him. More. He wanted more.

Chapter 20.

Emmy could barely think as Harland's tongue laved her skin. She'd been close to swooning with his kisses, but *this?* Words failed her.

Heat spread throughout her body and the muscles of her stomach contracted as his wicked mouth sent a spearing sensation down between her legs. He caught her nipple between his lips and the gentle tug almost buckled her knees. It was exquisite torture, one that somehow both satisfied and created more of an ache at the same time.

She vaguely registered the loosening of her coiffure. Pins were falling, the heavy coils sliding down, but it was of no importance when Harland was doing such wondrous things. It was only when the metal comb that secured her feathered headpiece jabbed painfully into her scalp that sanity returned in an unwelcome rush.

Good God! The ruby!

Emmy made a desperate grab for her hair, but there was no stopping its downward momentum; the heavy mass slithered to one side and began to unravel. She arched her back, offering herself even more shamelessly to Harland's mouth in the process, and tilted her head to prevent the gem from falling to the floor. With only the faintest of thuds, the ruby tumbled into the foliage behind her.

Emmy let out an inaudible sigh of relief and a thrilling wave of recklessness engulfed her. Harland could search every inch of her now and he'd never find it.

She frowned into the darkness. Was *that* why his hands were roving all over her? Was he searching her?

A stab of indignant outrage was swiftly followed by a smile. Who cared what his motives were? This might be the one and only time she ever got to experience the wonderful things he was doing. She certainly didn't want him to stop.

Emmy pulled his face back up to hers and kissed him, hard. He groaned against her mouth.

"Sweet," he murmured almost accusingly. "You taste so bloody sweet."

His hand stroked her unbound hair and she shivered as he coiled it around his fist and tugged. The possessive, almost barbaric, gesture pebbled her skin. He opened his hand and slid his fingers down her spine, from neck to waist, then farther still, spreading them wide to cup her bottom. He bunched the fabric of her skirt, drawing it slowly upward, and the warm air was a shocking caress against the bare skin above her stockings. An achy, excited feeling bloomed at the apex of her thighs as he slid his hand up over the heated silk of her drawers.

Emmy understood his destination. She and Sally had discussed the things a man could do to a woman, but Sally had never adequately described the sheer wanton pleasure of it. The urgency.

His fingers found the slit in her drawers. Emmy gripped his shoulders and squirmed in mortified bliss as he stroked the sensitive folds between her legs, sliding in her body's natural slickness. He skated around the tiny nub of pleasure, teasing her mercilessly with the promise of more, and she rocked against his hand, urging him on. He kissed her deeply, claiming her with his mouth as his finger circled the entrance to her body, hovering so close that Emmy bit back an agonized moan. Every inch of her was hot, desperate. Aching.

Yes, there. More. Please.

The click of the door was the most dreadful sound she'd ever heard. For a split second both of them froze, a tableau of scandalous debauchery. And then Emmy gasped and straightened while Harland stepped away from her with almost unnatural haste.

Her skirts fell demurely back around her legs, and Harland, already a respectable distance away, turned his back to the door and cleared his throat loudly.

"And *that*, Miss Danvers, is how the exotic pineapple came to these shores. In the wild, of course, they are pollinated by hummingbirds, and occasionally bats, but here, I'm told, different methods must be deployed to ensure a successful harvest."

Emmy blinked. He sounded so *normal*, as if the past few minutes had left him completely unaffected. She could barely remember her own name.

He turned, as if he'd only just become aware of the elderly couple who'd entered the conservatory and inclined his head in casual greeting. "Ah, Lord Travers. Lady Travers. Good evening. I was just discussing the ambassador's famous pineapple with Miss Danvers. She is an ardent horticulturalist."

Emmy managed to murmur an earnest agreement. *An ardent whore, was more like it.* She was certain her cheeks were a betraying shade of scarlet, and her hair a shocking mess, but the grey-haired couple clearly noticed nothing amiss. She sent up a thankful prayer for the concealing darkness.

Harland turned back to her and gave her a precise bow. "I do hope that satisfied your curiosity, Miss Danvers." The edges of his lips quivered in a secret smile. "Do let me know if you require further clarification on the matter."

He strode from the room without a second glance, and Emmy fought the desire to applaud his performance. He exuded arrogant indifference. Had he reacted any less quickly, they would have been steeped in scandal.

Lady Travers sent her a vague smile, devoid of speculative interest. Perhaps the thought of the notoriously selective Lord Melton seducing a nonentity like Emmy Danvers was just too preposterous to contemplate, despite the slightly dubious circumstances.

With her own show of unconcern, Emmy turned back to the flowers and feigned a rapt fascination in a tiger lily. Better to be thought an insufferably dull bluestocking than a woman who'd been on the verge of being debauched in the shrubbery. Her knees still felt weak.

Lord and Lady Travers began to stroll down one of the alternative paths, so Emmy bent and retrieved the ruby from where it had fallen in the dirt, then felt around on the floor for her hairpins and feathered comb.

She couldn't go back into the ballroom with her hair in such disarray. She twisted it up, stabbing herself with several of the pins in the process because she was shaking, and hurried to the dressing room set aside for the ladies. With the help of a mirror, and one of the ambassador's maids, she managed to make herself look halfway presentable.

There was nothing to be done about her lips—they looked redder and plumper than usual. Her cheeks were flushed, and her eyes sparkled with devilry. Danger obviously agreed with her. Did she always look like this during a heist? She'd never taken the time to stop and peer in a mirror. Shaking her head, she made her way back to the ballroom.

There was no sign of Harland, and she told herself she was relieved. What *had* that been about? At first she'd thought he'd known she had the ruby. But then he'd started kissing her, and if his goal had been to search her and find it, then he'd failed.

It would be lovely to think that he'd been so caught up in kissing her that he'd become distracted, but she didn't think that likely. Still, what other explanation was there? That he'd simply happened on her in the conservatory and decided to kiss her because he wanted to? Even more unlikely. A man like Alexander Harland always had an ulterior motive. Maybe he'd been hoping to befuddle her so much, she'd blurt out her crimes?

Either way, she'd been granted an unlikely reprieve, and she wasn't about to look a gift horse in the mouth. She caught Luc's eye across the ballroom, and he made his way over to her.

"Run into trouble?" he asked casually, raising his brows as he noticed her different coiffure.

Emmy fought a blush. "Nothing I couldn't handle."

Oh, she'd handled Harland, all right. And he'd handled her. Most proficiently.

Mortification mixed with frustration coiled inside her. Thank heavens they'd been interrupted. She'd been shamefully close to giving herself to him. Instead of thinking of ways to get away from him, she'd kissed him back, then lost herself in the taste and scent and feel. She could still recall the texture of his hair under her fingers, the incredible sensation of his hands on her breasts. His *mouth* on them.

Camille bustled up. "Are we ready to leave?"

Emmy could only nod.

When the carriage arrived home, she went straight up to her room. She barely glanced at the ruby, throwing it carelessly onto her bedside table before she collapsed facedown on her bed with a groan of dismay.

What a night. She was exhausted from the sheer range of emotions she'd encountered, from nervous excitement to dread, elation to panic, then guilty, reckless pleasure. Kissing Harland had been the real triumph, not successfully stealing the ruby. He'd warned her not to play with fire, but sparring with him was so full of paradoxical pleasure, it was hard to stop.

Chapter 21.

"He's back," Sally said ominously.

Emmy glanced up from her solitary breakfast and her heart started to pound at the thought of seeing Harland again. "Who's back?" she croaked.

Sally sent her a dire look. "Danton, that's who. He's down in the hall, cooling his heels."

Emmy's spirits plummeted and dread replaced anticipation. "Where's Luc?"

"Out for his usual walk around the park."

Emmy cursed. Hellfire. She didn't want to have to deal with Danton on her own, but Camille was still upstairs asleep, and she didn't want to rouse her.

"Show him up. And leave the door open."

When Danton entered, Emmy studied the man who'd made her life a misery for almost a full year.

Sally had described him well. He was of average height and of stocky build, perhaps a decade older than Emmy herself, and his features had a childish, petulant cast to them. He reminded her of a baby about to have a tantrum, except for the calculating gleam in his eyes. There was nothing innocent in his gaze. His eyes roamed over her face and figure, lingering lasciviously at her bosom and lips as if he had the right to examine her. As if he owned her.

Emmy felt a chill sweep over her skin when he smiled. This was a man who knew the cost of everything and the value of nothing. And he clearly relished his role of puppet master, making her family dance to his tune.

"Miss Danvers. We meet at last." He inclined his head. When Emmy sank back into her seat, he settled himself in the chair opposite her, making himself at home with a familiarity that made her bristle.

"I have been all curiosity to meet the thief who took up the Nightjar's mantle."

Emmy nodded stiffly.

He picked up a butter knife and toyed with it between his fingers. "I will admit to a certain hesitancy when I heard a *female* would take his place, but I own I have been delighted by your success. You have, I believe, recovered the Regent's diamond and the French blue?"

Emmy nodded again. She didn't trust her tongue. It would be foolish to antagonize this man, but she couldn't think of a single thing to say that wouldn't make her lose her temper. What gave him the right to force her to do things? And how dare he suggest that as a woman she was somehow less capable of doing the job than a man?

She was glad Luc wasn't here. He might have been goaded into doing something foolish. Like trying to stab him with that butter knife.

Her cool silence didn't seem to affect Danton. He raised his brows and helped himself to a bread roll. "And what about the ruby?"

Emmy found her voice. "I have that too. I retrieved it last night."

If Danton had come to collect the jewels, she might as well hand all three of them over to him. No need to give him another reason to call. "I'll go and get them now."

She rose and hurried out of the room, leaving Sally to keep an eye on him from the hallway. She retrieved the two diamonds from inside one of her shoes and collected the ruby from her bedside table.

When she placed the three gems in front of Danton, his delighted smile made her want to slap his face. She'd sweated blood and tears to get those jewels. Faced danger and possible arrest. It wasn't fair that he simply got to take them away. Selling them had never been part of her father's vision. Giving them to Danton simply so he could sell them for profit felt like a betrayal of the cruelest sort. Her stomach cramped in misery.

She watched, biting the inside of her cheek, as Danton examined first the Rundell & Bridge diamond and then the smoky blue from the museum. Rainbow shards scattered over the white tablecloth as he held them up to the morning sunlight, and the jewels fragmented the pale beam like a prism.

But when he picked up the ruby, he sucked in a breath. His features hardened and his mouth turned down in displeasure. "Is this your idea of a joke, Miss Danvers? What do you mean by giving me this?"

Emmy frowned. "You asked for Lady Carrington's ruby. That's it."

His eyes flashed in temper. "This is no ruby. Look at it! It's paste. Worthless!" He threw the stone across the table toward her.

Emmy stared at him, dumbfounded. She hadn't taken a good look at the jewel last night; it had been dark, and she'd been too distracted by what had happened between herself and Harland. Was it possible she'd been tricked?

Surely not.

Danton's voice, filled with fury, broke into her thoughts like a dreadful echo. "Do you think to trick me, girl? Do you take me for a fool?"

Emmy leapt to her feet and snatched up the stone from where he'd tossed it. "No! Of course not. I—I—"

She couldn't explain it. Now she looked at the stone in the daylight, it was painfully obvious it was colored glass. It was a fine paste copy, one of the highest quality, but she'd seen enough of the real thing to know what to look for. She squinted at the surface of the jewel and with a sinking heart identified the tiny white spots that indicated gas bubbles, the fine lines of surface-reaching fractures, neither of which were found in true rubies.

As if she needed further confirmation, she ran the edge of her knife across it and watched as the blade left a telltale scratch on the surface. True ruby was hard, second only to diamond. It should not have yielded to the scratch.

Damn. Damn. Damn!

When had the ruby been exchanged for glass? Where was the true ruby?

Danton rose to his feet. He gathered the two diamonds and tucked them in his inside coat pocket. His face was mottled red with anger.

"You will get me the real ruby as soon as possible, Miss Danvers, or your family will pay the price. I do not make threats lightly."

Emmy didn't bother answering him. When he sauntered out of the room, she collapsed back into her chair and stared at the fraudulent stone in front of her, her mind a barrage of questions. Someone had swapped the ruby. But who? And when?

She took a deep breath and tried to think rationally. The Carringtons, either one of them, could have replaced the stone. Lord Carrington could have done it before he presented the necklace to his wife, but it was unlikely.

Too many people had seen Lady Carrington wearing the necklace in public—and had a chance to inspect it at close range—for it to have been paste. The eagle-eyed ladies of the *ton* would have gossiped and speculated about it for weeks.

Lady Carrington could have done it herself. She could have pawned the original and had a paste replacement made if she needed funds and didn't want to tell her husband. Emmy bit her lip. Or perhaps another thief had beaten her to it? Plenty of people had access to Lady Carrington's bedroom, if rumor were true.

But none of those explanations took into account the evil genius that was Alexander Harland. He was by far the most likely culprit.

Damn him! He had the real ruby safe somewhere, she was certain. That's what he'd been doing at the Carringtons' that day—arranging for its replacement. No wonder he hadn't set anyone to catch her in the act; he hadn't needed to. He'd been perfectly content to let her steal something that was almost worthless.

Bastard. She'd *known* he'd been taunting her with his double-layered words. He'd enjoyed playing with her, watching her sweat. She quashed a wave of reluctant admiration for such a sneaky maneuver. It was precisely the kind of thing she would have done.

Had he been trying to find the fake ruby on her person when he'd kissed her in the conservatory? Had he been feigning desire while she'd been practically swooning in his arms, panting with eagerness?

Emmy took a calming sip of tea. No. She might not have had much experience with men, but his desire hadn't been feigned. She'd felt the rigid evidence of it pressed against her stomach, heard it in the desperate, throaty groans he'd made against her skin.

So, where did that leave them?

Whatever Harland's reasons for kissing her, the fact remained that he obviously knew she was the Nightjar. He'd correctly surmised she would steal the ruby. He was probably on his way here right this very moment, to arrest her, with a search warrant.

Emmy stared into the deep red facets of the fake gem and a strange calm slid over her. Where was Luc? The two of them had discussed what they would do if she were ever caught, but it had always been in general, abstract terms. Camille had wanted to avoid all discussion of the subject, thinking it tempted fate to even say the words out loud.

Emmy had always said she'd take the blame. What was the point in *all* of them being punished? She'd made Luc swear that if she were exposed as the Nightjar, he would take Camille and Sally to France or Spain, anywhere to escape English justice. But that had been years ago. Camille was strong-willed, certainly, but she was over seventy years old. The rigors of travel would exhaust her.

Emmy stood. She wasn't caught yet. There was still time for them all to leave the country. It would be a wrench, certainly, to leave behind the only life she'd ever known, and running away from a problem had never been her style. But better life as an exile than sentenced to death or transported halfway across the world on a prison hulk.

Decision made, she hastened to the door of the parlor and shouted out orders, even as she started down the stairs.

"Sally! I'm going to the park to get Luc. Wake Camille. Tell her we need to leave. Pack all her jewelry and a couple of dresses and—"

The crash of the door knocker silenced her tirade. Emmy skidded to a halt on the polished marble tiles.

Too late! A sense of fatalistic acceptance washed over her, and she straightened her spine. Very well. The game might be up, but she would accept the consequences of her actions with grace and poise. Her hand barely shook as she unlatched the door and braced herself to meet Harland's penetrating gaze.

The youth who stood on the doorstep was not the man she expected.

"Letter for you, miss. From Bow Street."

Emmy accepted it with a frown as the lad tipped his cap at her and scampered off. She ripped open the seal, scanned the contents, and let out a howl of furious disbelief.

Luc had been arrested on suspicion of being the Nightjar. He was being held for questioning at Bow Street regarding the recent break-in at the British Museum. She glared at the arrogant slash of ink at the bottom of the message. It simply read *"Harland."*

Double, triple damn.

By the time Camille came downstairs, Emmy had decided what to do. Harland's arrest of Luc—presumably while her brother took his customary early-morning stroll around Mount Street Gardens—was clearly designed to provoke her.

She'd initially thought of marching straight over to Bow Street, demanding to see Luc, and then haranguing Harland with a furious diatribe about harassing innocent citizens on the basis of insufficient evidence.

But Harland knew he had the wrong man. Luc's physical disability ruled him out as the active participant in any of the Nightjar's recent crimes. He clearly wasn't the one who'd been leaping between balconies, hiding in barrels, and stowing away in musty sarcophagi. No. Harland, the duplicitous swine, had correctly surmised that threatening her family was a far more effective weapon against her than threatening her own person.

Emmy drummed her fingers on the table. He must have known he planned to arrest Luc when he was kissing her senseless last night, the rotten scoundrel. He probably expected her to race over there, beg for her brother's release, and give herself up to his tender mercies with a full confession.

Not a chance. The game wasn't over yet.

The best way to prove Luc's innocence would be to have the Nightjar commit another crime while he was still incarcerated. Harland couldn't possibly pursue a conviction then. But what could she steal? Excluding the ruby—which she highly suspected was in Harland's possession—the only other jewel that remained from Danton's list was the Ruspoli sapphire. But she and Luc hadn't even confirmed its location, let alone started to plan for its removal.

Emmy bit her lip. Harland's persecution of her brother had made this personal.

So she would retaliate in kind.

There was no way of knowing how long Bow Street would hold Luc, so she had to work fast. She still had the key she'd stolen from the Tricorn's doorman. Tonight, she would break into the club, find a way into Harland's private domain, and taunt him by leaving a black feather on his pillow. That would prove not only Luc's innocence, but also provide the arrogant Lord Melton with humbling evidence of his own vulnerability.

Emmy smiled, delighted with the plan. When Camille entered the room, yawning politely behind her hand,

Emmy decided not to tell her about Danton's visit, Luc's arrest, or her own decision. Camille would only worry about all of them.

Sally could go to Bow Street later and reassure Luc that Emmy had things well in hand.

Emmy only hoped it would be true.

Chapter 22.

Emmy shivered in the predawn mist as she slipped into the mews behind the Tricorn Club. She was wearing her dark shirt and breeches, with short stays underneath.

The Spanish had a word for this time between late night and early morning: *madrugada.* The English called it the witching hour. It was a strange, lonely time, when the great beating heart of London lay unnaturally still. The only innocent people awake at this hour were the sleepless mothers of newborns and the odd night watchman or ferryman. The night was for criminals like herself—the ne'er-do-wells and cutthroats, prostitutes and thieves.

The Tricorn's upper windows were satisfyingly dark. It would have been nice to have waited until she was certain of Harland's absence, but she didn't have the luxury of time. She'd have to make sure she didn't wake him; she'd leave the feather on his desk, not on his pillow. She wasn't foolish enough to breech the sanctity of his bedroom just to make a point.

She inserted the iron key she'd pilfered into the lock

on the back door. A tentative jiggle revealed it was not the right one, and she swore under her breath, even though she hadn't really expected to be that lucky. She tiptoed down the set of steps that led belowground and tried it in the kitchen door instead. The metal tumblers creaked and ground, and she winced at the noise, but the lock opened with a yielding click.

Success!

The hinges didn't squeak when she pushed open the door, and there was no growling Brutus to impede her progress this time.

She found herself in the club's extensive kitchens. Copper pots, pans, and huge bunches of herbs hung from an iron rack suspended above an enormous kitchen work table. Emmy navigated the looming shapes and crept up the stairs into the private half of the house.

None of the wall sconces had been lit, but she recognized the sumptuous corridor she'd been dragged into by Harland. She glanced toward the door at the far end which opened into the public part of the building. *He'd kissed her up against that wall*. Her pulse rate increased even more.

Ears attuned for the slightest sound, she padded along, peering into a breakfast room and a sitting room. The heartbeat tick of a mantel clock measured out the seconds with satisfying regularity. No doubt this household ran with similar precision. Harland and Wolff were both used to military regimens. She'd bet every need was smoothly anticipated by their staff. Insubordination such as hers would not be tolerated. She bit back an irreverent snicker.

At the top of the stairs, she listened at the first door, but heard nothing. That was expected: Benedict Wylde's rooms had been empty since he'd moved in with his new wife a couple of months ago.

Emmy had confided her plans to Sally that afternoon, and while the other woman had cautioned her to be careful, she hadn't tried to talk her out of it. Instead, Sally had disappeared off to Covent Garden and returned with her friend Molly, the actress.

Molly, it transpired, had recently been invited back to the Tricorn's private salon by Sebastien Wolff, Lord Mowbray, and thus had an excellent insight into who slept where. At first, she'd been reluctant to share the information, but when Sally said that it was Harland's bedroom Emmy wanted to find, and not Wolff's, Molly was more forthcoming. The actress clearly still had a soft spot for Wolff.

Harland's bedroom was the third door on the right.

Emmy tiptoed down the hall and put her ear to the door. Her stomach knotted in mingled excitement and fear. Molly had said that each of the men had their own suite of rooms, consisting of an outer sitting room and an inner bedchamber. All Emmy had to do was open the door without waking Harland and leave the feather on his desk. She could just imagine his shocked face when he discovered it lying there in the morning.

The door opened with a tiny click, and she slipped inside, hardly daring to believe her own audacity. The fire in the grate had been banked for the night, but a few embers still glowed red. She could just make out the door to the bedchamber beyond, closed except for a thin sliver of darkness.

Perfect.

She strained to listen over the pounding of her own blood in her ears, but no snoring or mumbling came from the other room. Harland must be a quiet sleeper. An image of him in bed, his dark hair disordered against the pristine white of his pillow, assailed her.

Think of something else.

She prowled forward. What did this room tell her about him as an opponent? She stroked the top of an upholstered wing chair, then crossed to a dressing stand with a mirror for shaving. A porcelain jug and bowl sat on the top, with a folding razor, leather strop, and a bottle of his cologne. She leaned in close and took a sniff. *Mmm.* Pine and a hint of brandy. He'd smelled her perfume. Quid pro quo.

In truth, the whole room smelled nice, no, more than nice, as if Harland's irresistible essence had infused every piece of fabric and leather. She quashed a swirl of yearning in her chest.

Get the job done, Em.

A desk stood in one corner of the room. Emmy reached between her breasts, pulled out the black feather she'd stashed inside her stays, and kissed it for luck. She placed it dead center of the otherwise-clean desk. Mission accomplished.

She turned to go, but a flash caught her eye; her own perfume bottle, right there on the side table. It was almost empty, but she reached out to steal it back anyway. And then her hand stopped, arrested in midair, as she recognized the faceted lump that lay next to it.

Lady Carrington's ruby.

Hell and damnation! She'd *known* it was him!

It was the size of a pigeon's egg, glinting and beautiful even in the dim light. Emmy reached for it just as the rasp of a tinderbox ricocheted through the silence.

Chapter 23.

Emmy twisted around in horror as Harland calmly set a flame to the wick of an oil lamp and turned it up so a warm glow filled the space between them. The door to the bedroom behind him was open—how long had he been watching her from the shadows?

A million permutations of what might happen next flashed through her brain. Words sprang to her lips: *I can explain! It's not what it looks like!*

Except she couldn't explain. Not without dragging Luc and Camille down too. Better to hold her tongue.

The look Harland sent her pierced her to the core. It was filled with such accusation, such knowledge. He wasn't surprised, damn him. He'd known all along that she'd come. *God, she was so stupid!* He'd laid a trap, and she'd walked right into it.

He was wearing a shirt—barely. It was open at the neck and the untucked front extended to midthigh. He still wore breeches, thank God, but his feet were bare. Had he been lying in wait for her? Emmy could barely draw in a breath.

It was he who broke the agonizing silence. He leaned against the doorjamb and crossed his arms casually over his chest.

"You know, Bonaparte once said 'Never interrupt your enemy when they're making a mistake,' but in this case I felt compelled to intervene. We can't have you stealing that ruby now, can we, Miss Danvers?"

His voice was a deep growl, scratchy with sleep. He sounded pleasant enough, amused even, but beneath this outward show of courtesy, he was furious, Emmy was sure.

"Do you know what I hate, Miss Danvers?" he continued softly. "I hate being blind."

Emmy drew her brows together. "I thought you'd only lost—"

He waved that away. "No. I mean that I have been blinded by *you*. But no longer. The real Emmeline Danvers stands before me."

His mocking gaze made a slow, thorough inventory of her outfit, from the V of her dark shirt to the way her breeches clung to her legs. Her skin heated. He gestured toward the chair that was stationed in front of the desk. "Have a seat."

Emmy stepped sideways and dropped into the chair as her legs gave way beneath her.

Oh, God, what would happen to her? Would she hang? Be transported? Sentenced to hard labor?

Harland prowled forward and took the comfortable armchair opposite her, lounging back in it like a king as he regarded her with cynical interest. Emmy dug her nails into her palms. He tilted his head, as if a thought had just occurred to him. "You're so small," he mused aloud. "Do dressmakers charge you less because of how little fabric it takes to make your outfits?"

She blinked at the unusual topic. She'd assumed the interrogation would begin immediately: *Tell me where the jewels are hidden. Tell me why you did it. Tell me how you did it.*

She wouldn't tell him a thing.

He didn't wait for her to answer. "Not that I don't approve. You in breeches is quite possibly the finest thing I've seen all year." His eyes clashed with hers. "A brand-new fantasy to add to my collection."

Emmy was sure her heart stopped beating. She sucked in a breath. The interrogation *had* begun; he meant to scandalize her into submission.

"I have scores of them," he said darkly. "Of you and me together." His gaze lasted five whole beats of her heart before he looked away.

Good God.

Something dark and dangerous shivered in the air between them, a mutual awareness. Hunter and hunted. Predator and prey. Emmy's heart raced, but mixed in with the fear was a sharp, unwelcome stab of desire. She must be mad.

He was watching her with a smile that was hard to define. She regarded him warily, as she would an unpredictable wild animal, uncertain of his mood.

He tapped his fingers on the arm of the chair. "Can I just take this opportunity to say what a pleasure it's been having you as an opponent? Truly."

The way he said "pleasure," slightly drawn out, with his perfect lips pressing together and his tongue rolling around his mouth, sent a shiver of heat through her.

Ugh. She was a twit. A brainless twit with sawdust for brains.

"For weeks you've led, and I've followed. But now you've had a rather delightful comeuppance. No more running, Emmy Danvers. You've been caught." He stretched his long legs out in front of him, ankles crossed. "This is where you profess your innocence."

The cynicism in his tone made her flinch. Gone was the passionate lover from the ambassador's conservatory. Here was the hard lawman, the Runner who'd cornered his prey and was about to go in for the kill.

"Aren't you going to beg me to release you?" he taunted mildly.

Emmy almost snorted. As if that would do any good. There was no softness in him, no forgiveness. Nothing she could say would change his mind.

He rested his elbow on the arm of the chair and stroked his lips thoughtfully. A wicked gleam entered his eyes. "It might be interesting to see how far you'll go." His pleasant tone held a vibrating undercurrent of anger. "Some females, when faced with the death penalty, plead their bellies."

Emmy frowned in confusion.

"Women who are pregnant at the time they're sentenced have their punishment delayed until after the baby is born," he explained. "In theory, the sentence is then supposed to be carried out, but in practice, there's so much sympathy for the newborn child that the mother is often pardoned."

His gaze flicked down her body, and Emmy sucked in a breath as she grasped his implication. Her skin heated with anger and embarrassment. "I wouldn't sleep with a man just to save my neck!"

He seemed amused by her outrage. "No? You won't offer me your body in exchange for your release?"

Heat rose at the thought of them together in that way. If he'd been desperate and dishonorable, easily swayed from his goal, she might have stood a chance with a tactic like that, but Harland was irritatingly upright. Getting him horizontal and trying to persuade him to free her would have no effect whatsoever. He was immune.

Emmy sent him her haughtiest glare. "If you think for one moment, Lord Melton, that I would stoop to such a level, then you are gravely mistaken. And besides," she added for good measure, "even if I *were* the sort of woman who would do that, I know perfectly well that nothing could sway you."

His low laugh made her stomach coil even tighter. "Are you sure? Why not try it anyway? What have you got to lose?"

What did she have to lose, indeed? Only her virginity. Only her pride, her honor, her personal integrity. Everything she had left.

"You never know," he said softly, and his voice was a wicked serpent tightening its coils around her heart. "Maybe I'll buckle under the onslaught of your ardor." His gaze bored into hers. "Convince me, Emmy."

"No!"

He raised his brows. "Why not? It worked last night, did it not? I congratulate you. If that was feigned passion, it was extremely convincing. You certainly had my body persuaded, if not my mind."

Her eyes widened at his unexpected admission. He smiled.

"Let's try something new, shall we? I call it 'honesty.' It's where you say things that are true. I'll start, if you like. I'm hard as a rock for you right now."

Her mouth dropped open.

He casually lowered his hand to his lap and readjusted the bulge that had appeared in the front of his breeches. It reached almost to his waistband. He made no effort to hide it; he simply looked down and laughed.

Emmy couldn't drag her eyes away. A terrifying wave of desire sizzled through her. He wasn't lying. He wanted her. And she wanted him too. Not because she thought she could persuade him to release her, but because for the very first time in her life, here was a man who knew the truth—the complete truth about her—and he still wanted her. Wanted her despite it. Maybe even *because* of it.

Her senses reeled. That, paradoxically, was freedom.

He stood abruptly, and she did the same, instantly alert. He prowled around the desk and she sidestepped the opposite way, retreating until her bottom bumped the table that held the lamp. He sent her a mocking, triumphant look that said, *Where do you think you're going?* He was blocking the path to the door and the only other choice was his bedroom.

Not an option.

She leaned back as he stopped in front of her and closed the distance until they were almost nose to nose. His breath warmed the skin of her cheek and something dangerous and ungovernable crackled in the air between them.

"Here's another truth," he growled, and this time she had no trouble reading the anger in his glare. His nostrils flared and his eyes grew impossibly dark. "You're mine now, Emmy Danvers. I will never release you. Not even if you begged me on your knees. Not even if you fucked me all night."

The coarse declaration dropped between them like an incendiary device. His storm-dark eyes dropped to her throat, to the dip of her clavicle exposed by her shirt, then travelled back up to her mouth. They were both breathing hard, as if there wasn't enough air in the room, and Emmy couldn't remember when she'd been so aroused. Every cell in her body burned.

"Damn you," he murmured.

Emmy licked her lips. There were times when stealing something wasn't *so* bad. Stealing a kiss, for example. "I—"

"Shut up," he groaned. "I can't trust a single word that comes out of your mouth."

Chapter 24.

Alex couldn't remember a time when he'd been so angry, so aroused, so full of contradictory emotions. He wanted to strangle the deceitful little wretch for proving his suspicions correct, to punish her for doing something so utterly foolish as to get herself caught like this, by him.

He was honor bound to turn her in—she was a criminal, one who'd stolen thousands of pounds' worth of property that wasn't hers. So why in God's name was he feeling guilty for tricking her? For *winning*? Why this ridiculous urge to protect her from the obvious outcome of her capture—death by hanging, or at the very least banishment to the colonies, which was tantamount to the same thing, only slower?

And where had the suggestion that she use her body to influence him come from? The words had been out of his mouth before his brain had even been consulted. Had he been testing her? He told himself it had been to shock her, to goad a reaction, because he'd *never* be swayed in that way. Except he wanted her so badly, he might actually have been tempted to break his own strict moral code and let her escape. Christ, what was the matter with him?

He would have been furious if she'd even looked like she was considering it, but maybe it would have been better if she had. If she'd tried to seduce him, his disillusionment would have been complete. He could have been disgusted with her, instead of grudgingly impressed by her integrity, even now, when she'd proved a liar and a thief.

Bloody hell.

Alex glared down at her. How could someone look both guilty and innocent at the same time?

He touched his thumb to her lower lip and a savage feeling swept over him, a primitive need to vanquish, to conquer. He wanted to devour her, to possess all that spirit and defiance, to burn her up in the force of his desire. Bloody woman. She drew him against his will. Against his better judgment. What the hell was he going to do with her?

He kissed her.

Heat sparked the moment his lips touched hers. He hadn't meant to do it—he was sure he hadn't—but kissing her suddenly seemed like the most sensible thing in the world. The most necessary thing. He'd caught her. He couldn't let her escape. Kissing her senseless was the perfect way to stop that from happening. There. He could still think logically.

Alex closed his eyes and embraced the darkness. Her lips opened under his—so soft, so sweet—and he swept his tongue inside her mouth with a groan of bliss. Deprived of sight, he savored every other sensation: the softness of her skin, the addictive scent of her, the little gasp she made against his mouth.

Bloody woman.

Emmy could barely make sense of what was happening. Why was Harland kissing her? Was this punishment? It didn't feel like punishment. It felt wonderful—which in itself was so wrong as to be laughable. His tongue delved into her mouth and tangled with her own, and she grasped the edge of the table to stop herself from throwing her arms around his neck and pulling him closer.

He murmured her name between kisses and a quiver started deep inside. Heat bloomed and spread. This was a mistake. A dreadful, glorious mistake.

A fatalistic recklessness swept over her. She was about to lose her freedom, maybe even her life. This was her last chance to grasp a moment of happiness. If she told Harland to stop, he would. He was enough of a gentleman that he would listen if she made an objection. But she didn't want to object. For once she was going to reach for something—*someone*—she desired for herself. Even if he was the author of her downfall, Alexander Harland could give her one of the highlights of her life.

"Wait!" she gasped.

He stilled, instantly suspicious, and pulled back.

Emmy leaned sideways and extinguished the lamp.

He cursed the sudden darkness and made a grab for her, presumably thinking she was about to try to escape. He caught her upper arms in a fierce grip, and Emmy laughed in sheer elation.

Oh, yes.

She threw herself against him, full-length, flinging her arms around his shoulders and tugging his head down. He staggered backward, caught by surprise, then grunted as she pressed her lips to his. For a moment, he stilled, and she thought he would push her away—then with a growl deep in his throat, he picked her up, anchoring her to him with his hands at the back of her thighs.

The room spun in the darkness. Emmy wrapped her breeches-clad legs around his hips and clung to him, crossing her ankles behind his back. He crushed her into his chest as their lips met in a kiss that burned right down to her toes.

She was Icarus, flying too close to the sun, Persephone being dragged down into the underworld. She didn't care. This might be a disaster, but it was a glorious, glittering, incendiary disaster. A crazy blur of seeking limbs and hot mouths in the dark.

"You're a liar," he panted against her lips. "And a thief."

She couldn't deny it. She tightened her fingers in his hair.

His teeth caught her lower lip and tugged. "I want you more than anyone I've ever met."

Emmy rewarded his admission with another long, desperate kiss.

His fingers tightened on the back of her thighs. "I want to be inside you. I want to fuck you all night."

Delicious filthy words in her ear. This was the Harland she'd wanted to find, lawless, uncivilized. Free. "Yes," she said fiercely.

He stilled and raised his head. She could barely see him, just the faintest outline, but she knew she'd surprised him.

"Yes," she repeated, more forcefully. "And not to make you release me. This has nothing to do with that. This is just you and me."

She had no hope of clemency. No expectation of anything but pleasure. It was just that she'd finally found someone she could trust with her body, if not her secrets. Harland wouldn't hurt her, however much she teased and tormented him. If this truly was her last night of freedom, then she would spend it well. She would burn up in the brightness. She'd go out in a ball of flame.

His arms tightened, squeezing her ribs. She could feel his labored breathing, the rapid rise and fall of his chest against hers. He seemed to be waging an internal war; no doubt his sense of what was proper police procedure was battling with the iron-hard arousal she could feel pressing against her stomach.

She wanted desire to win. Needed it to win. Her entire body was glowing, fizzing with anticipation.

"Take off your clothes," she said.

Chapter 25.

Her hoarse command seemed to free him of the last vestiges of control. In a flurry of movement, he turned and carried her through the doorway and into his bedroom. A rush of air, a falling sensation that made her stomach pitch, and Emmy was flat on her back with Harland's delicious weight pressing her down into a soft mattress.

It was even darker in here. She experienced a flash of disappointment that she couldn't see him, his expressions, that glorious body of his. But, oh, she could feel. His hands sliding over her, molding, squeezing, stroking. In a sudden move he rolled over onto his back, taking her with him, and she was on top, straddling him.

"Shirt," he rasped, and she grabbed the hem of hers and tugged it over her head. She wasn't entirely clear which one of them was in control now, but that hardly mattered when they both wanted the same thing.

The darkness gave her confidence. She was beautiful, invincible. Shameless.

His hand caught her hip, then slid up her side, and she

sucked in a breath as he traced the edge of her short stays. She struggled to release the ribbon tie at the front. He pushed her hands aside, caught the top of the corset, and tugged. The cotton gave way with a deafening rip. Emmy wriggled her shoulders and managed to get the thing off her arms, then gasped as his warm palms covered her naked breasts.

He hissed out a breath, the sound indicative of pure, unadulterated pleasure.

"Emmy," he groaned, and the way he said her name, almost as if it were a benediction, made her glow. "So soft."

He squeezed, and she threw her head back, savoring the abrasion against her peaked nipples. His stomach muscles tensed beneath her as he sat up. She caught a flash of white as he tugged his own shirt over his head and sent it sailing aside, and then there was only the extraordinary sensation of his hot, hard body against hers.

She was still sitting in his lap, her knees on either side of his hips, pressing him into the bed. She could hardly believe that she was skin-on-skin with a man. *This* man. The heat was incredible, the contours of his muscles even more amazing as she stroked her palms over his shoulders, down his biceps, across the front of his chest. He shuddered beneath her touch, and she shifted in his lap, trying to get closer to the intriguingly hard part of him that throbbed and burned between her legs.

"Wicked girl."

He bent his head and caught one of her nipples in his mouth, using one hand to push her breast up toward him. Emmy arched, offering herself as his tongue swirled and laved and his mouth provided a tantalizing suction. Yes! This was what he'd done in the conservatory. And this time, there would be no interruptions. She would give herself to him completely; no reservations, no regrets. She wanted this, needed this, with every fiber of her being.

He grasped her hips and moved her off his lap, to the side. The mattress dipped beside her, and she realized he was removing his breeches with brisk efficiency. She lay down next to him and did the same, wiggling her hips, less proficient than he was. Her elbow bumped his ribs and he grunted, half pain, half amusement.

"Wretch."

She'd never been completely naked with a man before. In spite of the darkness, she could feel her entire body suffusing with a blush. And then there was no time to think. Harland turned on his side to face her, and his greater weight made her roll toward him. Their bodies touched all the way down. His arousal pressed insistently against her stomach, and her heart leapt in mingled anticipation and fear. She was almost glad she couldn't see him.

Oh, God. She really was doing this.

His hand found her hip, and he uttered a hiss of satisfaction as he stroked up over her waist, her ribs, her shoulder and neck. And then he threaded his fingers in her hair and pulled her in for a scorching kiss.

"Mine," he murmured against her throat, and Emmy could only give a wordless moan in answer.

He pushed her onto her back and moved partly over her, stroking up her arms, coaxing them up over her head. He caught her wrists, but no sooner had he taken her prisoner than he released her to trace the sensitive skin of her inner arms down to her breasts and then lower still. His palm flattened over her belly, and Emmy bucked her hips, desperate for him to move lower, to put his hand where she throbbed and ached. There was a restlessness in her that only he could quell.

"Nothing but trouble," he groaned, and she wasn't sure if that was a complaint or praise.

His hand slipped between her legs, and the ache turned to sweet fire. The moisture from her body coated his fingers, and Emmy squirmed as he circled and teased. He gave a dark chuckle, as if he knew how much he was torturing her, and took her lips in a deep, openmouthed kiss.

Emmy gasped in delight and arched her back as he pushed his finger inside her, amazed by the intensity of the pleasure. Her body clenched around him as he teased; long, luscious slides that built a coiling, knotted tension in her belly. Soon she teetered on the edge of something momentous, something she needed, but couldn't quite catch. She lifted her hips, begging him with incoherent sounds to resolve the glorious confusion he'd created.

"Harland!"

He pressed the heel of his hand against her. "Now," he growled.

His order pushed her over the edge of some invisible abyss. Her entire body tensed, then shattered, as pleasure radiated over her in waves.

She was still shuddering when he rose up and covered her with his body, supporting the weight of his torso on his arms. The lower half of him pressed against her, a delicious, unfamiliar weight, and Emmy opened her legs to allow him to fit more snugly between her thighs. He enveloped her, overwhelmed her in the best possible way, and the musky scent of him, of them, increased her arousal even more.

Here in the dark, they were equals, both as blind as each other. She couldn't see him, but she could hear his throaty growl; it resonated in his chest and down into her limbs.

"I want to be inside you. Is that what you want?"

"Yes," she panted.

He caught her hand and drew it down between them. Emmy sucked in a breath as he curled her fingers around his shaft and covered them with his own. He let out an impassioned groan and his fist gave an involuntary squeeze.

"Trouble," he muttered thickly.

Emmy widened her eyes at the feel of him. Velvet soft and truncheon hard. With him guiding their joined hands, he positioned himself at the entrance of her body, sliding against her slick folds, and she shivered in anticipation.

Alex was shaking with the need to join his body with Emmy's, but there was one thing he needed to know.

"Am I your first?" he breathed raggedly. "Are you a virgin?"

He heard her surprised exhale. "Yes, I—"

"I'll go slowly," he heard himself promise, then could have bitten off his own tongue. Despite his words, he hadn't meant to go this far. He'd planned to make her climax with his hand and then let her do the same for him. A satisfactory quenching of this ridiculous, inconvenient desire. But suddenly, being inside Emmy Danvers seemed vital to his continued survival.

The fact that she was a virgin should have cooled his ardor—she'd only confirmed what he'd already suspected—but the thought that he would be the first to show her pleasure this way gave him an unreasonable rush of satisfaction.

He told himself this wasn't making love. It was just sex. Lust. Fucking in its purest form. But that didn't explain the tendrils of affection that had become entwined with the attraction. He wanted to both conquer her and protect her. To capture her *and* keep her safe. He didn't even begin to understand it.

She must have taken his silence for hesitation. "Changed your mind, Harland?" she whispered, and he could hear the breathless challenge in her tone, alongside the bravado.

Cheeky little minx.

He tilted his hips and entered her just a fraction, and felt her tense. Sweat broke out on his forehead. He wanted to plunge forward, to bury himself to the hilt, but he forced himself to keep his promise. He didn't want to hurt her. He wanted her to experience the same heart-bursting pleasure he did. *But God, the feel of her.*

He slid his hand beneath her thigh, lifted her to a better angle, and clenched his teeth as he slid forward another inch. He withdrew, then pushed into her again, and this time, he heard her gasp. Her fingers encircled his wrists like manacles. She squeezed, and he found he loved the sensation; she held him captive with only a touch.

He hated that he couldn't see her. Being completely blind was his worst nightmare. It reminded him too forcefully of those moments right after the battlefield blast that had stolen part of his vision. He'd lain stunned on the ground, his ears ringing, all other sounds muffled by his perforated eardrums. For a moment of utter panic, he'd thought he'd lost his sight completely. Then his vision had cleared, and he'd seen smoke, and sky, and Seb stumbling toward him, blood streaming down the side of his face. Never had he been so glad to see his friend.

And now here he was, in the dark with Emmy Danvers, and his worst nightmare had suddenly become his hottest fantasy.

The darkness should have allowed him to pretend she was someone else, but it was impossible to forget who he was with. The maddening scent of her filled his nose. The taste of her skin was hers alone, floral and delicious. It was inescapably *her* pinned beneath him. Emmeline Danvers, the bloody Nightjar.

She wriggled, impatient, and he entered her full-length.

"Fuuuuck," he groaned.

He sucked in a breath, determined to give her time to get used to his body's invasion, but she squirmed beneath him again, and his brain went a little fuzzy. He rocked back and forth until he slid in easily, and reveled in her hum of delight when he found the perfect rhythm.

His usual finesse abandoned him. He was hungry for her. Desperate. Her hands roamed over his body, threading through his hair, clutching at his biceps. Her nails scored his back with a pleasure-pain that made him shudder.

"Who has you?" he heard himself growl.

"You," she panted, "Alex Harland." Her voice held a delight and disbelief that mirrored his own.

He increased the tempo, and she ground against him, unconsciously seeking her own climax.

"It's always been you," she choked out.

Alex caught his breath. He hadn't heard that right. He couldn't have done. But still, it almost sent him over the edge. Her body clutched his as she reached the peak again, and he was about to finish himself when sanity made a brief reappearance.

Not inside her. With a hoarse cry, he pulled out of her and spent himself on the bedsheets.

Chapter 26.

Emmy lay sweaty and panting against the rapidly cooling sheets. She stared into the darkness as her thundering heart slowly resumed its natural rhythm.

What had she done? That had been such a glorious madness, an impulsive flurry of passion. Everything Sally had described and more.

She wanted to laugh crazily, and maybe cry a little too. She felt shaky-limbed and breathless, as if she'd stumbled near the edge of a cliff and managed to right herself at the very last moment, just inches from the drop.

She was no longer a virgin. In society terms, she was ruined, but she couldn't bring herself to care. What did social standing matter when she was about to be incarcerated and tried for robbery? The gravity of that certainly put things in perspective.

Still, she had no regrets. If this was to be her one and only experience of lovemaking, then she was fiercely glad that it had been with Harland. She'd never imagined giving herself to anyone else; it had always been him.

The echo of that thought made her pause. Had she actually said that out loud? She'd certainly *thought* it. It was nothing more than the truth. She'd never wanted another man as much as she'd wanted him. Her feelings toward him were so complex, she didn't even try to understand them. She desired him, even when he opposed her. She thought about him constantly. She cared for his good opinion.

Was she was in love with him? It seemed ridiculous, impossible, and yet it was more than mere lust, more than simple attraction. The more she'd come to know him, the more she admired him.

There was absolutely no reason for *him* to know that, however.

Harland. She couldn't allow herself to think of him as Alex, despite the intimacy they'd just shared. She couldn't afford to forget who or what he was.

He lay next to her in the darkness; she could hear the deep exhalations of his breathing, feel the unfamiliar warmth of his body next to hers. She should be taking advantage of his exhausted lethargy. She should be leaping to her feet and running out of the room. But she felt just as exhausted. Her limbs were leaden, as if her bones had dissolved.

Besides, she had to face reality. Even if she managed to escape this room, this building, where would she go? She couldn't escape her fate. Luc was still in the cells at Bow Street. Sally and Camille were still at home. She couldn't possibly get them far enough away before Harland caught up with them again.

Emmy exhaled slowly. She was so tired. It was almost a relief to have been caught.

Almost.

The heavy weight of despair crushed her chest and squeezed the air from her lungs. No more running. Her life, as she knew it, was over. When dawn came, everything would be different. Worse. Infinitely worse. Would she even get to speak to her family before she was locked away?

She jumped as Harland shifted on the bed. The mattress bounced as he sat up and moved away, and she heard the rustle of sheets. What would happen now? Was he getting dressed? Was he about to put on the light? Interrogate her?

She heard the click of a lock as he turned the key in the door, shutting them in together, and her heart began to thump against her ribs. He paced over to the window and checked the latch was secure. Apparently satisfied that all the exits had been dealt with, he returned to the bed and perched on one side, his broad back to her.

Emmy swallowed and found her voice. "Now what?"

Alex didn't know how to answer that. He didn't know what the hell he was going to do with her. He should arrest her immediately, march her over to Bow Street and place her in the cell next to her brother. Hand her over to the proper authorities. Set the wheels of justice in motion.

But duty and honor seemed cold, abstract concepts compared to what they'd just done. There had been nothing cold about that. It had been heat—burning, fevered, *incredible*.

He imagined Emmy, cold and hungry in the cells at Bow Street, or worse, awaiting trial in the miserable conditions of Newgate, at the mercy of every vicious inmate, corrupt guard, and twisted official. She could be raped, beaten, killed.

Suspicion reared its ugly head. She'd said she wasn't sleeping with him to get preferential treatment, but was she lying? Surely she'd do anything to avoid punishment? Had this been a last-ditch effort? One desperate attempt to sway him from his course?

He raked his hand through his hair. God, he didn't know. Had she feigned her desire for him? He didn't think so. Her responses had been ardent, her body wet and willing. His cock twitched in memory.

He'd never slept with a virgin before. It should have been tiresome, her lack of experience, but he hadn't found the task onerous. He'd relished it. Her sweet enthusiasm had only made her more endearing. Alex frowned into the darkness. He should have gone slower. Been more careful. She was so small. Had he hurt her? Crushed something? Torn her inside? He'd heard some virgins bled the first time—

He stood and lit the lamp on the side table.

She blinked in the sudden flare of light and made a panicked move to cover her nakedness. "Wait!" she shrieked. "I'm naked!"

Her hands fluttered ineffectually, trying to shield her breasts and the dark triangle between her legs.

"*You're* naked!" she choked, stating the bloody obvious.

Before Alex could apologize, she caught the edge of the blanket, whipped it across herself, and disappeared beneath the sheets in a flash of pale skin. She pulled them up over her head.

He suppressed a reluctant smile. He was entirely at ease, being naked, as were the women he usually slept with. They were unashamed, proud of their bodies, and rightly so. The female form was lovely. Infinitely variable, soft and curved, with intriguing dips and hollows.

Emmy Danvers, recent virgin, was clearly mortified. She was a muffled lump under the covers.

He found his breeches in a rumpled mess on the floor

and shucked into them. "You can come out," he said. "I'm decent."

She made what sounded like a snort.

"I'm covered," he amended dryly. He might never be *decent*. What he'd done to her had been decidedly indecent. His worry returned. "I need to look at you. Is there blood?"

"What?"

Her voice was muffled by the bedclothes. He fisted the top of the sheet and pulled it down to expose her head. Her hair was tousled, shielding her face.

"Did I hurt you?" he asked again. "Sometimes, the first time—"

The skin he could see—part of her cheek and neck—turned a delicious shade of pink.

"Oh! No. I don't think so. That is, it hurt a little bit, at first, when you, ah—I'm fine. Really I am."

Alex frowned down at her, unsure whether to believe her. With no other choice, he sighed and extinguished the lamp.

He wasn't thinking clearly enough to question her now. He needed sleep. He considered locking her in here and going to sleep in Benedict's old room, but he didn't trust her not to attempt an escape if he left her alone. He couldn't let his guard down around her for one instant. Ergo, he would have to stay in here with her until morning.

With a deep sigh, he stretched himself back down on the bed. Before she could utter an objection, he snagged the covers from her, joined her beneath them, and gathered her into his arms. She froze.

Her back was to him and her naked form nestled perfectly within his own. Her small bottom was cradled sweetly up against his groin, and the top of her head fitted perfectly beneath his chin. Her bare back warmed his chest as he dragged the scent of her hair deep into his lungs.

God, he loved the scent of her.

His uppermost arm was around her shoulders and he made a gargantuan effort to fold it over her without caving in to the near-irresistible urge to cup her breast in his hand.

Perhaps noticing that he was still wearing his breeches, or perhaps because she knew escape would be impossible, she softened a fraction.

"I'm a very light sleeper," he warned. "I'll know the minute you try to escape. Don't even think it."

She made no answer, and Alex felt himself relax. He was filled with a deep sense of contentment, and yet torn between his head and his heart.

Or was it between his head and his *crotch*? Was this just temporary lust blinding him? He'd been fooled by an innocent-looking face before. Could he take the shot to bring Emmy down? Could he see her dead, like that bomber in Spain? He might not have to pull the trigger himself this time, but the end result would be the same.

He frowned into the darkness. The situations weren't the same. Emmy had never physically hurt anyone. She'd pose no danger to the public if she were free. Would he trust her word if she promised to never steal again? He wasn't sure. But something was clearly compelling her to keep stealing, even faced with very real danger. As soon as it was light, he would make her explain.

Emmy lay still, cradled in Harland's arms, hardly able to believe the way the night had unfolded. Being held like this, surrounded by his huge body, should have felt like an imprisonment, but instead, it felt like . . . safety.

She squeezed her eyes tightly. So wrong, to seek comfort from a man who could only bring her pain.

When she'd been younger, she'd dreamed of what it would be like to have Alexander Harland on her side—as an ally, not an adversary. He would make a wonderful partner, clever enough to scheme and plan. Strong enough to protect her from the Dantons of the world. If only she'd had him at her side when that first letter had arrived.

Unfortunately, a thief couldn't hire a Bow Street Runner to find the man who was blackmailing her. She almost snorted at the ludicrous idea.

She let her body relax a little more. Being held by a man was a foreign sensation, but it somehow felt completely natural, as if she'd curled up in his warm embrace a thousand times before. Such foolishness. This was a temporary truce, nothing more. When morning came, they would be enemies again. But just for a few hours she could pretend there would be no tomorrow.

"Sleep," Harland murmured, and she felt the rumble of it pass from his chest into her back.

What else could she do? Emmy closed her eyes and let exhaustion overtake her.

Chapter 27.

It was almost dawn when she awoke. She lay on her side and watched the light change, from dove grey to pearl white and wished they could have stayed in the darkness forever.

Harland had released her at some point during the night. He was still asleep beside her, lying on his back, and his features became clearer with every passing minute. He was so handsome, it almost broke her heart. His hair was rumpled, his bare chest visible above the sheet that had fallen around his waist. She remembered the silky feel of that hair beneath her fingers.

Several small scars marred his skin, and she resisted the urge to reach out and trace them, to smooth her palms over the defined ridges of his muscles. He reminded her of the statue she'd seen in the British Museum. Not the gladiator—although he was similarly muscled—but the dying slave. His austere face was relaxed, his beautiful lips soft and dreadfully tempting. He looked powerful and yet strangely vulnerable, almost boyish.

Emmy sighed.

No more dreaming. It was time to face the new status quo.

Her exhalation roused him. His slate-blue eyes snapped to hers. For a moment she saw confusion and then incredulity in their depths, before recollection came to him and he went from asleep to fully alert in an instant. That ability must be the result of so many years as a soldier.

He sat up in a swift move and was off the bed and standing by the door before she could even blink. He reached down and picked up her shirt and breeches from where they'd fallen on the floor, and her skin heated at the reminder that she was completely naked beneath the sheet.

He tossed them to her, his face expressionless. "Get dressed. I'll be waiting out there."

As soon as he left, Emmy made use of the chamber pot and splashed her face with water she found in the wash jug. The cotton drying cloth smelled of him. One glance in the shaving mirror confirmed her worst fears; she barely recognized herself. Her hair was a tangled mess and her lips seemed fuller than usual. She ran her hands through her hair, then braided it in one long plait and used a thread of cotton pulled from the washcloth to secure the end.

Muscles she'd never noticed before in her stomach and thighs protested as she bent to put on her breeches, but once she was dressed, she felt better armed to face whatever was to come. She straightened her spine, opened the door, and strode into the lion's den.

He'd taken up position in the chair behind the desk and gestured to the seat across the polished expanse of wood. Thankfully he'd donned a shirt; she doubted she'd have been able to think straight if she'd had his bare chest to distract her.

"Sit."

Emmy sat.

He cleared his throat and levelled her with a piercing stare. "I believe we need to clarify our respective roles in this play, Miss Danvers."

She winced at his return to formality but managed to match his tone. "Is it a farce? A comedy? A tragedy?"

"I haven't decided yet."

He placed his hands flat on the desk. *She would not think of those hands on her body.*

"Do you deny that you are the thief they call the Night-jar?"

She lifted one shoulder in an easy shrug and threw him an appeasing crumb. "That was my father."

He frowned at her. She raised one brow. Battle lines had been drawn. Last night she'd been too panicked to think clearly, but this morning she wouldn't go down without a fight.

"The only thing you can prove I'm guilty of is breaking into your bedroom," she said calmly. "And that's not much of a crime. I bet I'm not the first woman to visit your chamber uninvited in the middle of the night."

She quashed a hot flash of jealousy at the thought.

He sent her an impatient look. "Your father is dead. A dead man didn't break into Rundell and Bridge. A dead man didn't steal the blue diamond from the British Museum." He leaned closer. "A dead man didn't call me an *unresponsive lump of rock.*"

Emmy bit her lip to suppress a smile. So that still rankled, did it? *Good.*

"What do you want me to say? That I took over as the Nightjar from my father? Do you think anyone will believe that? I'm just a weak and foolish woman."

That, hopefully, would be the opinion of a bench full of judges, should she ever be brought to trial. She would play upon their standard male prejudices: A young woman like herself was too stupid to mastermind a string of audacious thefts, too feeble to carry them out.

"You didn't work alone. I know full well your brother is involved. And that housekeeper of yours, Sally Hawkins."

Damn. Emmy tried to keep her face impassive. She was prepared to take sole blame for the Nightjar's crimes, provided the rest of her family were spared. Perhaps it was time to divert his attention. She sent him a wistful smile. "I truly wish we'd met under different circumstances, Lord Melton. But the fact of the matter is, I'm—"

"A criminal?" he supplied smoothly.

She inclined her head but refused to admit it out loud. "And you're—"

"Not?"

"Indeed. So we shall ever be on opposite sides. Like Wellington and Napoleon. But I like to think we could have been friends."

He snorted. "As well ask a prosecutor and a defense lawyer to be friends." He gave her a look from under his lashes that made her stomach twist. "I think we're destined to be passionate enemies instead."

There was an awkward pause.

"There's no walking away from this," he said softly. "You know that, don't you?"

Her delight at their banter evaporated, replaced by a heavy sense of fatalism.

"Talk to me," he commanded. "Tell me how you became the Nightjar. This is not something you've taken on suddenly. Your skills must have taken years to hone. Who taught you? Your father?"

Emmy closed her eyes. So it began. The relentless questions designed to wear down her resistance. There really was no point in trying to wriggle out of it. He would break her eventually. He wouldn't stop until he had the answers, the evidence he needed. Even if she stalled him now, it would only be a temporary reprieve. It might even be a relief to finally confess.

She sat up straighter in her chair and tried to emulate Camille's worldly confidence. "I did everything in my power not to become a criminal, but it was inevitable, given my father's decisions. And since I had no choice in the matter, I decided to see it as a personal challenge. If I was going to be a thief, then I would be the best thief London has ever seen."

Harland's expression of surprise was delightful. He clearly hadn't expected to get a confession out of her so easily. She smiled. "I am a damned fine criminal, if I do say so myself."

"You *were*," he said brutally. "Until you got caught."

Her chest tightened at that irrefutable truth.

"Why jewels?" he asked. "And why only ones from the French royal collection?"

Ah, so he'd made that connection. She'd thought as much. How else could he have predicted she'd go for Lady Carrington's ruby and not some other prize?

She gave a sad half smile. "What is that phrase? 'The road to hell is paved with good intentions.'"

He leaned back in his chair and drummed his fingertips on the arms. "You do know the true, legal definition of stealing, do you not? As in, taking something that doesn't belong to you without intending to return it?"

A burst of righteous anger welled up inside her. "I have every intention of returning them! Just not to the people from whom I stole them. They will go back to their rightful owner."

"And I suppose you've determined who that rightful owner is?" The sarcasm in his voice could have cut glass.

"Of course. The people of France."

The silence that followed her pronouncement was profound. Harland stared at her as if the concept of her actually having a noble reason for stealing the jewels had never entered his head. She felt vaguely insulted. Had he really thought her so venal?

"You feel no remorse for what you have done?" It was more statement than question, but Emmy answered it anyway.

"Honestly? No. I feel pride. If you're expecting an apology, you'll be waiting until doomsday. I will never apologize for doing my duty. My duty to my father, and my patriotic duty to France."

Stealing back the jewels was morally the right thing to do. Emmy truly believed that. She just wished the responsibility had been foisted on someone else. Patriotism was all well and good, but in pitting her against Harland, a man she cared for, it had removed any possibility that they might have had a future together.

He sighed. "The diamond you took from Rundell and Bridge belonged to the Prince Regent. He wants it back."

"Well, he can't have it. It's not his."

"Tell me where it is."

"I can't," she said in perfect honesty. She had no idea what Danton had done with it.

A muscle ticked in his jaw. "You little fool! This isn't a game. It's a damn risky business. Who put you up to this? Your brother? Your grandmother?"

"Nobody. It was all me. Working alone." She curled her fists against her thighs. "You don't understand. I *had* to do it."

His eyes flashed, and she desperately tried to think of something that might appease him. "What if I collaborate?" she said quickly. "I'll return the diamond, and the blue from the British Museum, in exchange for immunity from prosecution."

She had no idea how she'd get the jewels back from Danton, but still—

"The Prince will never accept that. He wants the Nightjar punished to the full extent of the law. And what about all the other jewels that have been stolen over the years? We're just supposed to forget about those, are we?"

He let out a long, frustrated exhale. Emmy turned her face to the wall and focused on the bottle of her perfume that still sat on the side table. She was in no position to negotiate. She was doomed. But she could still drag Danton down with her.

"All right. I'll tell you who 'put me up to it.' A man named Emile Danton, a Frenchman."

She told him about Danton's letters. His threats and demands. The Rundell & Bridge heist and the one at the museum, making sure not to implicate Luc, Sally, or Camille in her testimony. To his credit, Harland didn't interrupt her. He just sat and listened, and when she'd finished, she felt strangely light and unburdened.

His chair scraped backwards as he stood, his expression impossible to read. "I have to go out."

"Where?"

"To Bow Street. I'll have your brother released."

Her shoulders sagged with relief, even though Luc was only being freed because she'd condemned herself so thoroughly. "Thank you."

He nodded, crossed to a handsome mahogany chest, and pulled out a cravat. Emmy thought he'd put it on, but he disappeared into the bedroom, and she was mystified to hear the splash of water in the porcelain washbowl. He returned with the dripping length of cloth twisted in his hands.

"Cotton is stronger when wet," he said by way of explanation. "Put your hands behind the chair."

Emmy gave a groan of protest, even though she hadn't truly expected him to leave her alone in the room, unsecured. "I promise I won't run."

He didn't justify that with an answer. She tried to ignore the feel of his warm breath on her neck as he crouched behind her and secured the wet cotton around her wrists.

"This seems to be a theme in my life recently," she said lightly, to cover her panic. "I am forever being confined in places I have no wish to be. Barrels. Sarcophagi. Gentlemen's chambers."

"I apologize," he said gruffly. "It won't be for long."

No, of course it wouldn't. He'd probably return from Bow Street with a set of Emmy-sized iron shackles. She was surprised he didn't have a pair lying around the place, ready to use in just such a situation.

He gave the bindings a final tug and stepped back, apparently satisfied. She gave her wrists an experimental twist and bit back a curse. They really were inescapable, damn him.

She heard the rustle of clothing from behind her but staunchly refused to look as he finished dressing. When he stepped in front of her, she had to suppress a scowl. He was unreasonably handsome. His broad shoulders and long thighs—both of which had been intimately pressed against her only hours ago—were outlined by his tan breeches and immaculately cut jacket.

She wanted to kick him in the shins.

His eyes rested for a moment on her flushed face, as if memorizing her features, then dropped to her chest where her breasts were pushed forward by the unnatural position of her hands. He raked his fingers through his hair in a distracted gesture and a flush darkened his cheekbones.

She raised her brows at him imperiously.

"Stay here," he ordered.

She sent him an exasperated look to remind him just how ridiculous that was. "Go away."

Alex locked the door, pocketed the key, and strode down the corridor, desperate to leave the confounding woman behind. He could barely contain his need to do violence. Not to Emmy, but to the bastard who'd placed her in such an untenable position.

The irony of the fact that he'd completely reversed his position, from being angry at her to being angry *for* her, did not escape him. The desire to protect her, from Danton, from herself, from her own foolish choices, was almost overwhelming.

He'd witnessed the infinite possibilities of violence in his three years of war. He knew the damage that could be inflicted on the human body. The thought of someone hurting Emmy made him break out in a cold sweat. If this Danton harmed a single hair on her head, he'd tear him apart with his bare hands.

Alex exhaled slowly and tried to calm the pounding in his blood. He needed distance. Not proximity. Emmy Danvers was dangerous. She sucked all the air from his lungs. No wonder he couldn't think straight; his poor brain was permanently deprived of oxygen whenever he was near her.

What did he want from her? He let out a despairing laugh. He wanted her to be a different woman. He wanted her to be the perfect, innocent girl he'd held fast in his memory for so long. He wanted her *not* to be a criminal.

What if she *hadn't* been the Nightjar? He forced himself to complete the thought. What if he'd simply recognized her across a dance floor as the girl from the garden and learned she was a paragon of virtue, perfectly socially acceptable. Would he have been contemplating marriage?

He doubted it. Because although he might have been

physically attracted to her, he couldn't imagine having much in common with a paragon. He'd have been bored with a perfect, automaton, society wife who only wanted to throw dinner parties and go shopping. It was Emmy's passion for adventure, her bravery, her brilliance, that attracted him.

He usually lost interest in a woman once he'd bedded her. The thrill of the chase was gone, the mystique shattered. He should have been immune to her by now. But he was even more drawn to her this morning than last night, if that were possible. Even *after* she'd confessed.

He should be feeling elated. He'd captured the Nightjar and made her admit her crimes. But that paled in comparison to the triumph he'd felt when he'd joined his body with hers, the satisfaction of holding her in his arms. He wanted her again.

No. Last night's lapse could be dismissed as temporary insanity brought on by shock and a whole host of other, contradictory emotions. Taking her to bed a second time would be a colossal mistake for which there was no excuse. He'd averted complete disaster by not finishing inside her last night, but he didn't trust himself to be able to repeat the task if he got carried away again. She made him forget his own name.

He regretted the need to restrain her. The sight of her, her chest rising and falling in anger, should not have filled him with such lustful thoughts. He knew there were places, clubs, in London that catered for those with such proclivities, and he'd never imagined he'd find it titillating to have a woman bound and at his mercy. Until now. He was still hard in his breeches.

Bloody woman. What was he going to do with her?

Chapter 28.

Harland didn't return for what felt like hours. Emmy could hear a clock ticking somewhere in the bedroom but couldn't see it. She shuffled her chair around in tiny increments to face the door. Several times she heard heavy footsteps outside—presumably the Tricorn's mountainous manservant, but nobody came in.

Her grumbling stomach reminded her she'd had no breakfast, and hunger did nothing to improve her temper. A procession of dire thoughts chased one another around her head. Not knowing what was going to happen to her was maddening. Finally, the door clicked open and Harland strode in, bringing a gust of pine-scented air with him. The grim set of his features did not suggest good news.

Her pulse spiked in alarm. "What is it? What has happened? Is it Luc?"

Instead of answering her immediately, he crouched behind her chair and untied her hands. They fell to her sides like lead weights, and she shook her wrists to restore the circulation.

He took the seat behind the desk. "Your brother is well. I went to Bow Street and had him released."

"And?" Emmy prompted, certain from his expression that there was more.

"While I was there, I met my colleague, Sebastien Wolff. He'd just returned from Gravesend."

Emmy sent him a mystified look. "Why had he gone there?"

"To check up on the one jewel you hadn't got around to stealing. The Ruspoli sapphire."

Her mouth dropped open. "You know where it is?"

"We had a little help from the French head of la Securité, Vidocq."

"I'm impressed. I hadn't even begun to trace it. Who has it?"

His brows lowered. "It was owned by a disgraced Italian diplomat by the name of Franco Andretti. Unfortunately, Seb arrived just in time to visit a crime scene. Andretti was murdered last night."

All the breath left Emmy's lungs. "What?"

"The killer left a black feather at the scene."

She choked back a gasp of horror. "It was made to look like the Nightjar's crime?"

It was one thing to be thought a jewel thief, quite another to be suspected of murder. Danton. It must have been him. He'd threatened violence, but she hadn't imagined he meant anything as serious as murder. The madman would clearly stop at nothing to gain the jewels. That he'd implicated the Nightjar in such a heinous crime was a clear warning. Her family would be next if she did not do what he asked.

Oh, God. How could she retrieve the cache her father

had hidden if she was imprisoned here, or locked in the cells at Bow Street?

Emmy suddenly couldn't breathe, no matter how quickly she inhaled. She bent forward and pressed her forehead to her knees in an effort not to faint. Harland's hand settled on the small of her back and rubbed up and down her spine in a comforting gesture so effective, she almost whimpered in gratitude.

"Take deep breaths," he commanded. "Slowly."

The dizziness eased and she sat back up. Harland returned to his position on the other side of the desk.

"Did the killer take the sapphire?" she asked, even though she already knew the answer.

"Yes. The safe was open, but empty. The thief forced Andretti to open it, then shot him in cold blood."

"So now the Nightjar is wanted for murder." Her lips felt numb. She could barely get the words out.

Harland nodded.

"Surely a judge will realize that this is the work of an imitator?" She could hear the desperate edge to her own voice. "The Nightjar's never even broken a window before. It's out of character." A knot of impotent fury balled in her chest. Danton had sullied her father's memory, his legacy.

Harland's slate-blue gaze burned her from the inside out. "I doubt a judge will bother to sift through the evidence. The presence of a black feather is damning. The thefts alone would be enough to send the Nightjar to the gallows. This just adds weight to the inevitable sentence."

He didn't need to say what that sentence would be. *Death.* Emmy leaned forward and reached across the desk toward him. Her heart felt like a stone in her chest. "Let me write to my family. I need to warn them. Please."

His eyes narrowed on her face. "You think Danton did this, don't you?"

"Who else could it be?"

Alex studied her from across the desk. Her eyes were huge in her pale face, the freckles on her nose more prominent than usual. Her lips, however, were bright pink, either from where she'd gnawed at them in worry, or from their passionate encounter last night. His body flushed in memory.

The look in her eyes was so fearful, so hopeless, it made his chest ache. He fisted his hands against the temptation to leap over there, drag her against his chest, and tell her that everything would be all right. He was no white knight. He couldn't promise her anything.

Her throat worked as she tried to speak.

"Help me," she said finally. Her eyes sparkled with a new determination. "Danton will contact me soon to see if I've managed to steal the real ruby." She glanced over at the jewel in question, still sitting on the side table next to her perfume bottle. "If he discovers I've been arrested, he'll hurt my family. Let me return home—just until he contacts me. I'll arrange to meet him with the ruby, and you can lay a trap for him."

Her eyes met his, and Alex experienced that now-familiar jolt. He couldn't help but admire the way she faced her problems head-on without flinching. She was like some poor, brave aristocrat proudly mounting the steps to the guillotine. Damned, but still defiant.

"I won't try to escape," she said, anticipating his next comment. "I'm quite prepared to be tried for the Nightjar's thefts, but I refuse to be punished for a murder I've had no hand in. Danton must be stopped. Catch him, and you'll have both your murderer and the jewels. You'll be a hero."

The curl of her lips made it clear he was anything *but* heroic if he returned the gems to the Prince Regent.

Alex was about to answer her when a commotion in the hall caught his attention. An agitated female voice merged with Mickey's much deeper tones in animated altercation. He opened the door just in time to see a beautiful, buxom woman duck under Mickey's restraining arm and sprint up the stairs toward him, advancing like an avenging fury.

"Alexander 'Arland?" she demanded, and just her way of shouting his name was enough to indicate she came from the East End. "What've you done wiv Emmy, you scoundrel? I know she's 'ere!"

"Sally!"

Emmy flashed past him through the doorway. Alex made a grab for her collar, but she was too quick. She launched herself into the arms of the disheveled stranger with a strangled cry of delight. The two women hugged, then separated, both of them talking at once.

"Sally! What are you doing here?"

"Em! Thank God! I didn't know what else to do."

"What do you mean?" Emmy clearly noticed the other woman's disarray; Sally's hair was loose around her shoulders and she hadn't bothered putting on either a bonnet or gloves. Alex noted, quite dispassionately, that she had a magnificent cleavage.

"What's happened?" Emmy demanded.

"Another letter," the woman said darkly. She shot a warning glance over Emmy's shoulder at Alex, who sent her a sarcastic nod in return.

"No need for discretion, Miss Hawkins," he said silkily, deciding this must be Emmy's housekeeper and co-conspirator, Sally Hawkins. How the woman had managed to disguise those feminine curves under the guise of a window cleaner was a mystery. "Miss Danvers and

I have no secrets between us." He enjoyed the way Emmy's ears turned pink at his unsubtle insinuation. "What does Monsieur Danton have to say?"

Sally shot Emmy an accusatory glance, as if disappointed that she'd caved in and told him, then reached inside her ample bosom and withdrew a folded note. Her chest swelled in misery, and her beautiful eyes filled with tears.

"He's got Luc!"

Chapter 29.

Sally thrust the crumpled letter at Emmy, who scanned it as quickly as she could. Luc, it appeared, had been released from Bow Street and almost immediately apprehended by Danton.

"I asked one of the sweeper boys," Sally said. "He saw Luc get into a carriage at the end of the street but didn't think anything of it. There weren't no markings or crests on it."

Emmy closed her eyes as the threatening note swam before her. Luc was Danton's hostage.

She let Harland take the paper from her nerveless fingers.

Oh, God. She hadn't thought things could get worse than her own arrest. But now Danton was demanding all of the jewels her father had collected, within twenty-four hours, or Luc's life would be forfeit.

If you doubt my claim, he'd written. *Take note of the example set by Signore Andretti. Such is the fate of those who defy me.*

Emmy shivered. Was that oblique reference enough to prove Danton had killed the Italian? Surely it was enough to convince Harland to help her?

"Does Camille know?" she asked.

Sally shook her head. "Not yet. She was still in her room. I came straight here. What should we do?" Her tears threatened to overflow, and she dashed them away with an impatient hand. "That bastard. If he hurts Luc, I'll—"

She didn't seem able to find a harsh enough expletive to finish that sentence. Emmy caught her elbow and tugged her into Harland's rooms, and the two of them dropped into the wing chairs that flanked the fire.

Sally looked around her with wide eyes, doubtless noticing the telltale rumple of sheets through the open door to the bedchamber and drawing her own—entirely correct—conclusions as to why Emmy hadn't returned last night. She sent Emmy a telling look, but thankfully forbore to comment.

Harland stepped into the room and turned his penetrating gaze on Sally. "How long ago was this letter delivered?"

"About an hour."

"By messenger?"

"Yes. One of them errand boys. There's no way to trace it back to the source. We tried that before. None of 'em know where 'e lives."

"Miss Danvers is currently helping Bow Street with its inquiries."

Emmy gave an inelegant snort at his linguistic circumnavigation—*helping with their inquiries, indeed.*

He ignored her. "Miss Hawkins, you should return to Waverley Gardens and await further instruction. You may tell the countess what has happened at your discretion."

Emmy opened her mouth to object to him giving such

summary commands concerning *her* family, but he sent her a quelling glare.

"Miss Danvers and I," he continued, "are going to discuss the location of the Nightjar's ill-gotten gains."

Sally sent Emmy another desperate look, and Emmy lifted her shoulders in a *what can I do?* shrug. In a choice between the Nightjar's jewels and her brother's life, there really wasn't a decision to make. Luc was more important than any patriotic whim. She'd loved her father dearly, but he was dead, whereas Luc—she sincerely hoped—was still alive and well.

She wasn't foolish enough to believe that cooperating with Bow Street would in any way lessen her eventual sentence, but she would do anything to save her brother. She sent Sally what she hoped was a reassuring smile. "He's right. Please go and sit with Camille. Tell her I have everything under control."

Sally nodded, apparently convinced by that outright lie. "All right. But you be careful, Em, you hear me." She sent another meaningful glance toward Harland and stood, shaking out her skirts. "Don't do anyfink I wouldn't do."

Emmy refrained from saying that didn't rule out much at all.

"Mickey will be delighted to escort you home, Miss Hawkins." Harland indicated the door with an expansive sweep of his arm, as if Sally were a duchess, and she bustled back into the passageway with a mollified sniff. "And Mickey," he added to the hovering manservant, "tell Sam to saddle up Bey."

As soon as the rustle of Sally's skirts and the thump of Mickey's boots had receded, he turned back to Emmy with a steely look in his eye. "Enough skirmishing. Where are the rest of the jewels?"

Emmy gave a disgruntled sniff. "Very well. They're buried in the grounds of a ruined abbey. In Rutland."

"Rutland?" he said aghast. "Near Lincolnshire? Dear God. Why there? I thought they would be here, in London."

She shook her head, rather enjoying his irritation. "My grandfather had a hunting lodge out there. You can't just go and dig the place up, though. Only Luc and I know the exact location of the cache." She sent him a sweet, triumphant smile. "If you want all the jewels, you're going to have to take me with you."

His eyes narrowed in displeasure. "How do I know you're not leading me on a wild goose chase? That you won't try to escape en route?"

"Apart from the fact that I give you my word?" she countered. "At least credit me with not wanting Luc to be hurt. I'm as keen to get those jewels to Danton as you are."

That logic seemed to satisfy him. "How far is it?"

Emmy suppressed a smile. "About ninety miles. It's near Stamford, straight up the Great North Road."

"Can we get there and back by this time tomorrow?"

"I believe so. It takes about six hours, with a change of horses."

"Can you ride?"

Emmy shook her head. "Not for that distance. I usually take the mail coach."

He gave a put-upon sigh and glanced at the clock on the mantel. "If we leave now, we should get there before dark. I'll have Sam ready the carriage for you."

"But not for you?"

He shook his head with a grimace of distaste. "I'll ride."

Emmy told herself the dip in her spirits was not disappointment. Was his grimace because he couldn't stand the thought of being in her presence, or simply because he hated to be confined inside when he could ride? Why did she even care?

He crossed to the side table, picked up the ruby, and made a point of placing it in the inside pocket of his jacket. "Stay here. I'll see about some food for you."

Emmy wrinkled her nose at his departing back, but it was hard to stay annoyed when he was being so considerate. She hadn't thought he'd care whether she'd eaten or not.

She was clearly still his captive, but she'd spoken the truth when she'd promised not to escape. With Harland's assistance, she could return to London with the jewels far quicker than if she'd been on her own, with the added benefit of his protection there and back.

As long as she delivered the gems to Danton by the deadline and saved Luc, she didn't care what happened to them after that.

Emmy shook her head. She'd have the dubious pleasure-pain of Harland's company until tomorrow. She must be a glutton for punishment. Even now, when she ought to resent him, she couldn't find it in herself to do so.

A few minutes later a brown-haired serving girl brought in a steaming tray of food, and Emmy almost groaned in delight. Coffee with cream and sugar. Bacon and eggs. Toast and jam. Harland was proving to be a very agreeable jailer. She'd just finished the last slice of toast when Mickey arrived with a carpet bag she instantly recognized as her own.

"Miss 'Awkins sent this over for yer," he mumbled. "'Is lordship said you got fifteen minutes to dress and meet 'im downstairs."

"Thank you, Mickey." Emmy smiled and watched the giant's ears turn pink in embarrassment.

She opened the bag and almost laughed. Sally had sent two of Emmy's most stylish dresses, along with a host of other necessary items. She donned a scandalously sheer chemise, stays, and silk stockings, then pulled the pale blue day dress over her head. At least it was cotton, and not some impractical featherweight gauze, but the tiny puff sleeves were hardly enough to keep an inch of her arms warm and the row of little bows along the neckline was pure frivolity.

Thankfully, Sally had included a matching spencer to wear over the top, in a dark blue velvet with military-inspired gold braid frogging down the front. It buttoned snugly over Emmy's bosom. She tugged a brush through her hair and secured it in a simple twist at the base of her neck with the pins provided.

As a final flourish, she crossed to the sideboard, reclaimed her bottle of perfume, and defiantly applied the last few drops to her wrists and neck. The familiar scent calmed her. She donned a pair of cream leather gloves and picked up the small drawstring reticule Sally had provided, which contained a handkerchief, a small circular mirror, a folding mother-of-pearl pocket knife, and a few coins.

A pistol might have made her feel a little more in control, Emmy reflected, but they'd never kept any firearms in the house, and she had no idea how to use one. Harland was used to serious weapons, rifles and muskets; he'd probably laugh himself silly if she threatened him with a muff pistol.

When she opened the door, it was to find Mickey waiting to escort her down to the mews. Harland was already out there, in a woolen greatcoat and riding boots, holding the reins of a bay stallion. Her heart quickened when she saw him, waiting with one foot propped up on a spoke of the carriage wheel and conversing with a groom who was seated behind a handsome pair of matched greys.

He took her hand to help her into the carriage. Her skin

tingled as his fingers squeezed hers, despite her gloves. Would she ever cease to be so acutely aware of him?

He sent her a baleful glare, his lashes a dark tangle against his blue-steel eyes. "Don't even think about trying to escape. If you run, I will chase you to the ends of the earth. Never doubt it."

Emmy suppressed a shiver. She was a fool to find such a declaration thrilling, but her heart was suddenly pounding with desire. The stupid organ clearly couldn't distinguish between a threat and a promise.

With a sigh, she sat back against the comfortable leather squabs and tugged a travel rug over her knees. The next few hours might be her last taste of freedom. She would make the most of every moment.

Chapter 30.

Emmy peered out of the narrow window as the coach rattled along. It hadn't taken long to reach the outskirts of London, and the jumble and chaos of the capital had given way to sporadic cottages, fields of swaying barley, and the occasional village turnpike.

Her chest tightened as bittersweet memories assailed her. She'd taken this journey many times in the company of her father, whenever there had been a new jewel to deposit in the cache. It was achingly familiar: the signposts for Letchworth and Biggleswade, the undulating sweep of English countryside. Never had the fields been so green, the songs of the birds so sweet. Life seemed infinitely precious, now that her days were numbered.

They stopped to change horses at a posting inn near St. Neots, but apart from providing her with a cup of coffee and a meat pie to eat in the carriage, Harland largely ignored her. She wasn't surprised that he didn't want her to show her face. If someone recognized him in the company of a lone female, they would either assume she was his mistress or—worse—that the two of them were eloping. They were, after all, heading north toward Gretna Green.

The idea should have been amusing, but instead, it added to the ache in Emmy's heart. She and Harland might have shared a night of passion, but they were far from being lovestruck swains. They weren't even friends. They were adversaries, under a temporary truce.

She hadn't really had time to think, back at the Tricorn, but now, trapped inside a carriage whose masculine scents of leather and horses reminded her so forcefully of Harland, she had plenty of opportunity. Her troubled thoughts were as inescapable as the man himself. Emmy shifted restlessly in her seat.

She'd given herself to him. His naked body had been next to hers. *Inside* hers.

The entire episode seemed almost too incredible to believe—as if she'd made love with some mystical creature who existed only in darkness and disappeared at daybreak—except her body remembered with excruciating clarity, even without visual corroboration. Her skin felt newly sensitized, invigorated, as if Harland's touch had introduced her to a new world of sensation. Her heart pounded whenever she thought about him, and not in fear or trepidation, but with a wicked kind of anticipation.

Had last night meant anything to him, or had she been just another willing body in his bed? Emmy wrinkled her nose. He'd *seemed* involved. His kisses had been ardent, almost desperate. His body had been hard and ready for hers. He'd murmured her name in the darkness too. A little of her tension eased. No, he hadn't been thinking of anybody else.

Last night had changed something inside her, changed

something between them, irrevocably. She felt as if she'd been pulled apart and put back together in an entirely new configuration.

Still, she was fiercely glad it had been him. No one else would have done. He was more than a match for her. His steadiness, his resourcefulness, even his bloody-minded determination to catch her, spoke of a strength of character she couldn't help but admire. Those traits that had led to her capture were the same ones she found irresistibly attractive. He'd outplayed her in this, the ultimate game of chase, and she couldn't begrudge him that. She had nothing but respect for him as an adversary.

Emmy smiled sadly. Alex Harland was just as much a thief as she was. He'd stolen her heart four years ago and never given it back.

His horse drew level with the carriage, and she sneaked a glance at his profile. He looked windswept and sinfully handsome, entirely at ease in the saddle. Although he'd been in the Rifles, not a cavalry regiment, he clearly felt comfortable on horseback. The muscles of his thighs rippled beneath his soft breeches, and the way his hips rocked with the horse's gait was positively indecent.

Emmy shoved the travel rug from her lap in irritation. It wasn't fair. He could discompose her without even trying.

The late afternoon sun slanted through the window, warming her even further. The brass buttons on his greatcoat flashed, and a wicked idea blossomed in her brain.

He'd called her aggravating, had he not? She'd show him.

She reached into her reticule, pulled out the small mirror, and tilted it so the sun's rays caught the surface. She trained the beam at the side of Harland's face. The patch of concentrated light danced over his cheek and jaw, then flashed into his eyes.

He shook his head, momentarily blinded, and turned to locate the source. Emmy hastily hid the mirror in her lap. He flashed her a dangerous, suspicious look, like Lucifer brooding on some secret fantasy of rebellion. Her heart pounded, but she sent him a cheerful smile and a wave. Annoying him was still a pleasure.

They passed Alconbury, then Stilton—a village famous for its cheese—and finally Wansford, the last stop before Stamford, and their destination. Emmy recalled an amusing tale her father had once told her about how the village had come by its full name: Wansford-in-England. According to folklore, it derived from a local man who'd fallen asleep on a hayrick and, upon awakening, found himself floating down the River Nene. Panicked, he'd asked a traveler on the riverbank where he was, and upon hearing the reply "Wansford," he'd asked, "Wansford in England?" The simple man had been afraid he'd floated out to sea and across to another country.

Emmy sighed. If only she could escape her current situation by floating away down a river.

Frothy white flowerheads of cow parsley and cornflowers the color of Harland's eyes bobbed in the hedgerows but Emmy glanced doubtfully at the darkening sky up ahead. Despite the sunshine, an ominous bank of clouds hovered on the horizon, threatening rain in the not-so-distant future. It wouldn't be fully dark until around ten, so they had a few hours before sunset, but she hoped they completed their task quickly. She wasn't dressed for rain.

When they stopped for a second time, at the George Inn at Stamford, Harland dismounted and indicated for the driver of her coach to climb down. She slid open the window as he came to the door of the carriage.

"We'll go on alone from here," he said. "Which way?"

She gave him directions and felt the conveyance tilt

and bounce on its springs as he climbed up front. It took another twenty minutes driving back out into the countryside before they reached the spot. "Stop here!" Emmy called.

He pulled the horses to a halt, and she didn't wait for him to help her down. She lowered the step herself and jumped into the narrow lane, glad to be out of the confining carriage. They were deep in the country, far from the town, and the road they were on was little more than an overgrown farm track. Trees flanked the high verges on either side.

"It's too narrow to take the carriage any farther," she explained. "We'll have to walk from here." She pointed uphill through the trees. "Grandfather's hunting lodge is just over there, but the ruins are this way. Come on."

Harland unhitched the horses from the carriage and secured them where they could crop the grass of the verge. He shrugged out of his greatcoat, threw it into the carriage, then followed her as she started along the narrow lane.

Emmy glanced back. His sinfully broad chest and shoulders were sun-dappled by the leaves, and his face wore an expression of resignation. She couldn't resist teasing him.

"Don't you have a shovel?" she asked innocently. "A pickaxe?"

He frowned. "What for?"

"To dig up the treasure, of course. We'll need to move a lot of earth and stones. Father always brought a crowbar. And a series of pulleys."

He sent her an exasperated glare. "You never mentioned needing a blasted—"

Her smile gave her away, and he stopped midsentence and fisted his hands on his hips. "You little wretch. I don't need anything, do I?"

"Only your hands and a little brute strength." She chuckled.

She beckoned him on, leaving the main track to push between the trees and into the wilderness of brambles, grasses, and ferns. She could hear Harland snapping twigs and rustling leaves behind her.

"Are you sure this is the way?" he asked.

"Oh, yes. It's not buried near the main house."

"Of course it isn't," he grumbled. "Heaven forbid it should be somewhere easily accessible. Knowing your family, I expect there's a series of booby traps and obstacles to maim us before we reach it. Don't tell me, we have to swim through an eel-infested moat and crawl through a pit of brambles just to get close?"

She grinned at his morbid humor. He certainly was grouchy. Was he experiencing the same sexual frustration as she was? The same impotent fury at being thrust into this impossible situation? She hoped so.

Acorns and beech nuts blanketed the ground and crunched underfoot, and Emmy sucked in a deep appreciative breath. She loved the clean country air. It was a world away from the capital's smoke-filled smog. Green leaves made a canopy above them, and the last of the day's warmth filtered through. It wasn't hot and lush, like the ambassador's conservatory, nor was it rigidly tended like the pleasure gardens at Vauxhall. It was nature, wild and unplanned.

Everything in London had been tamed. Not just the gardens, but every person too—hemmed in by society's rules, trained like vines over a trellis. Everyone was supposed to go in the same direction; any infringement would lead to exclusion and social ostracism. Anything too wild was forced back into line. Girls were scolded for laughing too loudly, for dancing too enthusiastically. For revealing they had a working brain. Part of Emmy's delight in thieving had come from the knowledge that she was subverting every expectation. Breaking all the rules.

Except breaking the rules came with a high price if you were caught.

She glanced around, and for a brief, panicked moment she thought she'd forgotten the way, but then the trees thinned out and she saw the clearing she'd been seeking.

The ivy-clad ruins were as picturesque as she remembered. Grey stones, green with moss, were interspersed with later portions of crumbling red brick. Emmy dodged a patch of stinging nettles and rounded a waist-high wall to enter a roofless nave, the far end of which contained a circular window with two arches but no glass. No wooden beams or rafters remained. Doorways on what would have been the upper floors opened onto nothing. A set of crumbling stone steps led up to thin air.

Once, this had been a proper church, full of color and life. Emmy imagined it decorated as if for a wedding, with a roof, and pews, flowers, and candles. Rays of sunlight would pierce the stained-glass windows and sprinkle their jewel colors on the white cloth of the altar. A man would be waiting for her at the end of the aisle with a kind-faced priest ready to join them in holy matrimony. Emmy would walk forward, jittery with excitement and nerves. The man's back would be facing her, his shoulders broad, but she knew his identity with a bittersweet certainty. Alex Harland would turn and smile at her as if he were the luckiest man in the world—

She tripped over a protruding stone and stifled a curse. Such foolish, impossible dreams. She turned and pasted a bright smile on her face as Harland stepped up behind her.

"What is this place?" he asked.

"It used to be an abbey, built by Cistercian monks. It

fell into disrepair in the 1500s when Henry VIII dissolved the monasteries and took all their wealth for himself." She shot him a glance over her shoulder. "Just think, all that social and political upheaval just because he wanted to divorce his first wife, Catherine of Aragon, and marry Anne Boleyn."

Harland's lips curved upwards. "*Cherchez la femme.*"

She raised her brows.

"It's a French saying," he said. "Surely your grandmother uses it? It means whenever there's a problem, or a man behaving stupidly or out of character, there's usually a woman at the heart of it."

She shot him an indignant glare. "Oh, that's typical—blame the woman! Men can make fools of themselves perfectly well on their own, without any help from us."

His expression hardened. "How very true, Miss Danvers."

Chapter 31.

Alex tamped down the wave of self-directed anger that Emmy's innocent comment had roused. He was no better than fat old King Henry, was he? In imminent danger of making a fool of himself over *her*. She'd twisted him up so much, he could barely distinguish right from wrong, madness from reason. Passion from love.

No. Not *love.* He wasn't even going to consider that dreadful possibility. His attraction to her was lust, nothing deeper.

As if the very heavens disputed his denial, a rumble of thunder sounded in the distance. Alex glared up at the overcast sky, then back at the tumbling ruins. No doubt a poet like Byron or Shelley would think the place was wonderfully romantic. It was certainly picturesque, in a gloomy, gothic kind of way. All it needed was some brooding, fever-browed lover stomping around, tearing his hair out and howling for his lost love.

He repressed a snort. He wasn't such a fool. That was why he'd refused to travel in the carriage: pure self-preservation. He hadn't trusted himself to be confined in such an intimate space with his prisoner for hours on end. He'd have started to sympathize with her.

He'd have made love to her again.

She was a siren, luring unsuspecting idiots like himself to their downfall. The French would call her a *femme fatale*—a woman fatal to his sense of reason. There was an enchanting sense of mischief about her, a playfulness that reminded him of a sprite or a fairy.

Alex cast another glance upwards, appealing to the heavens to deliver him from pert young women. He didn't hold out much hope of a positive response. He'd have more luck asking the devil for assistance in controlling one of his own. Except he suspected even Old Nick would find Emmeline Danvers too much of a handful. He'd thrust her back up top just for five minutes of blessed peace.

She was picking her way through the ruins now, lifting her skirts to show a tantalizing glimpse of silk-stockinged ankle. Alex clenched his fists.

"Are you sure we're not trespassing?" he growled, scanning the area with a soldier's eye for signs of life.

"No. All this land belongs to Camille. If anyone sees us, they'll assume we're lovers sneaking off in search of some privacy."

The mental images that glib little comment produced forced him to tug at his breeches in an unsuccessful attempt to relieve the throbbing discomfort there. He cast around for a less incendiary subject. "You like collecting words," he said at her retreating back. "Words that have no direct translation in English."

"I'm surprised you remember. But yes. The French have lots of words for things we don't. *Mie*, for example, is the soft inside of the bread. The bit that's not the crust."

She disappeared around the edge of another partly

ruined building, but her voice echoed off the stones. "*Empêchement* is an unexpected last-minute change of plans. It's the perfect excuse for when you don't want to be specific about being late."

"I thought of a Spanish word to add to your collection," he called after her. "*Sobremesa*. It's the time after dinner when the Spanish like to sit around the table to argue and talk."

He rounded the corner and caught sight of her again and the smile she shot back at him made his heart thud against his breastbone. "That is excellent!"

She climbed over a low wall and set out in a westerly direction. He knew it was west, because the setting sun was directly in front of her, and its departing rays rendered her skirts almost completely transparent. Alex counted slowly to ten and tried to ignore the glowing outline of her perfect derrière.

"Almost there," she called cheerfully. "Did you know the French crown jewels aren't the only ones to have been lost?"

"They weren't *lost*," Alex corrected dryly. "*Lost* implies they were mislaid. They were *stolen*. Most recently by members of your family."

She ignored the dig. "There are plenty of instances where new crown jewels had to be made because the old ones had gone missing. King John once lost the English crown jewels in a bog not far from here."

"That's not true," Alex scoffed.

"It certainly is. It was just after the famous Magna Carta was signed. Twelve hundred and something. King John was trying to suppress a rebellion and made a trip through the fens of eastern England."

She waved a hand vaguely down the hill. "Over that way. He and his entourage travelled with carts laden with supplies, including one holding all the crown jewels. John had fallen ill, and so was in a hurry to get across the Wash—it's a tidal area crisscrossed with creeks, streams, and treacherous patches of quicksand."

She grinned, as if the prospect of danger pleased her. "The riders got across safely, but the heavy baggage cart containing the jewels sank forever into the silt. King John died a few days later. His son, nine-year-old Henry III, had to be crowned with one of his mother's circlets." She gave a delighted chuckle. "No wonder he's remembered as 'King John the Bad.'"

She gazed out over the fields and a wistful look came over her face. "They're still out there somewhere, you know. Just waiting to be found. The landscape is always changing. A storm or high tide will uncover them eventually."

Alex's gut twisted at the yearning in her expression. If he turned her in, she'd never be free like this again. Never be able to stare out over the sunset, dreaming of treasure and adventure. She'd have no future at all.

He shook away the depressing thought. "Where exactly are we going?"

She continued a little way into the trees and then stopped in front of a shoulder-high stone monument shaped as an obelisk on a square-stepped base. It was clearly not as old as the ruins, but the lichen and weathering indicated it had been there for some time.

"What's this?" Alex squinted to read the inscription on the engraved brass plaque that was affixed to the pale limestone. "It looks like a gravestone."

"It is. Well, a monument, really. To Lily. She was my grandmother's dog." She pointed to the stylized floral carvings on the flat sides of the pyramid. "See the fleur de lis? That's 'lily' in French."

"It's also the symbol of the French Royalty," Alex said and was rewarded with a congratulatory nod for his perceptiveness.

"Father was inspired by Lord Byron, who did something similar for his beloved dog, Boatswain. The verse is his."

Alex leaned forward and read the inscription:

> NEAR THIS SPOT
> ARE DEPOSITED THE REMAINS OF ONE
> WHO POSSESSED BEAUTY WITHOUT VANITY,
> STRENGTH WITHOUT INSOLENCE,
> COURAGE WITHOUT FEROCITY,
> AND ALL THE VIRTUES OF MAN WITHOUT HIS
>   VICES.
> THIS PRAISE, WHICH WOULD BE UNMEANING
>   FLATTERY IF INSCRIBED OVER HUMAN ASHES,
> IS BUT A JUST TRIBUTE TO THE MEMORY OF LILY,
>   A DOG
> WHO WAS BORN IN PARIS MAY 1798 AND DIED AT
>   UFFINGTON NOVEMBER 18TH, 1810.

Alex glanced sideways at the woman next to him. Those same qualities could be applied to her. Beauty without vanity. Courage without ferocity. She'd accepted her fate without resorting to bitterness or treachery, with grace and even humor. What was he going to do with her? He had to make a decision by the time they returned to London.

"The grave of a dog wasn't Father's first choice of hiding place," she said, unaware of his seething thoughts. "He tried several others before deciding on this. He submerged them in a pond at first, in a tin box wrapped in oilcloth and weighted down with rocks. That proved very messy to retrieve. Luc and I eventually rebelled against wading through pond slime every six months to add a new jewel. In the winter, we had to crack the ice. It was awful."

She shook her head in memory. "Then he considered burying the box with a large number of truffles and using a specially trained truffle pig to find them."

"A truffle pig?" Alex choked out. "You're joking."

She grinned, enjoying his surprise. "I swear I'm not. Camille suggested it. Her first husband had them at his country estate near Périgord, which is, as everyone knows, the truffle center of France."

Alex gave a reluctant laugh. "And here I was, thinking things couldn't get any worse. I take it back. Imagine if we'd had to transport a great stinking pig with us."

"They're ill-tempered beasts, apparently. Camille used to say you could recognize the pig owners by their missing fingers."

"I wonder what it is about truffles that makes them so attractive to pigs?"

"To lady pigs," Emmy clarified.

He wrinkled his forehead. "Only female pigs like truffles?"

"Oh no, I'm sure male pigs like them too, but it's the lady pigs who are used to seek them out."

She sent him a cheeky grin, and he just knew she was going to say something outrageous.

"Females find them irresistible because they smell just like virile man pigs. The girl pigs work themselves into a frenzy, trying to locate the source."

"Good God." Alex shook his head, bemused. Then again, who was he to scoff? He fully understood the strength of desire that could be aroused by smell. One whiff of Emmy's blasted perfume was enough to drive him crazy. He'd probably break down doors to get to her.

His heart twisted in his chest as he realized how much

he enjoyed her company. She was an amusing companion, and he felt as at ease with her as he did with Benedict and Seb. He liked her. Were they becoming friends?
That would be a fatal mistake; it would only make it
harder when he had to turn her in. Damn it.

Emmy knelt on the ground at the foot of the steps,
heedless of the mud and her dress, and ran her fingers
along the mortar strips between the stones.

"What do we have to do?" Alex asked.

"Pry off the front of this stone."

With a sigh of regret over his pristine breeches, Alex
knelt beside her and nudged her aside with his shoulder. "Don't hurt your hands. I'll do it." He scraped away
some moss and tried to pry the slab forward. "There isn't
really a dog buried under here, is there? I'm not going to
come across bones?"

She chuckled. "No, you're safe. The real Lily's buried
up near the hunting lodge. This is more symbolic. Father
used to say it represented the death of the French monarchy, the end of France as it was before the Revolution."
Her face fell, and Alex kicked himself for making her
remember something that brought her pain. He wanted
her to smile.

The stone shifted beneath his fingers, and she made a
sound of delight. "Yes! There you go."

He pulled it forward and away, dislodging a bank of
dark brown soil that had been packed behind it. Emmy
started to scrape it away, and he did the same, their hands
touching occasionally as they worked. A dull metallic
thud sounded when his knuckles hit something hard, and
Emmy gasped in anticipation. She reached into the dark
hole they'd made and pulled out an unassuming black tin
box, about eighteen inches long and a foot square. She
rearranged herself to sit cross-legged on the grass.

Her cheeks were flushed, her eyes sparkled in excitement, and Alex curbed the impulse to lean over and kiss her.

She lifted the lid and he caught his breath. There, glittering in the dying rays of the sun like some magical hoard of leprechaun gold, lay a seething mass of diamonds, emeralds, pearls, and precious metals.

The missing crown jewels of France.

Chapter 32.

Alex could hardly believe his eyes. He reached into the tin and pulled out a gold crown, almost simplistic in design, with huge gems studded like barnacles around the sides and four large jeweled fleur de lis protruding from the top. He didn't know much about antiques, but it looked ancient.

"That's the crown of Charlemagne," Emmy said matter-of-factly. "Kings of France have been crowned with it for hundreds of years. It was rumored to have been destroyed during the Revolution, but Father managed to steal it before it was melted down."

She pulled out an earring and dangled it carelessly between her slim fingers. The pear-shaped diamond pendant was as big as a musket ball. "These were Marie Antoinette's favorite earrings."

She dropped the earring back onto the pile and withdrew a yellow-tinged faceted stone as large as a walnut and, in the other hand, a peachy-pink stone of at least twenty carats that was almost heart shaped. Tiny rainbows glittered on her palms as she held them up for inspection.

Alex whistled softly.

"The Sancy diamond," she sighed reverently, inspecting the jewel in her right hand. "A pale yellow, shield-shaped diamond. It weighs over fifty carats and was purchased in Constantinople in the sixteenth century by the French ambassador to Turkey, the Seigneur de Sancy. He brought it to France, where Henry III, who was sensitive about being bald, used it to decorate the cap he always wore to conceal his head."

She smiled at the jewel, clearly delighted by the history behind it. "During the next reign, when Sancy was made Superintendent of Finance, Henry IV borrowed it as security for a substantial loan to hire soldiers. A messenger was dispatched with the jewel, but never reached his destination; thieves had followed him. Knowing that the man was utterly loyal, Sancy searched for him, and when his body was discovered in a shallow grave, Sancy had him disinterred and cut open."

Her eyes widened at the gruesome tale. "And guess what? They found the diamond in the servant's stomach. He'd swallowed it to prevent it from being stolen!"

Alex grimaced. "I hope it's been thoroughly washed."

She grinned. "It ended up in the possession of Cardinal Mazarin, who gave it to Louis XIV."

She held up the pink stone in her other hand. "This is the Hortensia diamond, from India, named after Hortensia de Beauharnais, Napoleon's stepdaughter. Napoleon used to wear it on the fastening of his epaulette braid—until Father stole it from the Ministry of the Marine."

"Amazing," Alex muttered, and he wasn't sure if he was talking about the treasure or the woman in front of him. Her joyous spirit was infectious. He loved the way she was always game for an adventure. She was one of those women who would follow their man anywhere, even into battle, like the wives and mistresses who'd followed the drum around the Peninsular and even to the fields of Waterloo. He wanted to catch her up in his arms, swing her around, and kiss her.

She dropped the jewels back into the tin with a clatter and dusted the soil from her hands, then glanced over at him with a mischievous grin. Alex looked down to see what was so amusing and groaned inwardly at the state of his clothes. He'd absentmindedly wiped his muddy hands on his thighs. His breeches were covered in grass stains from where he'd been kneeling, and his boots were never going to be the same. His bootmaker, Hoby, would be horrified.

Her teasing laughter bubbled up. "What a sight! The illustrious Earl of Melton, covered in mud like a pig in a sty!"

Alex narrowed his eyes and feigned indignation, but all he could think of was how good *she* looked. Her skin was flushed, her pelisse molded to her figure in the most provocative way, and his body warmed despite the evening chill.

He took the box from her lap, placed it beside her on the grass, then took her hand and helped her to her feet. A sudden blast of wind shook the trees, and the first fat raindrops spattered around them, bouncing the leaves. Alex barely noticed. Her face was turned up to his, her lips parted invitingly. The impending storm hung in the air between them like a static charge, and anticipation made the hairs on his arms stand up. His gaze dropped to her mouth.

Her smile faded as a new awareness filled her face, a recognition of the fact that they were alone in the middle of the forest, with no one around for miles. She licked her lips and took a step back toward the cover of the trees.

He followed.

"We've had terrible weather recently," she murmured, and Alex almost smiled at the sudden nervousness in her voice. "They're calling it the year without a summer."

He closed the gap between them. She gave a little gasp as her back hit the trunk of a huge horse chestnut tree.

"Is that right?" he asked lazily.

She nodded, eyes wide. He regarded her from beneath his lashes and enjoyed the flush of pink that crept up her neck to her cheeks.

"Stop looking at me like that," she said breathlessly.

"Like what?"

She shook her head and gave another flustered laugh. "As if you've just come to a decision."

"Do I look like I want you?" His boots touched her skirts. "Do I look like I'm thinking of all the depraved things I want to do to you? Because I am."

Her mouth dropped open in surprise, and he would have laughed if desire hadn't been riding him so hard.

"I've wanted to join you in that carriage all day," he admitted, ruthlessly holding her gaze. "I wanted to climb in there, push you back on the seat, and make love with you again."

He leaned in, so his chest touched hers and he could feel her little pants of arousal. "I want to see you. All of you. I want to see my hands on your skin. Your nipples wet from my mouth. I want to see the look on your face when you come."

Emmy could barely catch her breath. The way Harland was looking at her made her heart hammer against her ribs and heat pool between her legs. She'd been fighting her attraction for him all day. It was impossible to watch the grace and power of his movements and not imagine the weight of him on top of her.

His eyes were the same blue-grey as the clouds above them. Thunder rumbled overhead, as if someone were rolling barrels over the flagstone floor of heaven. Another gust of wind shook the trees, and the rain started in earnest, a steady hiss pelting the leaves and hitting the ground.

A matching wildness rose up inside her. She loved storms, the ferocity, the drama. She reached up, caught the lapels of his coat in her fists, and raised herself on tiptoe.

It was all the encouragement he needed; he kissed her, deep and openmouthed. It was hard, almost bruising, and it released a flood of dark hunger so intense that Emmy shuddered against him. She could taste the anger in him, the frustration. The desire that matched her own.

She groaned into his mouth at the forbidden pleasure of it. Her knees buckled, and she clutched his coat in her fists just to stay upright. His hands pulled up her skirts with rough urgency, and she gave an excited whimper of assent.

A deafening crash of thunder sounded directly overhead and both of them jumped. The panicked whinnying of the carriage horses echoed through the woods.

"Bollocks."

Harland released her with unflattering speed and Emmy bit back a denial as her skirts fell decorously back around about her ankles. He bent to retrieve the box of jewels from the ground and sent her a look she found impossible to interpret.

"We have to see to the horses. Which way is the carriage?"

Her heart was still pounding, her lips still tingling, but she managed to gather her kiss-dazed wits. "This way. Follow me."

She lifted her skirts and ran back the way they had

come, careful not to trip on the sticks and rocks that littered the ground. The trees provided some cover, but they were still pelted with water droplets and by the time they reached the ruins they were both soaked to the skin. The rain streamed down, unpleasantly cold, and Emmy cursed as her feet were completely submerged in a puddle of muddy water.

When she finally spied the carriage through the trees, she let out a cry of dismay. The horses had been spooked by the storm. Even though Harland had tied them both, one had broken its strap, then either fallen against or kicked the side of the carriage. There was no sign of the animal, but the vehicle was tilted drunkenly to one side. The front axle was clearly broken, the spokes of the right wheel shattered.

Harland approached the remaining horse, making soft crooning noises to the terrified animal. Its eyes rolled back in its head, and he had to sidestep several times to avoid its plunging hooves before he managed to grab its halter and calm the beast by stroking its quivering neck.

He glared through the rain toward the entrance of the lane, seeking the missing horse, but Emmy suspected it was long gone.

"Bugger," he muttered. "Looks like we'll have to walk."

"Back to Stamford?" Emmy groaned. "It's miles." She dropped her sodden skirts against her legs and indicated the listing carriage. "Can't we just shelter in there until it passes?"

She tried to ignore the blush that rose in her cheeks as she remembered what he'd said about doing to her in that carriage.

He glanced crossly at the sky. "No. This doesn't look like it's going to stop anytime soon. I've spent far too many nights getting rained on and sleeping out in the open during the war, thank you very much. If I'm going to die of pneumonia, I'd just as well do it in a bed. We passed an inn a mile or two back, didn't we?"

Emmy sighed. "The Bertie Arms. But it has a dreadful reputation. No one of any consequence ever stays there. It's probably full of highwaymen and thieves."

"Then we're not likely to see anyone we know," he countered reasonably, "and you'll feel right at home in such company." He wheeled the horse around and started to trudge away down the lane.

Emmy scowled at his broad back. "We can't just leave the carriage here. What of my things?"

He shrugged, and carried on walking. "You can bring your bag if you like. And you might as well have my greatcoat. I'm already drenched."

With a sigh of defeat, Emmy reached up into the coach and pulled out her bag and his coat. The sheer weight of the heavy woolen garment almost brought her to her knees, but she managed to shrug it over her shoulders. The sleeves fell way past her hands and the hem dragged in the mud when she started after him.

His scent wrapped itself around her, infused in the fibers of the coat, and the musky, wet-pine scent made her insides curl. What would have happened if they hadn't been interrupted? Would she have let Harland take her up against that tree? On the ground in the mud and the rain? Her stomach gave a little flip. Most probably. She still ached for him.

She hastened to catch up. It was only a couple of miles to the inn. She could manage that. She wasn't a sensitive hothouse flower, like most of the young ladies of the *ton*.

Chapter 33.

The rain turned into a biblical downpour during the last agonizing mile. Emmy trudged alongside Harland and the horse, her shoes squelching in the puddles, her teeth chattering with the cold.

Darkness had fallen swiftly over the countryside, and there was little moonlight to help show the way. She followed them almost by sound, by the suck and splash of the horse's hooves in the mud, cursing the ache in her legs and the fact that the thin soles of her stupid slippers provided almost no protection against the rocky ground.

Her stockings were soaked, her sodden skirts a heavy encumbrance that made every step more difficult. She was so hungry, she was almost faint with fatigue.

No other travelers passed them on the road. No one else was foolish enough to be out in such weather. Emmy blinked through the teeming rain, which seemed to be going sideways rather than straight down, driven by a blustery, malevolent wind.

Harland's voice floated back to her. "It rained like this

on the morning of Waterloo. It was miserable. But the rain might have been what won the day for us. The French cannons got stuck in the mud. They left them behind when they retreated, and we were able to capture most of them."

One such cannon had injured him. Emmy sent up a brief prayer of thanks that he'd been spared. However miserable he was now, at least he was alive. Able to savor the rain on his skin. Able to harass poor innocent criminals like herself.

The higgledy-piggledy outline of the Bertie Arms finally came into view, and she let out a sigh. It was even worse than she remembered. Torrents of water streamed from the low-pitched roof and the timber-framed facade barely looked capable of supporting the upper floors. The entire structure seemed to be held up by a wish and a prayer.

Harland's features became more distinct as they staggered into the inn yard, lit by a feeble lantern flickering valiantly against the gusty wind. Emmy's stomach dropped at the thought of spending a night in such a place, but anywhere was better than being out here in the dark and the rain. Even if the place had fleas, rats, and cobwebs, at least it would be warm and dry.

A scrawny youth scurried out of the barn and led the horse away, and Harland headed for the ramshackle front door, which looked as though it was barely hanging on by its hinges.

"We'll pose as man and wife," he muttered. "We'll share a room."

Emmy scowled, but didn't argue. Whether it was for her protection, or simply because he didn't trust her not to run, she didn't care. She was too cold and too miserable. She clutched her travelling bag to her stomach.

In very little time, the greasy-haired landlord—

no doubt having ascertained the quality of Harland's clothing in one practiced glance, despite the mud, and identifying a wealthy patron—had shown them past a crowded taproom and up an unreliable set of stairs to what he proudly told them was "the best room in the inn." He clearly didn't believe Harland's introduction of them as "Mister and Mrs. Brown."

Harland took charge, ordering a warm brick to be placed in the bed, and a hot bath to be sent up immediately. Warm soup, bread. Candles—beeswax, not tallow.

The landlord touched his forelock respectfully. "Yes, sir."

The man had probably never had a member of the aristocracy under his roof before. Emmy kept forgetting that Harland was an earl in his own right, as well as the second son of a duke. Even without using his title, he had a natural air of command that elicited almost universal respect. It must be a result of his army training.

She exhaled in relief when she saw the fire in the hearth. Harland strode forward and kicked it with his foot to rekindle it, then added two more logs, and she held her hands out to the feeble warmth, pathetically grateful.

The room was small, with one canopied bed, a single drop-leaf table flanked by two chairs, a washstand, whose broken front leg was propped up with a gilt-edged Bible, and a rickety-looking chest of drawers that lacked all but two knobs.

Harland let out a deep sigh, then turned and extended his arm out toward her. "Grab hold of my cuff, would you? There's no way I can get this jacket off without assistance."

Emmy was still shrouded under his greatcoat, clutching the edges with fingers that seemed frozen in place. Her hair was wet through, the ends dripping mournfully down her back, and her skirts were making a puddle on the threadbare rug beneath her. Bracing herself for the rush of cold air, she shrugged the coat off her shoulders and let it fall to the floor in a sodden heap along with her bag, then grabbed Harland's sleeve and tugged hard as he pulled first one arm, then the other, from the wet garment.

He tossed it onto one of the chairs, then unknotted the rumpled cravat from around his neck and laid it aside.

"You need to get out of those wet things. You'll catch your death. Sit near the fire and dry your hair. I'll see about something hot to drink."

He left before she could frame a response.

Emmy sank onto one of the hard chairs. She'd never been so cold, nor so despondent. This storm was a disaster. Danton had only given her until tomorrow evening to get the jewels, and they still had a good six hours to travel in the morning—assuming they could procure a new carriage. She didn't want to imagine what would happen to Luc if she didn't get back in time.

Nausea racked her body. Could she persuade Harland to hire a horse and take the jewels back to London without her? Could she trust him to send them to Danton, so that he released her brother, before he set his trap to catch the Frenchman?

It was probably a moot point. He wouldn't leave her here alone and forfeit his capture of the Nightjar. He wanted both her *and* Danton.

Her teeth began to chatter, either in fear or cold, and she hugged her arms around her waist in misery. What she wouldn't give for a nice cup of tea. Her head was pounding, her fingers and toes aching now they were warming up again.

Harland was right. She couldn't stay in her wet clothes. With a grimace, she managed to undo a couple of the buttons at the back of her dress, then tugged the sopping gown over her head. Cotton ripped, and buttons bounced across the floor, but the thing was ruined anyway, so what did it matter? She stripped off her wet petticoat, stays, and chemise, and sent up a grateful prayer that she'd brought a change of clothes.

Fearful that Harland might come back at any moment, she pulled on a dry chemise and wrapped herself in the blanket that draped the bed. It covered her from shoulder to ankle.

The door opened, and she glanced up to see Harland with a maid behind him, carrying a tray. The girl set it on the table and lit a candle on the corner of the dresser. "Your bath'll be up shortly, ma'am."

Harland nodded, and she bobbed a curtsey, and left.

He gestured toward the tray. "I got you tea," he said gruffly. "With milk and sugar. And soup. I hope that's all right."

Emmy almost scowled at him for being so kind. She was used to high-handed, imperious, Harland. Thoughtful, solicitous Harland was so much harder to keep at bay. Tears prickled her eyes, and she blinked them away. She hated crying. Weakness. She was just at a low ebb, that was all.

Thankfully he'd already turned away and didn't see her shameful lapse. The bed creaked as he sat on the edge and removed his boots with great difficulty, leaving him in shirt, breeches, and stockings. Emmy averted her gaze from the way his wet breeches clung lovingly to his legs.

"Drink the soup," he ordered.

Against all expectations, the stew was hot and delicious. Emmy felt better with every mouthful. Harland took the chair across the scarred table from her and made quick work of his own bowl, and Emmy had the strangest thought that this was what it would have been like if they really had been married: Mister Brown and his wife, sharing their meal in quiet companionship.

Harland looked so approachable, so human. In his open-necked shirt, with his hair damp and tousled, he could have been a rugged laborer fresh from the fields, instead of one of the most elevated members of society.

A feeling of regret, of wistfulness, slid over her as she watched him eat. If she'd been an ordinary girl instead of a criminal, able to choose her own destiny, she would have wanted something exactly like this: a husband, a family, a home. Her stomach clenched in misery. This was a cruel glimpse into a future she could never have.

She wanted a man she could trust with her secrets. Someone with a quick wit and a wicked sense of humor. A contradiction of a man—strong shoulders and gentle hands. A man who wouldn't bore her, or belittle her, or mock her, except to tease in a loving way. A good-hearted man who would open doors for her and was kind to dogs. A man like *him*, who would give up his coat and shiver just to keep her warm.

She trusted him. She *loved* him. She was an idiot.

Chapter 34.

Emmy accepted a cup of tea with a murmur of thanks and added milk and sugar to the chipped cup, acutely aware that she was wearing only a bedspread and a thin cotton chemise. Never in her life had she imagined she would be taking tea with Alex Harland like *this*.

A knock on the door saved her from further introspection. The scruffy young man who'd taken their horse in the courtyard positioned a small copper tub at the foot of the bed, then helped the maid pour several buckets of steaming water into it. The girl sent shy, flirtatious glances at Harland as she placed clean bath linens on the bed, but he ushered them out without acknowledging her.

His mouth curled upwards as he surveyed the tub. It was clearly too small for him to sit in. "You can go first."

Emmy shook her head. Her throat closed at the thought of stripping naked in front of him. "No, I'm fine, really. I don't want to bathe."

He chuckled. "You clearly haven't looked in a mirror. You're so splashed with mud, it's hard to tell what's freckle and what's dirt."

He took one of the washcloths, dipped it in the steaming water, and wrung it out. Emmy's heart began to pound as he stepped up in front of her, caught her chin, and started to wipe her face clean.

She stilled, too stunned to do anything, as the warm cloth laved her cheeks, her temple, the sides of her nose. His eyes never met hers. He seemed engrossed in the task, as if he were her servant. It was a ridiculously erotic experience. The cotton was thin, and she could feel his fingers through the fabric as he wiped it across her lips. Blood pounded in her ears.

"Close your eyes." He passed the cloth gently over her closed eyelids and down the bridge of her nose.

"If you rub harder, you might remove some of those cursed freckles," she joked weakly.

He stilled, then resumed stroking. "I like your freckles." He applied slight pressure to her chin and tilted her jaw to expose the side of her neck.

Emmy suppressed a shiver as the cloth slipped over the sensitive skin behind her ear and then slid down to her collarbone. She was so aware of him, of the faint warm disturbance in the air as he moved about her. Each tiny hair on her body prickled, and she almost groaned when he lifted the now-cool cloth from her skin and stepped back.

"Better," he said gruffly.

He turned his back on her, and Emmy closed her eyes. Everything the man did seemed designed to lower her defenses, to turn her into mush. Staying near him all night was going to be torture.

The low hum of conversation filtered up through the

floor from the taproom below, mingling with the crackle of the fire in the grate.

"Well, if you're not going to use the water, I will," he said.

Emmy opened her eyes in shock. Before she knew what he was about, he reached his arms over his head, grasped his shirt between his shoulder blades, and pulled the material over his head. The maneuver revealed the tawny skin of his back and a pair of deliciously muscular shoulders.

Her mouth went dry. He turned, utterly unself-conscious, and provided her with a front view that was even better than the back. The shirt bunched over his forearms and gathered at his wrists as he lifted each one and flicked the button to release the cuff. His biceps and forearms rippled in the candlelight, and her avid gaze roamed over the expanse of pectoral muscles and an abdomen as ridged and troughed as a furrowed field.

Good lord, he really was magnificent. She'd known he was muscular, had felt him in the darkness at the Tricorn, but she hadn't imagined how incredible he'd look in candlelight. His nipples, like small bronze disks, were hard and pebbled from the cold.

He threw the shirt aside and picked up a fresh linen cloth, and she must have made a strangled noise, because he glanced over and lifted his brows in a questioning lilt.

"What?" he said. "Don't tell me you're shy. Not after last night."

Her tongue felt like leather in her mouth, but she tried to think of something flippant and sophisticated to say. "I've never seen anyone remove a shirt in such a manner," she managed.

"Seen lots of men removing their shirts, have you?"

She narrowed her eyes at his slightly sarcastic tone.

"I haven't seen any, as a matter of fact. Not even my brother."

A spark of amusement kindled in his expression. "You wear masculine clothes for your thieving." He tilted his head in challenge. "How do *you* do it?"

The blanket slipped from her shoulders as she stood. "Like this." She crossed her arms in front of her at the waist and mimed lifting her chemise up and off, over her head, uncrossing her arms as she did so.

He shrugged. "Women's shoulders must be different. I'd dislocate something if I did it that way." His lips twitched in a wicked smile. "In fact, I don't believe it can be done. Show me."

Emmy laughed. "Oh no. I'm not falling for that. You're just trying to get me naked."

His expression changed from playful to intent in a heartbeat.

"I can't deny it," he said softly. "I meant what I said back in the woods. Last night was good, but I never got to see you. Never got to savor."

The huskiness of his voice robbed her of breath. Desire, swift and fierce, clenched her stomach.

"I want you, Emmy Danvers. And I want to take my time."

How on earth was a woman supposed to resist that?

He was still wearing his breeches. Emmy couldn't prevent her gaze from dropping to the proud bulge that strained against the fabric. He wasn't lying; he wanted her quite desperately.

Sally had always told her that virginity was overrated. "Men make such a fuss over being the first," she'd said blithely. "But think of how many times you'll make love in your life. Hundreds, if you're lucky. The first time's always a trial because you don't know what to expect. It's like riding a horse. At the start, it's more daunting than enjoyable. But with a little practice, and the right mount"—she'd giggled softly at that—"you'll soon find it extremely pleasurable. If something feels good, make sure he keeps doing it. Don't just lie there and expect him to read your mind. Tell him. Move him. Or move yourself into a better position."

Emmy's face had been as red as a beetroot by that point, but Sally had chuckled bawdily. "Telling him what you like, what you want him to do, can be half the fun, believe me. Men love it when a girl does that."

Emmy had been a virgin last night, but she'd found the whole thing intensely pleasurable. Harland was clearly an accomplished lover, one who cared for the enjoyment of his partner. She couldn't have wished for a better introduction to the sensual arts. The idea that there could be more than she'd already experienced was something she both doubted and prayed was true with equal fervor.

She wanted to experience it all. Everything he had to give. Even if it was only for one night.

Her heart pounding, she took a step toward him. "Yes."

He opened his arms and tugged her against him, trapping her in his embrace. She rested her cheek against his sternum. His heart beat, steady and sure, beneath her ear. Giving in to temptation, she opened her mouth and tasted him with an experimental flick of her tongue.

He tightened his arms. "Emmy. You're killing me."

His hand came up to her hair and she lifted her face, silently demanding a kiss. This was madness, weakness, stupidity. She didn't care.

He dipped his head and kissed her with slow deliberation. "You taste like honey," he groaned. "And smell like heaven. God, you drive me mad."

They were nose to nose. Heat radiated from him, despite the chilly room. His hardness pressed insistently against her stomach.

"I haven't forgiven you for your British Museum taunt, you know," he growled against her lips. "You naughty girl. You implied I was dense."

"And hard," she added mischievously.

He rocked against her. "Allow me to demonstrate just how hard I can be."

Wicked heat coiled through her, burning her from the inside out. He drew her hand down between them and pressed himself into her palm. Her fingers tightened around him of their own volition, and he groaned, a deep rumble in his chest.

"Is that hard enough for you, Emmy?"

He slipped the edge of her chemise off her shoulder and kissed the skin he'd exposed. He teethed her lightly, a nip that sent shudders racing through her. She made a wordless sound of assent and tilted her head to give him better access, but he stepped away with a rueful shake of his head.

"Wait. I need a bath. I've ridden all day. I'm filthy."

She opened her mouth to tell him she didn't care; she wanted him exactly as he was, all sweaty and rain-slicked, but he sat on the edge of the bed and removed his stockings. She stared in fascination at his bare feet, at the hair that grew on his legs below the knee. He was so undeniably masculine.

With a mocking, challenging glance he stood and slowly flicked open the fall of his breeches, as if daring her to tell him to stop.

She didn't.

He caught the waistband with his thumbs and pushed the damp buckskin down over his narrow hips, and she caught her breath as he stepped out of them and tossed them carelessly onto the chair.

Naked. He was wonderfully, gloriously naked.

She'd caught a tantalizing glimpse of him that morning in his bedroom, but now she looked her fill. He was beautiful, a creature built for pleasure and sin. The candle glow flickered over him, and her gaze followed the intriguing line of hair that ran down from his navel to surround the part of him that reared up straight and proud between his legs.

He didn't seem embarrassed by his nakedness. He stepped into the tub, wet the cloth he'd used to clean her face, and washed his own face and the back of his neck.

Emmy watched transfixed as he rubbed it briskly over his shoulders, arms and chest, sending rivulets streaming down his body. The water found the grooves between his ridged muscles, following the path of least resistance. She wanted to trace the same route with her tongue.

She gave a sympathetic wince when she saw the long scar that bisected the muscle of his thigh. She'd nursed Luc's terrible injury, so she knew just how long that must have taken to heal, how much it must have hurt. Her heart clenched for him.

"Did you get that at the same time as you lost your vision?"

He glanced down, as if he'd forgotten it was there. "Oh. No. That was courtesy of a French saber at Badajoz. It hurt like the devil."

Gathering her courage, Emmy stepped forward and took the washcloth from his hand. "Let me help. Turn around."

After an instant's surprise, he turned and presented his back. She had to go up on tiptoes to reach his neck, then she slid the washcloth over his shoulders and down the twin ridges of muscle that bracketed his spine. He fisted his hands at his sides. His muscles twitched as she washed his ribs and the triangle of muscle that overlaid them, then swept the cloth down over the perfect globes of his backside.

He sucked in a breath.

She knelt beside the tub and trailed the cloth down the back of his thighs, over the back of his knees, fascinated by the way the hairs diverted the water in dark swirls. He shuddered like a fine, impatient stallion as she stroked his calves. A heady power filled her. He was giving her permission to explore. She could do whatever she liked.

"Turn around," she commanded softly.

She was still on her knees, so when he complied, his rigid erection was right there in front of her. It bobbed as if it had a life of its own.

"Touch me." His voice was gravelly with need.

Emmy felt light-headed. She'd heard about this from Sally, dreamed about it in the dark recesses of the night. Whatever happened after this, she would know the taste of him, the feel. She leaned forward.

Chapter 35.

Alex gripped the sides of Emmy's head as his eyes rolled back in his skull. She pressed a tentative kiss to his tip, then swirled her tongue around as if she were licking the last traces of a Gunther's ice from a spoon.

His knees almost gave out. She was going to kill him; he was going to die of pleasure and he didn't even care. Nothing had ever felt so good as her sweet, inexpert touch.

After enduring her innocent explorations for as long as he could stand, he leaned down and pulled her to her feet. Her cheeks were flushed, her eyes sparkling with mischief.

"Enough of that," he rasped, "or it'll be over before it's begun."

He stepped out of the tub, caught the hem of her chemise, and drew it over her head. Before she could protest at being naked, or become embarrassed, he maneuvered her onto the bed and followed her down, half lying over her. His breath caught in his chest at the incredible feel of her soft skin against his own, the fragrance of her in his nose. *God.* He braced himself on one elbow and gazed down at her, utterly enchanted.

Beautiful.

This was what he'd been missing last night: the sight of her alabaster skin, a glimpse of those perfect breasts and long legs. He'd felt her body, heard the breathy little sounds she'd made in the darkness, but he hadn't *seen.* Now, he feasted his eyes.

She was sleek and smooth; slight and intensely feminine. In the flickering candlelight, her nipples were dusky pink, tight buds in the cool air. The long hair spilling over the pillows matched the dark curls at the junction of her thighs, and his mouth went dry in anticipation. She was spread out beneath him like a banquet.

He wanted to set upon her like a wild beast, to taste and to ravish, but there was no urgency this time. There would be no groping around in the darkness. He would see every nuance of her expression, watch every shiver and stroke. They could both take delight in discovery. His body hardened to the point of pain. *God, he wanted her.*

Giving into temptation, he stroked down her side to her waist and spread his fingers wide, gauging the distance across her navel. He could probably encircle her waist with both hands if he tried.

"You're so small," he murmured, almost to himself. "God, I'll hurt you. Crush you."

Her chuckle brought his gaze back to her face, and she stroked his arm from shoulder to wrist with a light touch that made him want to arch like a cat.

"And you're so big," she teased, wrinkling her nose. "The terrifying Alexander Harland of Bow Street, known to show no mercy."

He mock scowled at her, but she met his eyes, and he felt himself being sucked down into their depths.

"You won't hurt me," she whispered confidently. "You didn't last night, did you? I'm stronger than I look, Harland. I can take whatever you give."

She slid her hand to his nape and pulled him down for a kiss, and Alex groaned into her mouth. With a giggle of delight at how much she obviously affected him, she kissed her way down his chin, his neck, then across his collarbone. When she reached his shoulder, she bit him lightly, a string of teasing nips, then flicked him again with her tongue. It was heavenly torment.

Alex leaned back and threaded his fingers through hers, noting with a kind of detached despair how much larger his own hands were. Her fingers were so delicate, her nails neat ovals. His hands looked like bear paws in comparison. How could such a tiny thing have caused him so much trouble? She was mischief and lawlessness in a tiny, irresistible package.

He brought her finger to his mouth and enjoyed the way her eyes widened as he sucked it between his lips. He released her hand and cupped her breast, savoring the sweet, slight weight of it, and watched as she bit her lower lip in an unconsciously provocative gesture. He'd never felt this desperate for a woman before in his life. Hell, he was no better than a randy schoolboy. The scent of her skin coiled in his head and the only thought he could manage was: *I have to taste her.*

It didn't matter that they were on opposite sides of the law. What mattered was that they were on the same side of this bed.

He planted a trail of kisses down the center of her body. *Roses and peonies. Madness and sin.*

She arched as he took her nipple into his mouth and

sucked hard, but he didn't allow himself to dwell too long.
He kissed lower, shifting down her body, and she tensed
as he swirled his tongue into her belly button then kissed
lower still. He wedged his shoulders between her thighs,
spreading her open to his gaze, and she instinctively covered herself with her hands.

"Wait—!" she gasped. "What—?"

"We didn't get to this last time," he said, gazing up her
body. Her cheeks were pink with embarrassment, and he
sent her a teasing, confident smile. "Trust me, Emmy.
You'll like it. I promise."

Emmy lay back against the sheets as Harland placed
a soft kiss on the inside of her thigh. She trusted him
completely. If he said she would enjoy it, who was she
to argue? He clearly had the greater experience. Even
so, she squirmed as his hot breath laved her feminine
core.

He chuckled and lifted one brow in amused inquiry.
"May I?"

She managed a dazed nod and gave an incoherent
groan of pleasure when his tongue swept over her sensitive flesh. His eyes were closed, his lashes lowered
as if he were tasting something infinitely sweet, to be
savored.

He licked her again, a lazy swirl, and she shuddered. It
was different to the touch of his fingers, but equally maddening. Sensation flickered hot and cold over her skin,
little tongues of ice and flame. She arced off the bed,
grabbing hold of his hair as pleasure swelled, a throbbing ache that built like a wall of water pressing against
a dam.

She reveled in his strength, his skill. He had such mas-
tery over her body, and yet it didn't feel like restraint.

It felt like freedom. Like soaring, infinite power. Emmy dug her heels into the bed as he worshipped her with his mouth. No mercy—only surrender. She'd never expected anything else from him.

She climbed higher and higher, teetering on the edge of the abyss, desperate to take the leap into soaring oblivion.

L'appel du vide.

She so wanted to jump.

"Harland. Oh. God. Pleeease."

Alex wanted her lost, as mindless as himself, begging for what he burned to give.

She groaned in frustration when he pulled away and rose over her and he sucked in a steadying breath, fighting the need to spread her open and simply thrust into her. She incited him to mayhem, to madness. Instead, he slid into her so slowly, they both gasped. He ground his teeth until his jaw ached.

So good. So good. So good. She fit him like a glove.

He was dangerously close. He closed his eyes, determined to bring her to completion before reaching it himself, and was rewarded with a breathless cry as he rocked his hips. He repeated the move, building a rhythm that had her clawing at his back.

"Yes. That. More," she cried.

Suddenly desperate, he cupped her face and kissed her deeply, his tongue probing in harmony with his thrusts. *Sublime.* She was with him, all around him, and he felt his climax building as she flung her head back and reached her own peak with a hoarse little cry.

The feel of her convulsing around him was enough to set him off. He pulled out of her at the very last second as stars exploded behind his closed eyelids and he was hit with a punch of pleasure so strong it almost knocked him senseless.

He collapsed against her in blissful, panting exhaustion and buried his face in her neck, his heart hammering against his ribs.

Bloody hell. What a woman.

Chapter 36.

Emmy held Alex against her as they both struggled to catch their breath. She stroked his back and broad shoulders and stared up at the canopy above her with a kind of dazed wonder.

Blissful lethargy suffused her body. She was boneless, and yet she hummed with a purring, contented energy. She felt invincible. As if she'd stolen fire from the heavens or conquered some impossible mountain peak.

Her heart turned over in her chest as the world came back into focus. Despite that final, frenzied climax, it hadn't felt like mindless coupling. *It had felt like making love*. The teasing expression on Alex's face, the gentle way he'd coaxed her toward pleasure, the ardency of his kisses all spoke of something deeper and more complicated than mere lust.

Or was it just wishful thinking on her part? Maybe he looked at every woman he bedded with that same tender, exasperated expression. Maybe he kissed all his lovers as if they were the only woman in the world.

And when had she started thinking of him as Alex, instead of Harland?

Emmy closed her eyes in despair at her own foolishness. She was in love, but she had no idea how to define their relationship. Theirs had been such a strange courtship. A wicked, flirtatious game of cat and mouse brimming with mistrust and reluctant admiration. Some wishful, stubborn part of her insisted they were becoming friends, as well as lovers, but the pragmatic side of her knew how ridiculous that was.

I don't think we can really class ourselves as friends, he'd said.

It was true. Her crimes, though committed under duress, were inescapable, and Alex's adherence to the law was strict. She couldn't expect him to change, nor would she want him to. His loyalty to his profession, to seeing justice done, was one of the things she loved most about him.

She doubted her reluctance would count for anything in a court of law. The fact that she hadn't *wanted* to steal those jewels would be of no interest to a judge.

She stroked Alex's hair as he rolled off her with a mumbled apology and dragged the sheets over them both. He gathered her into his arms and pulled her back against his body in an embrace that brought bittersweet tears to her eyes.

She was well and truly caught, in a snare of her own making. Alex had no need for cuffs or physical restraints. He'd bound her with passion. With love. And like an opium addict, or a hardened gamester, she couldn't stop craving more, even when she knew it would lead to ruin.

From her position, lying on her side, she could see the tin containing the jewels resting on the window seat. Time was running out. She could almost feel the noose tightening about her neck. A dreadful sense of finality weighed down upon her, and she felt the sudden, urgent need to wring out every precious moment that remained, to impress it upon her memory like a brand.

The candle still flickered on the chest of drawers, and the fire lent a primitive glow to the room. She turned within Alex's arms. He lowered his chin to look down at her with a sleepy, quizzical expression, and she stroked her thumb across his cheek, marveling at the fact that she was free to do so. The right to touch him was still a novelty.

"Did you know that your eyes are the precise color of the Bleu du Roi?"

She had no idea where that nonsensical thought had come from, but he smiled, apparently not displeased by her desire to talk. He traced the worry lines that had appeared between her brows with the tip of his index finger, then stroked the length of her nose.

"I have another word for you," he murmured. "Have you ever wondered what the space just here, between someone's eyebrows, is called?" He found the place again, and Emmy frowned instinctively, creating a furrow beneath his finger.

"I've never really thought about it."

He smoothed her eyebrows. "The English don't have a word for it, but the Spanish do. *Entrecejo.*" He tapped her on the tip of the nose, as if he were scolding a naughty puppy, and she fought a smile. He looked so pleased with himself.

She raised one eyebrow and tried to adopt a condescending tone. "All right. I'll admit that you've proven far more useful than I ever imagined in providing me with new and interesting words."

His lips twitched. "Oh, I do hope I've proved educational in several other areas as well, Miss Danvers," he drawled.

She managed a weary chuckle, and he pulled her close. "Sleep now," he ordered.

He gave a jaw-cracking yawn and closed his eyes, the epitome of sated masculinity, and Emmy gazed at him in wonder. His hair was ruffled, his lips pink from kissing. He looked younger, more boyish than usual, and she felt a sudden rush of affection. It was odd, to see him like this, so unguarded. She had a feeling that only a select few had been allowed to see the coolly controlled Lord Melton so at ease. An aching sweetness filled her. She was glad she'd been permitted to see it.

Without opening his eyes, he pulled her even more snugly against him and tucked her head beneath his chin. They fitted together perfectly. Emmy rested her hand on his chest and closed her eyes, listening to the steady rhythm of his heart.

Would he regret these moments they'd spent together? Would he remember her with affection, when she was no longer a part of his life?

He made love to her again just before dawn.

Emmy had been having a blisteringly erotic dream in which she'd been under him, his big body pinning her down, his wicked hands exploring every inch of her. *I have plenty of friends,* he'd whispered in her ear. *What I require is . . . an adversary. Do you think you can do that for me, Miss Danvers? Do you think you can keep running forever?*

She'd surfaced hot and frustrated, wrapped in the sheets, only to discover Alex—real Alex, not dream Alex—cupping her breasts and kissing the nape of her neck as he pressed up against her back. The hard length of him slid between her bottom cheeks, and she sucked in a surprised gasp as he rubbed himself between her thighs.

Her blood heated. In an instinctive move, she tilted her

hips and he pushed into her from behind. She rocked herself back against him and delighted in his throaty groan and the new sensations the position offered.

He withdrew and rolled onto his back, coaxing her to sit on top of him. With her knees pressing into the mattress by his hips, her hands flat on his chest, she quickly grasped the concept. She slid slowly down onto his shaft, enjoying the heady sense of power as she learned to control the pace.

After a while he pulled her forward and she stretched out on top of him. Her breasts brushed his hair-roughened chest, a delicious foreign abrasion. Her toes brushed the front of his shins. He caught her hips and moved within her, and the new angle hit a spot deep inside her that promised ecstasy. She ground herself against him, desperate to fan the flames, and it wasn't long before she was holding her breath and plunging headlong into that whirlpool of bliss.

She never wanted the sun to rise.

Chapter 37.

Alex drifted into consciousness slowly, becoming aware of a pleasant lassitude, a general feeling of well-being. Sunlight warmed the side of his face. Without opening his eyes, he let the sensation bubble up inside him and spread out, and he realized with a slight shock that he was happy. Not merely content, but joyful. He wanted to leap out of bed, fling open the window, and shout out his happiness to the world. He felt invincible, as optimistic as he could ever recall.

Last night with Emmy had been extraordinary. He slid his hand sideways, searching for her, and encountered only cool sheets. He sat up, seized with sudden panic, and glanced around the room.

Where was she? Had she played him false? Sneaked back to London without him? The little—

No. She was sitting in the window embrasure in her chemise, her knees drawn up to her chest, looking out at the inn yard. She turned when she heard him move and gave him a shy, tentative smile as if unsure of her reception.

The morning light behind her made a halo of the soft curly fuzz of her unbrushed hair, a red-orange glow around her head, and Alex was momentarily struck dumb. With that peachy glow to her cheeks, pink lips, and those damnable freckles, she was the most beautiful thing he'd ever seen. He wanted to cradle her against him at the same time as he wanted to overpower her. He tamped down a fierce tide of lust.

Sometime over the past twenty-four hours, he'd come to a decision. He couldn't turn her over to Bow Street. She needed his protection. Not just from prosecution, but from Danton too. And the best way he could think of to do that, after catching Danton and having him tried for the Italian's murder—was to give her the protection of his name.

He was the Earl of Melton. If she married him, even if Bow Street *did* decide to prosecute her for the theft of the jewels, as the wife of an earl she could claim "privilege of peerage." As a countess, she couldn't be arrested or imprisoned, except at the request of her fellow peers. She would have the right to be tried by a jury of peers in the House of Lords, who would determine her sentence, and—since she wouldn't be accused of either treason or murder, the two exceptions to the rule—even if she were found guilty, she could escape punishment if it was her first offence.

Alex was hoping she could avoid prosecution altogether if they returned all the jewels to the Prince Regent, not just the diamond she'd stolen from Rundell & Bridge. Prinny was immensely fond of grand, dramatic gestures, and he never tired of opportunities to flaunt his benevolence. He'd be thrilled at the idea of being able to present the missing French crown jewels to the French ambassador or to the newly reinstated King Louis at the next state visit.

The Prince was also a fan of settling feuds by marrying enemies off to one another. A secret romantic at heart, he abhorred violence and always preferred a peaceful solution to any problem. Alex would personally vouchsafe his wife's future good behavior and swear to keep her out of trouble.

He almost laughed aloud. Good God. Was he mad? He'd never thought he would marry, at least, not for another decade or so. And yet the idea of being wed to Emmy Danvers wasn't unappealing. Quite the opposite.

He was attracted to her in ways he hadn't experienced with any other woman. If he married her, he could kiss her whenever he wanted. And yet his desire wasn't completely sexual. Lust was undeniably a factor, but there was more to it than that. He loved her strength, her bravery, her quick wit. He loved catching her eye in a shared joke across the room, the way they seemed able to engage in silent communication. He appreciated her humor, and even the quiet moments, holding her in the darkness, just standing next to her without speaking. She engaged his mind. His heart.

Alex blinked. *Good God. Was he in love? The kind of thing the poets went on about?*

It definitely wasn't the moping, gloomy love of Shelley, or the quiet admiration of Keats. Nor was it the desperate, soul-rending agony of Byron. But the prickly, teasing, exasperating love of Shakespeare's Beatrice and Benedick, or Katherina and Petruchio?

Maybe.

There were so many things he didn't know about her, things a man ought to know before considering a woman for his life partner. What foods she liked and disliked, whether she could play a musical instrument. How she took her tea.

But they were minor, of no real import. At her core, he knew her. Despite her crimes, he believed in her intrinsic goodness. She was not unkind or unfeeling. She cared deeply for those who had her trust, and she would defend those lucky enough to be in her inner circle to the death.

She would have made a bloody good soldier.

He couldn't wait to learn all the tiny inconsequential things about her. Things that would doubtless drive him mad, or fascinate him, or delight him in equal measure.

She was pragmatic, a realist. She wouldn't refuse him. She would recognize that this was the best option available to her. The one that would cause her family the least amount of distress.

He supposed it could be called a marriage of convenience—at least for her. He'd always thought that a singularly stupid phrase. Everything about the woman was *inconvenient*.

His own family would doubtless say he'd made a dreadful mésalliance, but he had a reputation for doing things out of the ordinary. This might well prove to be his greatest scandal yet. They'd recovered from the disgrace of him owning a gambling club, however. They would recover from this. His father had been after him for ages to settle down and start providing him with grandchildren. And besides, who cared what anyone else thought? He wanted Emmy, with that clever mind and tart mouth. He could do far worse for a wife.

Maybe marriage would be good for him. He'd seen a change in Benedict since he'd married his Georgiana. He was happier, more settled, as if Georgie had added an extra dimension to his life that had been missing.

Alex had grown so accustomed to living with partial sight that he was barely conscious of the lack. But what if he suddenly regained his complete field of vision? Maybe marriage was like that? Like gaining something you never knew you'd been missing and finding your life immeasurably richer because of it. He prayed it would be so.

"You don't seem to be much of a morning person, Harland."

Emmy's amused greeting jolted him from his thoughts, and he realized with some chagrin that he'd just been staring at her like an idiot for the past few minutes.

"Morning," he croaked. His voice was almost an octave lower from sleep, and he cleared his throat and tried again. "Morning, Miss Danvers. I trust you slept well."

He took pleasure in the delicate pink flush that warmed her cheeks. He didn't think he'd ever tire of embarrassing her. He ran his fingers through his hair, then over his jaw, testing the need for a shave, which was a pointless move considering he didn't have a razor with him and there was no way he'd trust a blade provided by this establishment. It would probably be rusty and blunt. He'd slice his own ear off.

"We should go," she said briskly. "We need to get back to London so you can organize your ambush for Danton. We don't have much time." She glanced away from his bare chest and looked out of the window with a worried frown. "What shall we do about the carriage? I doubt we'll be able to find a wheelwright who can fix it in time. I can't ride all the way back to London."

Alex flipped back the covers and put his feet on the floor. She kept her gaze primly averted. He suppressed a smile. He found his breeches and tugged them on, along with his stockings and shirt. His boots were a disaster.

Though dry, they were almost impossible to pull on, but he managed it at last and turned to her.

"I'll go down to the taproom and see if there's anything to eat for breakfast. And I'll enquire about hiring a vehicle of some sort."

He made a point of looking inside the jewel box to make sure it was still full, and she sent him a withering look.

"Do you really think I've had time to hide them somewhere?"

He hefted the box in his arms and gave her a charming smile. "Better safe than sorry. I know the dangers of underestimating you, my love. You should be flattered."

She sniffed, only partly mollified.

He paused, one hand on the doorknob, and looked back at her. "Don't worry about Danton. I spoke to Seb—Lord Mowbray—before we left and told him to be ready. Believe me, this isn't the first ambush we've ever set. Get dressed. Come down when you're ready."

Chapter 38.

The trip back to London was uneventful.

The horse that had escaped during the storm had been discovered with its reins caught in a bramble bush a few miles down the road and had been brought to the inn, apparently none the worse for its adventure. Alex had managed to procure a shabby but serviceable closed carriage from a Reverend Blythe, a local clergyman.

It was a decrepit old thing, with moth-eaten curtains, metal springs, and horsehair stuffing poking out of the seats. It smelled of mildew and wet dog, but its wheels were sound, and Emmy didn't care how awful it was, provided it got them back to London in time to save Luc.

At Stamford, Alex collected his original mount, a handsome stallion named Bey, and their original coachman. As before, he rode alongside the carriage, leaving Emmy alone with her tumultuous thoughts.

There had been no one else in the taproom when they'd taken breakfast, save the obsequious landlord, and they'd endured an excruciatingly polite meal. Alex would reach for his silverware, or lift his coffee mug, and her attention would be drawn to his wrist, or his lips. A brief image of last night's lovemaking would flash into her brain. She'd spent the entire meal trying to will the embarrassed heat from her cheeks.

Harland's amused, knowing looks, as if he knew exactly what she was thinking, hadn't helped matters at all.

Emmy sneaked a glance at him beyond the carriage window. His jaw this morning was faintly darkened with beard shadow. He looked more disreputable, like a highwayman or a pirate—a fitting mate for a jewel thief.

The carriage bounced through a rut, and the box of jewels slid across the floor and bumped painfully into her ankle. Alex had placed it next to her with a significant look, as if she were being honored by his trust. Emmy snorted. Where did he think she was going to go with it? She couldn't very well leap out of a moving carriage and start running across the fields. He'd ride her down in no time.

Alex had told her not to worry about the meeting with Danton, but it was impossible. He and Mowbray might well have set similar traps during their army days, but had any of them involved hostages? She doubted it. If anything happened to Luc, she would never forgive herself. And what if Danton didn't contact them, as he said he would? What if he'd already killed Luc? Her head began to pound. Ignoring the lumpy, uncomfortable seats, she lay down and tugged Alex's heavy greatcoat over her, awash in misery. The scent of him provided a little comfort and eventually she slept, worn out by worry and exhaustion.

It was midafternoon when they clattered into the mews behind the Tricorn. Sebastien, Lord Mowbray, must have been listening out for them, because the back door opened, and he bounded down the steps.

He gave a lordly grimace when he caught sight of the shabby conveyance. "What the hell did you do to our carriage?"

Alex dismounted. "It's somewhere in deepest, darkest Lincolnshire with a broken axle. I've arranged to have it taken to a wheelwright in Stamford, then delivered back here when it's mended."

Mowbray raised his eyebrows. He opened the door to the carriage and extended his hand to help Emmy down, but Alex pushed him out of the way with his shoulder and took his place. Emmy sent them both a smile of thanks.

Mowbray's eyes were sparkling with interest. He was clearly dying to know what had happened. "Sounds like you had an eventful trip," he prodded.

Alex sent her a smile that made her innards liquefy. "You could say that," he murmured.

"Did you retrieve the jewels?"

"Yes." He reached into the carriage and withdrew the box. "Come inside and I'll show you."

Mickey was waiting in the hall to relieve them of their cloaks. Alex started toward the drawing room, then turned to Emmy.

"Why don't you go upstairs and freshen up? I need to have a little talk with Lord Mowbray."

Emmy refused to be so summarily dismissed. She turned and addressed Mowbray. "I assume you've been in contact with my grandmother? Has Danton sent instructions about exchanging the jewels for Luc?"

Mowbray grinned at the way she ignored Alex's suggestion. "Yes. He sent a note to Waverton Street this morning. He wants to meet at Kew, in the grounds of the palace that's being constructed there, at ten o'clock this evening."

Emmy nodded. "Very well. I will be ready." She turned back to Alex. "I would like to let Sally and Camille know that we have the jewels. I don't want them to worry unnecessarily."

"You can write them a letter now. I'll have it delivered straight away. There's paper and ink on my desk."

She nodded, like a queen bestowing favor upon her lowly subjects, and turned to the massive doorman. "Good. In that case, Mister, er, Mickey," she amended, when she realized she had no idea of the man's surname, "I would very much appreciate some food. And a nice cup of tea, if that wouldn't be too much trouble."

The giant's ears turned pink as she gave him her sweetest smile.

"Of course, miss. I'll go tell Mister Lagrasse. It'll be his pleasure."

Alex rolled his eyes and she just knew what he was thinking: What kind of prisoner ordered people about in such a manner? She didn't care. She was cross and worried and altogether out of sorts. If she was going to be his captive for another few hours, at least, until they met Danton, then he could damn well provide her with a decent meal.

She swept up the stairs in high dudgeon.

Seb let out a quiet laugh as Emmy stalked away from them. "That's quite the subdued prisoner you have there. She seems properly terrified of you."

Alex shot him a filthy look. "I'd like to see you do any better. The woman's a handful."

"I'll just bet she is." Seb chuckled again, his eyes on Emmy's pert bottom as she mounted the staircase, and Alex quashed the urge to put him in a chokehold to give him something else to think about. He turned and strode into the study, where he discovered Benedict Wylde, Earl of Ware, ensconced by the fire.

"Benedict's here, by the way," Seb said belatedly.

Ben rose from his chair. "I hear you've been having adventures without us." He eyed the box with undisguised interest.

"I'm amazed you've managed to tear yourself away from your wife," Alex countered sarcastically. "We count ourselves honored by your presence."

Benedict laughed. "One day, the two of you are going to find yourselves happily leg-shackled, and we'll see how willing *you* are to traipse around the countryside in the rain."

Seb sent him a doubtful look. "There's not a woman alive who can make me willingly enter the parson's mousetrap."

Benedict grimaced. Seb had certainly made no secret of his views on the subject: marriage was for idiots. In all fairness, Alex thought, Benedict's marriage was probably the first happy one Seb had ever encountered. His own family certainly bore no shining examples of matrimonial bliss. Seb's father, the Duke of Winwick, was one of the loudest proponents *against* marriage Alex had ever met.

It was the worst kept secret in the *ton* that Seb's father had not been married to his mother at the time of his conception. The duke's first wife, a dull, dutiful woman, had died giving birth to Seb's older half brother, Geoffrey, who was only eight months older than Seb himself.

Seb was the result of an affair the duke had had with a volatile Italian contessa. When his first wife had died, the duke swiftly married the already-pregnant contessa to legitimize his son and ensure he had a "spare," in case Geoffrey proved as sickly as his mother.

The marriage had not proved a happy one. The contessa was far too spirited to be content to stay in the country and play duchess. She'd returned to London and taken a series of lovers, and the duke had continued his rakish ways with a steady succession of ever-younger actresses and courtesans.

Seb's mother had died of smallpox when he was six, and the duke had vowed there and then never to remarry. Women, he declared, were just not worth the bother.

It was no wonder Seb's views on the subject were jaundiced.

Alex glanced over at Benedict. Marriage did seem to agree with *him*, though. He'd been disgustingly happy with his new wife for months. He'd barely stopped smiling since the wedding, and he'd had this smug, self-satisfied expression on his face, as though he'd discovered some secret Alex and Seb had yet to fathom.

Not that Alex begrudged his friend happiness, of course, but he knew the chances of himself finding similar happiness in the married state were exceedingly remote.

Seb and Benedict both let out slow, impressed whistles when Alex lifted the lid of the box and showed them the jewels. Seb picked up the peach-colored diamond, the one Emmy had called the Hortensia, and held it up to the light.

"Bloody hell. That's enough to make even Prinny's glitter-loving heart beat faster." He replaced it and poured out three glasses of brandy from the decanter on the sideboard. He offered the first to Alex. "Drink? You look as if you could do with it. Stayed up all night making sure our little thief didn't abscond with the goods, did you?"

"Something like that."

Seb shot him a knowing look. "I'm sure you went above and beyond the call of duty. We all know how conscientious you are, Harland."

Alex sent him a hard glare and Seb grinned. "While you were enjoying your bucolic interlude with our delightful captive—"

"Recovering stolen property," Alex amended.

"As I said. While you were showing the lovely Miss Danvers the error of her larcenous ways, *we* found a witness to the Italian's murder."

Alex let out a shocked breath. "You did? Bloody brilliant!"

Seb shrugged, pretending a modesty he most assuredly didn't possess. The man was as arrogant as they came. "Why, thank you. It was rather well done, if I do say so myself."

"Tell me everything."

"Well, when we got to Gravesend, we poked around a bit and heard mention of a servant missing from Andretti's household. The local constabulary hadn't been able to find him and assumed he was either party to the murder, or had himself been killed and his body disposed of by the murderer."

Alex shook his head as he lowered himself into one of the comfy wing armchairs that flanked the fire. "That makes no sense. The black feather at the crime scene points the finger squarely at the Nightjar. Why would he kill the servant and hide his body when he made no attempt to conceal the murder of the Italian?"

"I didn't say the locals were the sharpest nibs in the inkpot, did I? I begin to see why Conant holds them in such contempt."

Benedict nodded. "They really were a bunch of amateurs. Couldn't find a clue if it was tied to their coattails."

Seb sent him a droll look. "But we digress. We told the locals we didn't believe in the missing servant's guilt and let them know that if he ever presented himself at Bow Street, he would receive a fair hearing. I even hinted there would be a financial reward for information."

Alex nodded. "Good thinking."

"Yesterday, an Italian by the name of Stefano Mancini

sent a message to Bow Street to meet at a tavern down by the East India docks." Seb's mouth kicked up in a mocking grin.

"Mancini witnessed the entire thing," Benedict said. "He was about to deliver his master's usual post-dinner tipple when an 'Eenglish gentleman' arrived and was shown into the study. Mancini, the perfect servant, heard raised voices and decided to listen at the door. Since it was good, solid English oak, he could hear very little, so he sneaked around the side of the house to see what was happening through the study window. It was dark outside, so he was fairly certain he wouldn't be seen from within."

"Very commendable," Alex said snidely.

Seb glared at Benedict for taking over the tale and continued. "He saw his master remove a painting from the wall and open the safe that was hidden behind it. Unfortunately, whatever the English gentleman wanted was not inside. The Englishman grew agitated. Mancini saw him pull a pistol from his cloak and threaten Andretti. Andretti held up his hands and went to his writing desk, one he'd brought over from Italy. He reached inside a drawer, released a secret compartment, and withdrew a large, blue stone.

"This, apparently, was what the Englishman had been after. He pocketed the stone, gestured for Andretti to sit, and calmly shot him in the head. Mancini, quite justifiably, believed he would be next. He ran away and hid in a nearby farmer's cowshed. When he was certain the murderer had gone, he returned to the house, packed his few belongings, helped himself to the contents of the safe, and hightailed it to London."

"His plan," Benedict interrupted again, "was to catch a boat back to his native Genoa, but he was robbed and beaten on the way back to his lodgings. With no money, and no other options, he decided to contact Bow Street and claim the reward for information about Andretti's killer."

Alex leaned forward. "Can he positively identify Danton?"

"Without a doubt," Seb said. "And he's willing to testify. He's keen to see his master's killer brought to justice. Conant's put him in a safehouse in Whitehall under guard until we catch Danton."

Alex nodded. "Along with Danton's oblique written admission in that note he sent to Emmy, Mancini's testimony should be enough to convict him. Good."

"So all you have to do now is catch him and retrieve the sapphire," Benedict said happily. "Easy."

Seb frowned. "What will you be doing?"

Benedict slapped his palms on his knees and stood. "I'll be getting back to my wife. It pains me to miss an adventure, boys, but I promised Georgie I'd escort her to the theatre. You're going to have to do this one without me. Remember not to get shot, all right?"

Chapter 39.

Alex swallowed the rest of his brandy and frowned into the fire as Benedict took his leave. "Danton's expecting Emmy to meet him—alone—at ten o'clock, correct?"

"Yes."

"Then we'll go with her and take up position close by. I don't want her near that murderous bastard any longer than absolutely necessary. She's a witness. There's no chance he's going to let her live. He'll try to shoot her, just as he did Andretti. As soon as either of us gets a clean shot, we take it, understood?"

"We can't kill him," Seb said, his expression grim. "I know it's tempting, but we need him alive to face trial."

Alex scowled. "I know."

"If you want her to have some extra protection, why don't we borrow that guard dog from the British Museum? He certainly looks fearsome enough."

"Brutus? Good idea."

"So, assuming we succeed in capturing Danton, what are your plans for the fair Miss Danvers? A carriage straight to Newgate?"

Seb's expression was pure mischief. He and Emmy would get on extremely well, Alex thought. He tried to school his features into revealing absolutely nothing, but his old friend knew him far too well.

"I know that look!" Seb said, suddenly incredulous. "It's the one you get when you're about to do something stupid but heroic. Like when you leapt in front of me and saved me from that sniper's bullet in Spain." His smile widened. "You're not going to turn her in, are you? I knew it! What *are* you going to do? The prince demands a culprit."

"He'll have one. Danton."

"You're going to claim Danton's the Nightjar? Conant won't believe that."

"No, but the prince will."

"You're going to lie to him?"

"Danton's the reason the Nightjar went after the gems. The most recent ones, at least. If we hand the jewels over to the prince and tell him the perpetrators have been dealt with appropriately, it won't be a lie. Danton can stand trial and receive his just punishment for murdering Andretti. And I'll personally vouch for Emmy's continued good behavior to Conant if she's spared prosecution. Case closed."

Alex stared into the fire. Emmy wouldn't like Danton taking credit for her heists. She was proud of her talents, and rightly so. But if this solution stopped her from being imprisoned, he would do it, her pride be damned. Danton would hang for the Italian's murder. He might as well take the blame for the thefts too, and let the Nightjar die with him. Emmy would be free from her father's legacy once and for all.

Seb wrinkled his forehead. "Vouch for her? How are you going to do that? Sail her off around the world? Keep her chained up at the Tricorn for the next sixty years?"

"By keeping a close eye on her for the rest of my life. I'm going to marry her."

Alex derived a great deal of satisfaction from the way Seb's mouth dropped open in shock.

"You're going to *what*?"

"Marry her." It got easier every time he said it out loud. Alex smiled. "I'll swear to Conant to keep her out of trouble. I'll keep her so busy, both in bed and out of it, that she won't have time to steal."

Seb slouched back in his chair and took another sip of brandy. "Does *she* know about this brilliant plan of yours? You've actually asked her to marry you? And she's agreed?"

"Not yet. I was going to tell her, once tonight was over with."

Seb gave a bark of laughter. "Tell her? Good God, man! I might not be married, but from everything I know about the fair sex, you don't just *tell* a woman you're going to marry her. You ask. You grovel, in fact. You get down on your knees and beg. And then you pray she's either foolish enough, desperate enough, or pitying enough to say yes."

Alex shifted in his seat. "She won't refuse me."

Seb's disbelieving chuckle made him want to punch him in the face. "This is the same woman who still thinks you're about to lock her away and throw away the key? That one?" He shook his head.

"I'm doing it for her own protection," Alex growled, inexplicably feeling the need to justify his decision with rational argument. "As my countess, she'll be far better off, both socially and financially. That alone should convince Conant that she won't need to steal anymore."

"She never stole for profit in the first place," Seb pointed out, with irritating logic. "That's the worst excuse I ever heard. Why don't you just admit the real reason?"

Alex felt heat creep up his neck. "What reason?" Seb's teasing smirk made his hands itch to close around his neck. He clenched them into fists.

"That blind spot of yours is an extremely good metaphor, you know," Seb drawled. "Physically, you can't see to your right. Mentally, you can't see what's been bloody obvious to everyone else around you for weeks. You can't take your eyes off her. You can't stop thinking about her. You can't stop talking about her. You can't stop *chasing* her. You are, in fact, one hundred percent *in love with her.*"

Alex opened his mouth to deny it, but Seb raised his hand.

"Admit it. You're head over heels in love with her, and you're too much of an idiot to tell her so." He shook his head mock mournfully. "Oh, how the mighty have fallen."

"It'll happen to you too, someday," Alex growled.

"Not in a month of Sundays. Love is for fools."

"You don't need to tell me. I know. We're from opposite ends of the legal and—might I add—*ethical* moral spectrum. I'm sworn to uphold the law. She's committed heaven knows how many crimes and shown not a shred of remorse for any of them. In fact, she seems to exhibit an unholy glee at having outwitted us all for so long."

"She brings out the best in you. And just think, life will never be boring."

"Well, that's true. I never know what the hell she's going to do next."

Seb sighed. "I wish you luck, my friend. That woman has been one step ahead of us for months. You might have the upper hand right now, but she has a lifetime of tricks up her sleeve."

Deciding to give Emmy a little space, Alex made sure her letter was delivered to her grandmother, checked that her request for food had been accommodated, and joined Seb in the Tricorn's private dining room for a meal provided by the wonderful Monsieur Lagrasse.

When he finally entered his rooms, it was to find Emmy looking ridiculously attractive in a moss-green velvet dress he hadn't seen before. She'd obviously had a bath—her skin was pink and rosy, and her hair had been put up in a complicated-looking twist. That damnable perfume of hers swirled in the air.

Instead of striding over there and kissing her senseless, which he very much wanted to do, he frowned and took a seat behind his desk to hide the telltale bulge in the front of his breeches. "Where did you get that dress?"

"Sally sent it over." She took the chair across the desk from him and placed her hands neatly on the top. "She thought I might need something clean and warm for tonight. So, do we have a plan?"

"We do. Danton wants you to meet at Kew, in the grounds of the castle King George has been constructing for the past decade." He glanced over at the mantel clock. Eight thirty. "It's about eight miles as the crow flies, across the river from Brentwood. It should take about an hour with the carriage, so we need to be leaving soon. Dan will drive you, but when you reach the gatehouse, you must get out of the carriage and go on alone with the jewels. Don't worry. Seb and I will be hidden in the undergrowth. We'll always have you in our sights."

"That's reassuring," she said dryly. "I'm sure I'll feel much more relaxed knowing you're tracking my progress with the barrel of a Baker rifle."

"It's not you we'll be aiming for. It'll be Danton. And you won't be completely alone. Seb spoke to Franks at the British Museum. He's lent us Brutus, the dog, as extra protection."

Emmy bit her lip to prevent a smile, but he saw it anyway.

"Considering your success at the museum, I'm assuming you and Brutus have an understanding?"

Emmy nodded. "He's particularly fond of steak."

"All right. We'll ride with you until we're almost there, and then we'll flank you and lie in wait. Do whatever Danton says. As soon as an opportunity presents itself, we'll run in there and arrest him."

Her face was pinched with worry, but she pasted a brave smile on, and Alex impulsively leaned over the desk and squeezed her hands. "It's all right. We'll get Luc back unharmed, I swear."

She nodded.

He stood, and she did the same. "All right, let's go."

She disappeared into his bedroom and returned, pulling on a velvet pelisse. Its many buttons fit snugly over her breasts and fastened up her white throat. All completely proper, but just the hint of those feminine curves had Alex thinking dissolute thoughts. He gave himself a mental slap on the head. He needed to concentrate. There would be time enough to do all the things he wanted to do to her after tonight's trial was done.

He ushered her out and down the stairs. Mickey stood in the yard, feeding a delighted Brutus a strip of Chef Lagrasse's finest sirloin. The dog bounced around and barked in excitement at the end of his leather leash. When he saw Emmy, he leapt forward, almost pulling Mickey's arm out of its socket, and reared up on his hind legs to give her an enthusiastic greeting.

Emmy yelped in alarm and stepped back so the enormous animal's paws fell back to the cobbles.

"Down, Brutus!" she commanded, half-laughing. "Yes, it's good to see you too, but do stop licking me. It's disgusting."

Mickey managed to coax the giant beast to jump into the carriage and secured the leash to one of the sconces. After an investigative sniff of every inch of the carriage, the beast sat down on the threadbare seat, facing forward just like a human passenger, ears pricked and ready to go. Alex was intensely glad they were still using the run-down vehicle he'd purchased in Lincolnshire. It didn't matter if the monster shredded the seats or drooled on the upholstery.

He'd already packed his trusty Baker rifle in his saddlebag, and he knew Seb had done the same. He'd sent a message over to Benedict's town house to see if he'd changed his mind about coming to help, but Alex didn't expect it. Benedict adored adventures like this, but he enjoyed the company of his wife even more. He and Georgie were a rarity amongst the *ton*—a couple who genuinely liked each other.

Alex hoped he and Emmy would be able to emulate their example. He'd do everything in his power to make sure she'd be happy married to him.

With that thought, he handed her into the carriage and accepted the box of jewels from Mickey. He placed it on her lap, then fished in his jacket pocket and withdrew the Carrington ruby. Her eyes widened in surprise as he opened the tin and added it to the glittering pile.

"Just in case Danton wants to see it," he explained. "What? Did you think I was going to keep it for myself? Some of us have principles, Miss Danvers," he couldn't resist teasing. He closed the carriage door with a snap.

"Just remember, when you meet him, keep him talking. That way, he'll be focused on you."

She nodded again, and he left her and mounted Bey. The Tricorn's coachman clambered up in front of her, and Seb mounted his own horse.

"Let's go."

Chapter 40.

They travelled west out of London, through the Knights-
bridge turnpike and down past Bayswater. Emmy tried to
quell the anxious churning of her stomach as she thought
of the ordeal ahead.

She was grateful for Brutus's distracting presence. The
dog poked his huge head out of the open carriage window, tongue lolling, delighted by the novelty of travelling
in such a way. He barked at every late-night passerby,
rider, coach, and animal they passed.

Reaching down, Emmy slid open the catch on the tin
box and took one last look at the jewels. Apart from the
sapphire Danton had stolen, all the other major gems her
father had wanted to recover were here, on her lap.

So near and yet so far.

Tears pricked her eyes. She and her father had taken
such pains to amass this collection, but they would never
be returned to France. Still, better the British government have them than that murderous, blackmailing swine
Danton. The self-absorbed Frenchman was no match for

Alex. Harland was a seasoned, wily strategist with years of experience. He would defend her.

Emmy closed the lid with a snap and secured the latch.

Never had she felt so unprepared. If this had been a heist, she and Luc would have done meticulous research on the location to anticipate every eventuality. If only they'd had time to visit this meeting site, to assess all the exits and entrances, to find the places of elevation and blind corners. If only she'd learned how to shoot a pistol or wield a knife.

The coach rattled over Kew Bridge and rocked to a stop. Alex's dark shape appeared at the window. "This is where we leave you."

Emmy managed to nod, even though she felt almost nauseous with nerves. He nudged his mount closer and reached his gloved hand through the open window to stroke her cheek.

"It'll be all right, Emmy. Trust me."

She allowed herself the brief indulgence of pressing her cheek into his palm, then pulled away. She refused to think that this might be the last time she ever spoke to him. "Go."

A few minutes later the coachman angled the vehicle through an arched red brick entrance, and they started down a tree-flanked lane. Emmy peered through the darkness. After half a mile or so, they pulled over and she looped Brutus's leash around her wrist and jumped down from the carriage, then turned and hefted the tin.

The coachman pointed through the trees to where the partly constructed battlements of a great stone edifice gleamed pale in the moonlight. "'Is lordship told me not to get too close. But don't you worry none, milady. 'E'll 'ave yer back, all right and tight." He saluted her with a finger to his cap.

Emmy started down the dark lane. The trees arched

overhead, their branches dark and menacing, and she tried to regulate her breathing. *Just a nice walk in the moonlight, that's all.* Brutus tugged at the leash, eager to investigate everything, snuffling in the shifting undergrowth. A gust of wind brought the distinctive smell of the river to her nose, and she realized they weren't far from the Thames. She spied the silver-grey sliver of water between the trees.

The main building came into view: white stone crenelated walls, round turrets, and small windows in the Gothic style. In the moonlight, it looked like a medieval ruin, a folly, but Emmy knew it was in the process of being built, not falling down.

King George's "new palace" had been featured in the newspapers for years. Still unfinished more than a decade after construction had begun due to the king's many bouts of madness, it was a constant source of derision, outrage, and scorn. Its detractors decried it as ruinously expensive, ugly, and tasteless. A monument to folly and unfinished dreams. A prime example of the foolishness and profligacy of the monarchy. One politician had even likened it to the Bastille.

Building work had clearly been at a standstill for some time. Brambles and weeds had overgrown the joists that protruded from the unfinished walls. Emmy shivered, hating the place with an instinctive dread. Danton had chosen his meeting place well; there were a hundred places he could be hiding, dead ends and shadowy corners. He could be watching her even now.

Brutus let out an excited bark. Nose to the ground, he tugged her down a path that led through the trees toward the river, a muddy track obviously once used by the workmen. Emmy almost turned her ankle in one of the wheelbarrow ruts before she hauled him to a stop.

She glanced around, her heart thumping against her

breastbone as she tried to decipher the dark shapes in the darkness. Every rustle of leaf, every snap of a twig, made her want to scream. Was Danton lurking in the shadows? Did he have a gun trained on her even now? She clutched the metal box tighter to her stomach, almost numb with terror. What was to stop him shooting her and taking the jewels from her corpse?

She clenched her jaw. No. He would want to be certain she had the jewels before killing her. And Alex was somewhere out there too. She tried to guess where he might be hiding but could see nothing.

Her heart leapt as the undergrowth rustled and Danton's squat figure materialized from the shadows.

"Miss Danvers," he called out, his tone genial, as if they'd just met on the street and not in some terrifyingly isolated piece of woodland. "I'm glad you came." He took a step forward and glared at Brutus. "But not alone, I see."

"Brutus needed some air." The dog gave a short, unfriendly bark and strained at the leash. Emmy wrapped it around her wrist and clutched the heavy tin box in front of her like a charm to ward off evil. "Where's Luc? I want to see him."

Danton's wide lips curled in a derisive sneer. "He's not been harmed. He's aboard my yacht, which is moored down by the water." Without taking his eyes from her, he half-turned and shouted, "Danvers!"

His voice echoed through the trees, and Emmy strained her ears for an answering shout. Her knees almost crumpled in relief when a reply—undoubtedly Luc's voice— came from afar.

"Emmy! I'm well."

She glared at Danton's impassive face. "All right, then. I have the jewels."

He stepped forward eagerly. "All of them?"

"All except the Ruspoli sapphire. You stole that your-self, I hear." she added caustically.

He gave a careless shrug, and anger began to replace her fear.

"You killed a man for it," she pressed. "And made it look like the Nightjar's crime."

He smirked. He was a monster, utterly unfeeling. He'd taken a human life, kidnapped her brother, blackmailed and threatened her, and clearly felt no remorse. She was almost shaking with the urge to throw the box at his head.

"You need not fear that I shall ask you to steal again," he said calmly, mistaking the look on her face. "Once you hand me that box, our acquaintance will be at an end. I'll have no further tasks for you. The Nightjar can retire gracefully."

Emmy narrowed her eyes. She didn't believe him. She was a witness; what incentive did he have to let her live? He'd already killed the last man who could identify him.

Brutus, apparently an astute judge of character, strained toward him and growled. Danton flicked the animal an irritated glance. "Tie him up."

Emmy looped the dog's leash around a tree branch.

"That's better. Now, the jewels. They're in that box?"

"Yes."

"Good." He indicated a spot about six feet in front of him. "Put it down on the ground, then step back."

Emmy did as she was told. She watched as the French-man squatted awkwardly and lifted the lid. The gems sparkled, even in the dim moonlight, and his smile of tri-umph made her want to slap him. Where was Alex? Why wasn't he rushing forward to arrest him? What was he waiting for?

Chapter 41.

Alex was waiting for a clear shot. He inched forward, crawling on elbows and knees, cursing the abundant undergrowth. It was useful to disguise his own position, but the sheer density of it made it impossible to get a clean line of sight to Danton. The Frenchman had chosen a good place for his rendezvous.

He caught a glimpse of Seb moving around to the rear of Danton's position, and was reminded of all the times they'd done similar maneuvers during the war, belly-down in the dirt, hiding in the bushes with their rifles. It was good to have Seb at his side.

He squinted through the trees and tried to locate Emmy. That velvet dress of hers was fetching, but it made her bloody hard to see. She almost disappeared into the shadowy foliage. All he could make out were her pale hands and her equally pale face. She looked frightened but determined; her freckles stood out starkly against her cheeks.

He watched her put the box on the ground and say

something to Danton. The Frenchman ducked out of sight and Alex cursed silently. He glanced over at Seb, who shook his head in a silent message to indicate that he didn't have a clear view, either.

Alex inched to the right, trying to line Danton up with the V-shaped notch on the end of the Baker's barrel. Another tree blocked his aim. Bloody hell. He'd only graze the Frenchman's arm if he fired now.

Danton picked up the box of jewels. Alex held his breath, waiting for the bastard to step into his line of sight. He wasn't about to kill the man, but he could certainly incapacitate the bastard. He tightened his finger on the trigger.

Danton was almost in range when he drew a pistol from his coat and Alex's blood ran cold.

He leapt to his feet with a savage cry and fired. His bullet went wide, but Danton, as he'd hoped, whirled around and fired the pistol wildly in his direction, instead of at Emmy. The ball whistled past his head and embedded itself in a tree to his right with a dull thud.

The scent of spent gunpowder took him right back to the Peninsular and he started to reload his rifle without conscious thought. He'd already placed the butt on the ground and was reaching back for a paper twist of gunpowder when he remembered he had his dueling pistol in his belt. He threw down the rifle, pulled out the smaller gun, and started sprinting through the trees toward Danton.

Brutus had been thrown into a frenzy by the gunfire. He was barking wildly, twisting and straining on his leash. With an athletic lunge, he broke free of the branch and leapt toward Emmy. She shrieked in alarm, but he surged past her and headed straight for Danton, his teeth bared in fury.

Danton threw his spent pistol at the dog and turned

to run just as Alex fired. The ball caught the Frenchman midthigh, and with a high-pitched scream he went
sprawling to the ground. The tin fell from his arms and
burst open, spewing jewels onto the muddy ground.
Brutus was on him a second later, barking fiercely,
his front legs splayed wide to corner him and guard
Emmy.

Danton rolled over with a howl of fury. Alex grabbed
hold of Brutus's flailing leash and tugged the dog back
toward Emmy, who was standing frozen as if in shock.
He thrust the leash into her hand.

"Here. Hold him."

She grasped it automatically, still watching Danton's
writhing efforts to crawl away on his hands and knees.

A blinding fury seized Alex. He strode over, grasped
Danton by the collar, and dealt him a punishing blow
across the jaw. Panting through his teeth, he punched him
again and again.

He didn't fight like a gentleman. The bastard had tried
to shoot Emmy. He deserved no such courtesy.

Seb grabbed his shoulders and tried to pry him away,
but Alex shrugged him off. He hauled Danton to his feet,
ignoring his screams for mercy, and punched him in the
kidneys. His flabby stomach absorbed most of the blow.

The Frenchman doubled over with an agonized exhalation, gasping for breath. When Alex let him go, he
dropped to the ground and lay curled around himself, his
hands grasping his middle. Alex gave his injured thigh a
contemptuous kick for good measure.

"Easy, Alex. Enough!" Seb's urgent words pierced his
red haze of anger. "We need him alive to hang, dammit!"

Alex shook out his fists. His knuckles stung. He looked
down at the whimpering, cowering heap below him with
disdain. Threaten Emmy, would he? Bastard.

Seb stepped in front of him and ushered him a few steps away.

"Can't we just shoot him here?" Alex growled.

"You've already done that."

"Only in the leg. It's just a flesh wound. Let me try again. Somewhere really painful this time. The knee? The hand?"

"No! Conant wants him alive to stand trial. Leave it to the authorities. Let them decide what they want to do with the traitorous bastard."

Alex scowled at his friend.

"Nobody's shooting anyone," Seb repeated firmly. "Unless Emmy decides to shoot you, of course. That I'd pay to see."

"Some friend you are. You'd probably hand her the gun." Alex glanced around the clearing as a wave of belated shame swamped him. Oh, God, she'd seen him beating Danton to a pulp. She must be disgusted. Horrified at his barbarity. "Where is she?"

There was no sign of her or the dog.

Seb shrugged. "Probably gone to release her brother."

Danton had lost consciousness. Alex rolled him over and searched his pockets, but they were empty. "We need that sapphire to tie him to the Italian's murder."

Seb nodded. "I'll take him back to the coach. You find Emmy, her brother, and the gem." He grabbed hold of Danton's ankles and began to drag the unconscious man down the lane.

Alex scooped the jewels from where they'd fallen in the mud and replaced them in the tin. "Take these too." He balanced the box on Danton's stomach so Seb could use him as a human sled. "Don't feel the need to be gentle with the bastard."

Alex headed through the trees in the direction of the

Thames. An excited bark helped him pinpoint a small, sleek vessel secured to a wooden jetty. Brutus was tied to a piling. Emmy and her brother appeared, both ducking to avoid the craft's low doorway and then climbing back onto the dock.

Alex strode forward and held out his hand. "Still in one piece, Danvers? None the worse for your adventure?"

Luc Danvers returned the handshake with a smile. The man had a black eye and some ugly swelling on his eyebrow, but otherwise appeared unhurt.

"That's quite the shiner you have there," Alex said.

Luc grimaced. "Looks like I've gone six rounds with Gentleman Jackson, doesn't it? Danton kicked my good foot from under me and I fell." He shrugged. "Still, I've had worse." He glanced down meaningfully at his prosthetic leg.

Alex sent him a respectful nod. They were both men who understood the subtle gradations of pain. "I need the sapphire he took from the Italian."

Luc nodded toward the boat's cabin. "He showed it to me. It's in there. In the tea caddy."

Alex inclined his head in thanks and stepped aboard. Emmy's voice floated after him as he stooped into the untidy living quarters.

"Oh, Luc! I'm so glad to see you. You're not hurt anywhere else?"

"I'm fine. In fact, I probably should be thanking Danton for kidnapping me."

"Thanking him?" Emmys voice was incredulous. "What do you mean?"

"I haven't been on a boat since Trafalgar. I thought I'd never want to set foot on one again, to tell you the truth. But this whole adventure has reminded me just how much I love being on the water."

"What?"

Emmys voice was strangled, and Alex suppressed a smile. He could just imagine her horrified expression.

Luc's voice came again. "After what happened, I thought being on a boat would give me nightmares. But it's quite the opposite. My disability doesn't matter when I'm on deck. I can sway around as much as I want."

Alex listened for what would undoubtedly be Emmy's scathing response, but her answer was too quiet for him to hear. Or maybe her brother had finally rendered her speechless.

He'd like to know how to do that, himself. The only way *he'd* ever managed it was by kissing her. Come to think of it, he preferred his way. He couldn't wait to silence her again.

Luc let out a satisfied sigh. "Ahh, yes. The wind in my hair, the seagulls calling, the spray on my face. I'm going to get a boat, Em. I'll moor her at Southampton and take you and Sally on pleasure jaunts up the coast. Or over to France, if you like. I bet Camille would like to visit the old homeland."

Alex spied a metallic silver tea caddy on a shelf. He pulled off the lid, upended it, and a blue stone the size of a walnut slid out onto his palm. The Ruspoli sapphire—evidence to link Danton to murder. Satisfied, he pocketed it and started for the door.

"Hoi, Harland," Luc called out from the dock. "What do you suppose is going to happen to this ship, now Danton's in custody? Will Bow Street confiscate it? I'll give you a fair price for her, if so."

Alex exited the cabin and clambered back onto the jetty. Luc was alone. "Where's your sister?"

"Oh, she went back to the carriage with the dog."

Alex started toward the trees. Luc limped alongside him. Out of politeness, Alex slowed down and shortened his stride so the other man could keep up, even though he was desperate to see Emmy again. He had to speak to her. Had she left because she couldn't stand the sight of him after the way he'd beaten Danton? The blackmailing sod had deserved every punch, but he shouldn't have lost control like that in front of her. Thief she might be, but she was still a lady.

The dark bulk of the carriage finally came into view, with Seb and Dan the coachman standing at the horse's heads, deep in conversation.

Alex tilted his chin at the vehicle. "Danton's in there?"

Seb nodded. "Making the acquaintance of a pair of Bow Street's finest shackles."

"Where's Emmy?"

Seb frowned. "I thought she was with you?"

Alex glared at Luc. "Where is she?"

Luc shrugged. "How should I know? Maybe she needed a moment of privacy? She's had a few trying days, by the sound of it."

A rustle in the undergrowth had all four of them turning toward the sound, but it was only Brutus. He came bounding between the trees, his leash dragging on the ground behind him. Alex narrowed his eyes as a sudden wave of suspicion crashed over him. "Where are the jewels?"

Seb opened the door of the carriage. "In here. With Danton." He slid the black metal tin across the floor—and cursed. "What the devil—? It's too light."

He lifted the lid. All four men leaned forward to look, but Alex already knew what he would see.

A single black feather.

He stared down at it in disbelief. How in the name of all that was holy had she—? Fury such as he'd never known pulsed in his blood. He snapped a murderous gaze to Luc, who tried and failed to look innocent. "Where's your bloody sister, Danvers?"

Seb started laughing like a madman. "My God, I love this girl! She's marvelous. I hope you do marry her, Alex, because if you don't, I will. What a sneaky little—"

"Marry her?" It was Luc's turn to scowl. "Who said anything about marrying her?"

Alex stopped listening. She couldn't get far on foot. She knew that. He'd track her down and— Another dreadful thought occurred to him. He started running down the lane toward the clearing where he and Seb had left their mounts. She wouldn't—

She would.

Seb's horse was happily chomping the foliage, but a patch of trampled grass was the only indication that Bey had ever been there.

Alex raised his fists to heaven and counted to ten, then exhaled slowly, but he could still feel a muscle ticking in his jaw and the blood pounding in his temples.

The thieving little baggage! She'd stolen his horse, and *all* of the jewels. The only one she didn't have was the sapphire in his pocket.

Bloody woman!

He stalked back to the others.

Did she think she could hide from him forever? He'd chase her down. And not because of the jewels—he truly didn't care who had the bloody things anymore—but because he simply couldn't imagine life without her. She was a brilliant, conniving, sneaky little weasel. And he was fatally in love with her.

Alex kicked a stone with the toe of his boot. Seb was right. Marrying her to protect her was just an excuse. He wanted the daily battles marriage to her would provide. The teasing and the banter and the irritation. He wanted her, body and soul.

He'd do whatever it took to get her back. He'd find her and *make* her marry him, dammit. If nothing else, she should accept him out of sheer gratitude for sparing her from imprisonment. For getting Danton off her back.

He kicked the stone again, harder, sending it skittering into a tree stump. No. That wasn't true. He wanted her to accept him because she returned his feelings. Because she loved him, too.

Did she? He thought she might. She'd given herself to him, hadn't she? She desired him physically. But could that make up for the resentment she bore him for catching her? Was it completely idiotic to imagine they could ever make a life together?

Where the hell had she gone?

Chapter 42.

Emmy hadn't visited her parents' graves for months. It took her a little while to locate them, even in the pale morning light.

The grass was wet with dew. A few tendrils of mist snaked eerily around the tombstones as she unfolded the rug she'd brought with her and sat. She wasn't afraid; the dead couldn't hurt her. Only the living could do that. And besides, at this hour, there were only a few servants and tradesmen about in the streets. No one would bother her.

She leaned forward and placed a tiny bunch of violets on each grave—the little purple petals were already drooping.

She hadn't slept since she'd stolen the jewels from the coach and galloped away on Alex's magnificent Arabian stallion. She'd gone to the one place she, Luc, and Sally had always agreed she would go in just such an emergency: the lodgings of Sally's actress friend Molly O'Keene.

Molly's small apartment was, ironically, less than a quarter mile from Bow Street, conveniently near Covent Garden and Drury Lane, but it was a world away from the refinement of St. James's Square. It was the perfect place to hide—under Harland's very nose.

Molly hadn't asked any questions when Emmy had arrived close to midnight, her hair a tangled mess from her wild gallop, her cheeks red from the wind. She'd welcomed her inside, summoned a lad she trusted to deliver Bey back to the Tricorn without being accosted, and had shown Emmy upstairs to a cramped but comfortable attic room.

Emmy had collapsed on the small truckle bed, her body exhausted but her mind spinning. So many schemes. Her brain was practically bursting with them. She'd lain awake, trying to sort through all the endless permutations of what to do next. Dawn had found her no closer to an answer, but she'd been seized by the need to come here, to her father and mother, for clarity.

Father had been very specific about where he wanted to be buried, next to her mother, here in this quiet London churchyard. Emmy sighed. Her parents had loved one another deeply. Her mother had died trying to bring her younger brother into the world, and while Emmy could barely remember her, perhaps her father's decision to become the Nightjar had been an understandable way for him to channel his grief and frustration at the loss of his beloved wife into something positive. It had given him something to live for, just as planning the heists had sustained Luc during his long convalescence.

Emmy settled the tin box on her knees and lifted the lid. The jewels gleamed softly within.

"We did it," she whispered. "We got them back." Tears tightened her throat as she tilted the box toward the unresponsive stones. "I wish you could both have been here to see it, but I know you'd be so proud of us. We miss you so much."

A tear spilled over and trailed down her cheek. She brushed it away. "You know how you always said you wanted us to be happy? Well, I'm not. I thought I would be, once we had the jewels, but to tell you the truth, I'm miserable."

She glared down at the fortune in her lap, then over at her father's headstone. "This was your dream, not mine. It was a good dream," she added hastily. "A noble dream. I don't blame you for pursuing it. But it wasn't mine."

She closed the lid of the box.

"Do you know what my dream was? It was to meet someone who loved me right down to my toes, the way you loved Maman. And do you know the worst thing? I found him. He's worth more than any treasure I could steal, but I found him too late."

Emmy wiped the corner of her eye on her sleeve.

Too late.

The French had a word: *dépaysement*. It described the feeling of not being in your home country. It was similar to homesickness, except with the added disorientation of being strange and foreign, like a fish out of water. That was how she felt now, without Harland. He was her country. The place she most wanted to be. She wanted him with a fierce, soul-deep yearning.

What on earth was she going to do now?

With a cry of anguish, she pushed the box aside and buried her face on her bent knees. Why had she even taken the jewels from the coach? She hadn't been thinking. It had been a reflex action—steal the gems, escape. It was what she always did.

But to what end? Even with Danton in custody and implicated in the Italian's death, she couldn't avoid being punished for the rest of the Nightjar's crimes. Having the jewels was of no use to her. Alex would simply persecute her family until she returned them. She should have just left them next to Danton and accepted her fate. Now, she'd ruined everything.

The click of the gate and quiet footsteps on the path made her lift her head in panic. But instead of Alex coming to arrest her, it was Camille walking between the rows of neatly tended stones. She was wearing a straw hat with a blue silk ribbon and carrying another equally fetching bonnet in her hands. She smiled fondly when she reached Emmy.

"I thought I'd find you here, darling. I'm glad to see you safe and sound."

"Have you seen Luc? Harland?"

Camille nodded. "Both of them. Lord Melton escorted your brother home last night. Luc told me what happened with Danton, and Lord Melton seemed under the impression that you might have preceded them to the house. He was most put out when I disabused him of that idea." She sent Emmy a dry look of understanding. "I assume you followed our contingency plan and went to Sally's actress friend instead?"

Emmy nodded. "Yes. Are you sure you weren't followed? I can't believe Harland didn't set a watch on the house."

Camille's gray eyes twinkled with mischief. "Oh, I'm sure he did. A scruffy-looking lad was lounging around on the corner when I left. The poor thing must have been there all night. But I took a very circuitous route, changed carriages twice on the way here, and swapped hats too, just for good measure." She flapped the bonnet she held in her hand. "I lost him somewhere around Piccadilly. I must say, Lord Melton does seem rather keen to speak with you. I assume it's because of that?" She tilted her head toward the box on the grass.

Emmy flipped open the lid to expose the contents, and Camille sighed in rapture.

"Ahh! The Hortensia! And Marie Antoinette's pearls. How lovely to see them all together again, just as your father wanted. But they have been the cause of much heartache, *n'est-ce pas*?"

"What are we going to do with them? I don't even know why I took them again last night."

Camille shot her a sly sideways glance. "Do you not?" she said softly. "Was it not to prolong the game you have been playing with Lord Melton?"

Emmy scowled. "That would be idiotic. I'm too tired to keep on running. I don't want to be a fugitive for the rest of my life. But how can I give them over and let Bow Street return them to the fat Prince Regent and the undeserving Lady Carrington?"

"From what Lord Melton told me last night, there might be another option."

Emmy raised a skeptical eyebrow. "Like what?"

"Well, he didn't go into detail, but he did suggest that if I were to contact you, I should tell you he had a proposition to make to you. One that doesn't involve you being prosecuted, and one that would see most of the jewels handed over to the French government."

Emmy sent her a derisive, disbelieving look. "You don't think it's a ruse to get me to give myself up? You think he means it?"

"As a matter of fact, I do," Camille said pensively. "He said to tell you he trusts you to do the right thing."

"Ha! That's rich. He doesn't trust me as far as he could throw me. Why on earth should I trust him?"

"Because you're in love with him?"

Emmy dropped her head back onto her knees with a choked sound "Oh, God. I am. It's awful."

"Come here, darling." Camille settled herself on the

rug next to her and put her arm around her. Emmy rested her head on her grandmother's shoulder.

"Do you know the precise moment I knew I was in love with your grandfather?"

Emmy shook her head.

"It was the day I found him hunched over next to an open window, looking at something on the sill. Anthony—your grandfather—glanced up with a guilty start when he heard me enter the room, and his cheeks turned a delightful shade of pink. He angled his body to try to hide whatever he was up to, but when I demanded to know what he was hiding, he moved aside so I could see."

Emmy lifted her head and Camille smiled in fond reminiscence.

"A bumble bee lay on the sill. It was almost dead, but he'd placed a teaspoon of honey next to it. As we watched, the bee stuck out its little tongue, or antenna, or whatever it is bees have, and started to suck up the honey. Within a minute it had recovered enough to wander around, albeit a little drunkenly. Within two minutes it started to buzz its little wings, and then it was off, into the sky. Anthony was obviously highly embarrassed at having been discovered undertaking such an unmanly task, but the smile he gave me melted my heart. That's when I knew. He was handsome, of course, and quick-witted, but more than that, he was *good-hearted*. He was the kind of man who helps grumpy old dowagers across busy streets. I knew then that I would love him forever."

Camille stroked a lock of Emmy's hair from her cheek. "This man, Alexander Harland. A blind man could see the attraction between the two of you. He has a handsome face and a strong pair of arms. But you know what they say: 'handsome is as handsome does.' What of his heart,

Emmeline? What do you think his attitude is toward bees? And grumpy old dowagers?"

"He would give the bee some honey, and the dowager his arm."

Camille gave a decisive nod. "Well, then. I approve wholeheartedly."

Emmy managed to snort. "Even if I *am* in love with him, what does it matter? He doesn't feel the same way about me. I'm just unfinished business, a criminal who must be brought to heel. I've hoodwinked him and hidden things from him since the day I met him." She gave a watery sigh and squeezed Camille's hand. "I know I have to face him. But I need a little time. Do you think you can keep him away for a day or two?"

"Of course, darling. Take as much time as you need. Oh, I almost forgot to tell you the other news! Luc and Sally are engaged."

"They are?"

"Yes. As soon as Lord Melton left last night Luc asked for a private word with Sally. I took one look at his face and knew exactly what he was going to ask her. There's nothing like a near-miss to put everything in perspective. I'm just surprised he's taken so long to do it."

"And she said yes?"

Camille nodded, clearly delighted. "She took some persuading, by all accounts. Said she was too low-born for the likes of him, but he convinced her that was nonsense. He wouldn't take no for an answer. He's talking about buying a boat and taking her sailing around the Greek islands."

Emmy laughed. "Oh, that's wonderful! I'm so happy for them both! I wish I could come back home with you now and congratulate them."

Camille got to her feet and shook out her skirts. "Take

a few days to think about whether you trust Harland enough to hear him out. If you don't, we'll have to come up with a new plan to spirit both you and the jewels out of the country."

Emmy was already shaking her head. "I don't want to be a fugitive for the rest of my life, separated from everyone I love. I know I have to face the consequences of my actions."

"If you *do* decide to trust him," Camille continued, "then you can decide where and when you want to meet him. Send a message to Sally via her friend."

"All right."

Chapter 43

Emmy had just come to a decision when Harland forced her hand.

A note from Camille, passed via Sally and Molly, informed her of his masterstroke: Bow Street had told the Prince of Wales that they'd successfully recovered the French crown jewels. The delighted prince had decided to hold an impromptu celebration at Carlton House. On Friday.

Harland had sent her an invitation.

Emmy sucked in a horrified breath. As a gesture of "solidarity and friendship between two great nations," the prince would be holding an "intimate gathering" to present the missing crown jewels of France to the French ambassador. Miss Emmeline Danvers was most cordially invited to attend.

It went without saying that she was expected to bring the jewels too.

Emmy sat heavily on the edge of the lumpy mattress in Molly's attic and stared at the invitation in her hand.

Harland was a fiend. He was calling her bluff, as if this were a game of faro, demanding that she put all her cards on the table. All or nothing. The ultimate dare to see which of them would fold.

She should have expected nothing less from the owner of a gambling club.

Irritation roiled in her breast. The nerve of the man! She could practically feel the weight of his expectation pressing down on her. What a risk he was taking. If she didn't show up with the jewels, not only would he be humiliated, but so would all of his colleagues at Bow Street, and the Prince Regent himself. His arrogant belief that she would "do the right thing" had given her the power to cause an international diplomatic disaster.

Emmy frowned at the neat, confident slashes of his handwriting. How could he trust her with something so monumental? She could ruin him, and his friends, and embarrass the monarchy, all in one fell swoop. What was he thinking? She'd betrayed him on numerous occasions. Why did he think this time would be any different?

Was his faith in her so strong? A tiny warm glow spread in her chest, but she beat it down ruthlessly. She'd already come to the decision to hand over the jewels on her own. If she returned them now, he'd think it was because of what *he'd* done. He'd be smug and arrogant and assume she'd caved in due to the pressure of his bold move.

She should call his bluff. She should catch a packet to Calais or sail off to the Americas with the treasure. That would teach him. But, of course, she wouldn't do that. He seemed to know her better than she knew herself. It was maddening.

She couldn't imagine what kind of deal he was going to offer her. In truth, she still didn't entirely trust that there would be one. She didn't have Camille's confidence. Even if Bow Street could prove Danton had been responsible for killing the owner of the sapphire, she couldn't believe they'd be willing to let a thief as prolific and infamous as the Nightjar go unpunished. Or remain at liberty. Still, she'd made her choice. Harland's confidence in her was not misplaced, damn him.

She rose and went to sit at the small desk in the corner. Molly had provided her with paper, ink, and quills. She dashed off a reply to her grandmother, confirming she would be there on Friday, but telling her not to inform Harland. The beast deserved to sweat a little. It would be a small victory, but she'd take whatever she could.

She would attend the party, even though it might be her last. And she would do it looking her very best. Camille was right about that. If one was going to be arrested and imprisoned, one might as well do it in style.

The Prince Regent always kept his apartments overly warm. Alex tugged at the folds of his neckcloth. He certainly wasn't nervous. Of course not. Emmy would come. She was fashionably late, that was all. She was making a point. He refused to believe the worst of her.

She *had* to come. He'd given his word to Conant the jewels would be here. He'd even persuaded the prince to give over "his" diamond too, in a grand gesture to the French.

If it ever bloody arrived.

His throat was parched. He grabbed a flute of champagne from a passing servant and took a healthy gulp. It wasn't just his employment at Bow Street that was at stake, it was his honor as a gentleman. The honor of the entire bloody nation. What had he been thinking, to let it all rest on the unpredictable whim of a thief?

The Regent had already settled himself in the Council Chamber under a crimson canopy to receive the French delegation. The French ambassador, René-Eustache, the

Marquis d'Osmond, had already arrived, as had half the French aristocracy. They'd all come out of the woodwork, despite the short notice, since half of them were still living in exile in London. Alex almost groaned when he saw the seventy-nine-year-old Louis Joseph, Prince de Condé, and his cousin, the thirty-eight-year-old Charles Ferdinand d'Artois, Duke de Berry. If Emmy didn't show, this could be a disaster of epic proportions.

Where the hell was she?

The rest of her family had already arrived. The Comtesse de Rougemont—Camille, as she'd begged Alex to call her—was over by the door with Luc and his new fiancée, the termagant who'd pushed her way into the Tricorn.

They'd been in contact with Emmy all week, Alex was certain of it, but they were all fiercely loyal. They'd refused to divulge her location, no matter how many times Alex had asked. Or demanded. Camille had been adamant that Emmy hadn't left London, but that was all she'd been prepared to say. She'd relayed Alex's invitation for tonight, but she couldn't, or wouldn't, say whether Emmy was coming or not.

Alex realized he was tapping his knuckles against his thigh and forced himself to stop. He'd felt this way countless times during the war, restless and jumpy. Knowing the enemy was out there and just waiting for the attack. Wishing it would come so he could get it over with.

He'd never been like this for a woman, so keen that every sound made him edgy. In the past, when other women had failed to show up at their appointed time, he'd been mildly irritated at the need to change his plans, but the inconvenience—and the woman—were quickly forgotten. He could never forget Emmeline Danvers.

He caught sight of Seb deep in conversation with Benedict and his wife, Georgiana, on the opposite side of the room. There must have been over two hundred people crowded into the place. Prinny's idea of an "impromptu little gathering" had swelled to include almost every member of the *ton* still in London. His household staff were probably all in various stages of apoplexy.

Alex couldn't shake the feeling that he was about to experience a very public humiliation. He glanced at an ornate gilt clock above an equally gaudy fireplace and cursed under his breath. She was over an hour late. Had he really misjudged her so badly?

Then he saw her, on the steps leading down from the entrance, and his heart seized before pounding back to life.

Thank God.

He blinked in slow appreciation. She'd clearly decided she no longer needed to blend in. No drab colors for Miss Danvers tonight. Her dress was a deep, rich burgundy, a ravishing, seductive color guaranteed to bring every man in the room to his knees. Alex felt the strangest desire to applaud. She looked incredible, as haughty and as regal as a queen. The low neckline of the dress showed to perfection the rubies—presumably *not* stolen—that glittered at her ears and throat. Her glorious hair was swept up in an elaborate coil to reveal the pale curves of her shoulders.

She was carrying a large reticule. Could all the jewels fit in there? He bloody well hoped so.

Alex pushed his way through the crowd, determined to reach her before she had a chance to speak to her family. There was no hint of the easy, laughing expression he knew so well. She was coldly beautiful, composed—like a prisoner going to the guillotine. She was fully expecting to be arrested and thrown into prison.

A warm glow of pride formed in his middle. She was brave, this girl. And ironically honorable, for a jewel thief. But her days as the Nightjar were over. It was time to end the game.

Chapter 44.

Emmy clutched the heavy bag tightly and swallowed the lump of terror that had lodged in her throat. Had she been invited here to be clapped in irons as soon as she'd handed over the jewels? It was possible. Perhaps they planned to make an example of her? A very public come-uppance for the thief who'd taunted them all for so long.

She would be brave. She would face her fate with dignity.

The ballroom was crowded and ridiculously warm. She glanced around for the rest of her family, but of course it was Harland who materialized at her side and caught her elbow in a firm grip. Her heart pounded at the sight of him.

He bent his head to her ear, and she tried to ignore the wave of longing that washed over her, the desire to push herself into his arms and hold on tight.

"Good evening, Miss Danvers. I'm delighted you could join us. This way."

He didn't seem to require a reply, which was fortunate,

because Emmy had lost the power of speech. He steered her through the crowd, navigating the crush of bodies with ease, and, nodding to two footmen standing guard at the door, propelled her into a small private room in which only two people were gathered.

The closing of the door dampened the noise as if they were suddenly underwater, and it took Emmy a moment to realize that she was in the presence of royalty. The rather plump gentleman lounging on a chaise beneath the red canopy was none other than the Prince Regent himself. She dipped a deep, belated curtsey.

Harland, without letting go of her arm, folded into a bow. "Your Highness, may I present Miss Emmeline Danvers." He straightened and gave her a little tug forward.

Prince George's appreciative gaze roamed over her face and figure in a way that could hardly be considered regal. His blue eyes twinkled, and he licked his red lips as though she were a morsel of food he wanted to sample.

"Ah, so this is the young lady you were telling me about, eh, Conant?" He turned his head slightly to address the gentleman standing on his right—a difficult task considering the dangerously high points of his shirt collar.

"Indeed it is, sir," the older man said. His expression was inscrutable. "Miss Danvers and her family have worked tirelessly for several years now to discover the whereabouts of the missing French crown jewels."

Emmy felt her brows rise. *That was a diplomatic way of putting it.*

Harland squeezed her elbow.

The prince gave a grunt that made his entire belly wobble and turned to Emmy. "And I hear you've been remarkably successful in finding the gems?"

Emmy found her voice. "Indeed, Your Highness. It was something of an obsession for my father before he died."

She gave another curtsey and offered forward the bag

of jewels to the man named Conant, who must be Sir Nathaniel Conant, the Chief Magistrate of Bow Street, and Harland's superior. He tugged open the drawstring and upended the bag of jewels onto a red velvet pillow beside the prince. The diamonds and other gems slithered out like some wondrous, glittering serpent.

The Prince Regent sucked in his breath. "Good lord. Just look at that." He clapped his hands like a five-year-old child on Christmas morning. "Always gratifying when we English succeed where the French have failed, what? Excellent work by Bow Street, Conant. You too, Melton."

Emmy sent him what she hoped was a winning smile. Harland might be planning to throw her into Newgate as soon as this interview was over, but she could at least try to ensure the jewels went where they belonged.

"It was my father's dearest wish to see these jewels returned to the people of France. May I say how glad I am that you have the wisdom and generosity to bring it about?"

The prince, apparently susceptible to flattery, puffed up his chest a little. "Quite. Quite. Not that it ain't useful to grease the wheels of diplomacy too, eh, Conant? Shame we had to do this quite so quietly, of course, in a private ceremony, but it wouldn't do to embarrass our French cousins in public. Not now we ain't fighting 'em."

He turned his attention back to Emmy and raised his brows. "I also hear, young lady, that you were instrumental in putting an end to the career of that blackguard the Nightjar."

Harland gave her elbow another warning squeeze, and Emmy shot him a quick look of irritation. What did *that* mean? Confess? Or keep quiet?

She chose her words with care. "You could say that, Sir. I think it's safe to say the Nightjar's career is over."

The prince chuckled. "I should say so. Got him in

Newgate, haven't you, Conant, awaiting trial? Not at all surprised to discover he's a Frenchie."

Emmy opened her mouth, then shut it again. What game was Harland playing? The prince clearly thought *Danton* was the Nightjar. And while she wasn't entirely happy with that attribution, she wasn't about to start admitting to the crimes herself.

Still, even if the prince hadn't been told she was the Nightjar, Harland and Conant knew the truth. They might not be forcing her to make a full public confession, but they would never allow her to go unpunished. They doubtless had some private torture planned.

The Regent nodded. "Good, good. Well, then. I believe Lord Melton has come up with a suitable reward for you, my dear."

Emmy's heart sank. Any "reward" Harland proposed would probably include her sharing a tumbril to the gallows with Danton. "Thank you, Your Highness."

The prince picked up the diamond she'd stolen from Rundell & Bridge and eyed it with a wistful look. "Shame we have to give 'em *all* back, eh, Conant? Surely the French wouldn't miss one or two—"

Conant coughed discreetly. "We have submitted a full inventory to the ambassador, sir. I'm sure we wouldn't want to disappoint them."

The prince's lower lip stuck out in a distinct pout as he dropped the diamond back onto the pile. "Shame. I do so like diamonds. Ah, well. I suppose you'd better let 'em in."

He turned to Harland. "Grateful to you, Melton, of course, but you've already had an earldom from me this year." He chuckled, sending his belly jiggling like a blancmange. "You ain't getting another. Chaps might get jealous." His eyes twinkled in merriment, and to Emmy's astonishment, he gave her a wink. "You two young things must go and dance. Think of it as a royal command."

He flicked his fingers at the two of them in clear dismissal.

Emmy ducked another swift curtsey, shot one last goodbye look at the jewels on the cushion, and was escorted from the room by Harland. It was only when the doors closed behind them that she realized she was shaking.

That was it, then. Ten years of work, and all she had to show for it was an empty reticule. No, she realized, she didn't even have that; she'd left her bag in there with Conant.

Harland still hadn't let go of her elbow. She was intensely conscious of him next to her, his height, his strength. She tried to pull away, desperate to join her family and say her goodbyes before she was whisked off for whatever new interrogation he had planned, but he stepped in front of her.

"I believe this dance is mine, Miss Danvers. We can't ignore a royal command."

Chapter 45.

Emmy could hardly look at him. Just being near him made her chest ache for all that could have been, and yet she found herself nodding in agreement. One last dance.

Instead of leading her onto the crowded dance floor, he pulled her through a doorway and into an unoccupied room whose curtains, walls, and furnishings were covered in dark blue velvet. He closed the door with an audible click.

"Dance with me."

The music was still faintly audible through the wooden panels. He pulled her close, and her body came alive with his touch. She felt light, almost transparent. As insubstantial as air, except for where he held her. Those points alone felt real, felt solid. They swirled into the familiar steps, and she concentrated on the pearl studs on his waistcoat. God, he danced so beautifully. Her heart felt heavy, almost to bursting. She forced herself to look up at him, then wished she hadn't, as his intense blue-grey eyes met hers.

The chandelier above them provided excellent illumination. She studied every detail of his face, trying to impress it upon her brain, to forge a memory she could hold in her heart forever.

The silence between them became pronounced. With a deep breath, Emmy decided to broach the subject at the forefront of her mind. "All right, Harland, out with it. The prince said you'd devised a suitable punishment for me. You might as well tell me what it is and put me out of my misery."

His lips curved up at the corners in that teasing way she knew so well. "I'm not sure he described it as a *punishment,* per se. I discussed the matter with Conant, and we both agreed the plan held merit."

She bit her lip and waited for him to continue.

"The charges against you will be dropped—"

She lifted her brows in silent astonishment and waited for the inevitable catch.

"—if you become my wife."

Emmy almost swallowed her own tongue. For a moment, she couldn't even begin to make sense of what he'd just said. She simply gaped at him.

"I've given Conant my assurances that as my wife, you will refrain from stealing. I have guaranteed your future good behavior. The Nightjar will be put to rest once and for all."

Emmy blinked. And then her confusion coalesced into disbelief and white-hot fury. Of all the mutton-headed, arrogant— She didn't know whether to laugh or cry. This *was* a punishment. A slow, heartbreaking humiliation. She'd learn the exquisite pain of having his attention for a brief time before he left her for another. Of having him marry her, and then abandon her in the countryside while he returned to his life in London.

It was the perfect revenge. As his legal wife, she

would have no recourse to complain against whatever he chose to do with her. He could lock her away in some musty old country estate and be perfectly within his legal rights.

Her heart felt as though it had been shredded. How many times had she dreamed of hearing a proposal from his lips? But never one such as this. He was clearly being coerced into offering for her. How humiliating.

"Isn't that as much a punishment for you as it is for me?" she choked.

Harland scowled, as if she'd mortally offended him. "I think you know me well enough by now to know that nobody can force me to do anything I don't want to do."

She raised her brows. "And if I refuse?"

He snapped his jaw shut, and for a moment she didn't think he'd answer, but eventually he ground out, "Then you'd still be pardoned."

She narrowed her eyes. "I would be free?"

"Yes."

"Safe from prosecution and imprisonment?"

"Yes, provided you never committed another crime."

"What about my family?"

"They would be safe too." He lowered his brows into a fearsome scowl.

"In that case, I decline."

He raked his hand through his hair in a gesture of frustration. "Let me rephrase."

She crossed her arms in front of her and gave him a look that clearly said: *As if anything you could say now would make it better.*

He gazed down at her, and she tried to ignore the traitorous quickening of her pulse. Why did he have to smell so good?

"It has occurred to me that I was mistaken in my previous assessment of our relationship. Do you remember when I said I didn't think we could ever be friends? I'd like to amend that."

She glared up at him, hating the way her stupid heart still fluttered with a tiny spark of hope. She must be deranged. "You think we could be friends?"

"Why not? We've already been lovers. I was hoping we could amalgamate both roles."

Her heart crashed to the pit of her stomach. Stupid rat of a man! "You want to make me your mistress? No, thank you."

She turned away, desperate to escape the suffocating misery that had descended on her like a shroud. She was almost at the door, her hand on the knob, when he spoke.

"Leaving me, princess?"

His soft voice stopped her in her tracks. He'd said those words to her in the same resigned, slightly teasing tone four years ago, at Lady Carlton's masquerade.

When he hadn't known who she was.

Emmy sucked in a disbelieving breath. *He knew!* He knew she was the one who'd danced with him and kissed him and left him alone. How? How long had he known? She swung around and was immediately caught in his smoke-grey eyes.

He sent her a crooked smile, cocky and heartbreakingly unsure all at once. "Don't leave me this time, Emmy. Stay."

Her throat was hot and tight. The end of her nose began to sting. She pressed herself back against the door. "Why should I stay?"

He took a step toward her, closing the distance. "The Nightjar only ever steals things that have already been stolen, is that correct?"

"Yes."

He shook his head. "Not true. Because you stole my heart, Emmeline Danvers. It's never belonged to anyone else since that night I danced with you at the Carltons' masquerade."

He took another step, and Emmy dragged in another shaky breath.

"And since you can't give me my heart back, I want yours, in exchange. I promise I'll guard it as well as I would my own. I will never bruise it or cause it to ache. I will love it forever." His eyes bored into hers, burning and intense. "Why should you stay? Because if you go, I'll be miserable for the rest of my life."

Emmy could barely breathe. She hardly dared believe the sincerity in his expression.

He took a final step, and they were chest to chest. "I don't know what qualities you think a husband of yours might need," he said softly. "A knack for scaling tall buildings? The ability to argue convincingly in front of a judge? I'm not sure I have those. I can't be your partner in crime. But I'd like to be your partner in life, if you'll have me."

With a sob, Emmy threw her arms around his waist and dropped her forehead onto his chest. His arms came around her, and she felt him kiss the top of her head and exhale as if in great relief. He spoke into the top of her hair.

"Don't cry. Just say yes. Say yes because you love me. As much as I love you."

She lifted her head. Tears pricked her eyes, but she managed a radiant smile. "That was a *much* better proposal, Harland. And in light of your recent admissions, I'd like to amend my earlier answer. I accept."

His smile was like a ray of sunshine breaking through a cloud. "Thank God."

Emmy closed her eyes in blissful surrender as his mouth came crashing down on hers. Joy bloomed within her. She was home.

Epilogue

Eight weeks later.

Emmy paused as she was about to sign the marriage document. Her heart was full almost to bursting. She and Alex had become man and wife just minutes ago, as part of a double wedding with Sally and Luc. Harland had obtained two special licenses from Doctors' Commons and the ceremony had taken place in the elegantly appointed drawing room of the Tricorn Club. All that remained was the signing of the register.

"What's the matter?" Alex leaned down and peered over her shoulder. "What are you waiting for?"

Emmy sent him a teasing smile. "Father always told me never to put anything in writing. Too incriminating."

Alex mock frowned. "It's too late, Lady Melton. We're married now. Signing that is a mere formality." He handed her the pen and lowered his voice so the vicar couldn't hear. "Sign the damn book, Emmy. I want no doubt at all that you're my wife."

She signed her name with a flourish, and his smile grew decidedly Machiavellian.

"What?" she asked.

"I've finally stolen something from *you*, Emmy Danvers."

"Oh really? What?"

"Your name. I've taken the Danvers and given you Harland in return. And, generous soul that I am, I've given you an extra name for good luck. The Countess of Melton. Are you happy now?"

Emmy smiled up at him. "Happier than I ever thought I could be."

"I can't wait for tonight," he murmured.

"Why?"

He raised his eyebrows with a suggestive leer. "Because I have my very own black feather, just like the one the Nightjar used to tease me with."

His eyes flared with desire and Emmy felt her cheeks heat in response. Really, the man was a devil, speaking to her like this in front of at least thirty witnesses, all of whom were dear friends and relations. She sent a weak smile toward Lord Mowbray's great-aunt Dorothea, the one he called the "Dread Dowager Duchess of Winwick," and tried to pretend that her husband wasn't seducing her in full view of everyone. The news that Alexander Harland was married would be all over town by teatime. No doubt the scandal would keep everyone gossiping for weeks to come.

"If you only knew how many dreams I've had about you and that feather," he whispered. "I've been carrying it around with me for weeks."

"We have the wedding breakfast to get through first," Emmy said primly, then sent him a look full of promise from under her lashes. "But after that, Lord Melton, I'm all yours."

His smile grew decidedly wicked. "Oh, yes, indeed you are."

AUTHOR'S NOTE

Emmy loves discovering foreign words that have no direct translation in English. I didn't use this in the story (because I thought it implausible that Emmy would have found out about it in 1816) but there's a wonderful Japanese phrase that's just perfect for her and Alex: *Koi No Yokan. The sense of inevitability upon first meeting a person that the two of you are going to fall in love.*

Coming soon . . .

Look for the next novel of
"genuine romance" (*Kirkus Reviews)* in
the Bow Street Bachelors series by
Kate Bateman

*The Princess &
the Rogue*

Available in 2021 from
St. Martin's Paperbacks